PREP
AGENT

JOE W. BOYOU SR.

Copyright © 2026 by Joe W. Boyou Sr.

All rights reserved. No part of this publication may be reproduced, distributed, or transmitted in any form or by any means, including photocopying, recording, or other electronic or mechanical methods, without the prior written permission of the author, except in the case of brief quotations embodied in critical reviews and certain other noncommercial uses permitted by copyright law.

978-1-965552-71-1 (Paperback)
978-1-965552-70-4 (Hardback)

Library of Congress Control Number: 2026905143

admin@bookwrightshouse.com
☎ (213) 286 6700

EPIGRAPH

"Be the hero in your own story."

This book is dedicated to the boys in blue.

This book could not have been completed without the support of those who walked beside me through long nights, endless edits, and moments of doubt.

To my family and friends, you give me the spark that keeps me going. Your encouragement carried me through every draft.

To the brave men and women in service, whether in law enforcement, military, or intelligence, your sacrifices inspire the spirit of this book, though the characters here are entirely fictional.

And most importantly, to my readers and supporters, thank you for stepping into this world with me. May you find suspense, laughter, and truth woven between these pages. You remind me that stories matter, and I promise to tell them all.

This story blends action, espionage, and personal drama, but at its core, it is about resilience-about ordinary people placed in extraordinary situations, forced to make choices that shape not only their lives but the world around them.

If at any point you laughed, clenched your fists, or simply paused to think about the nature of truth and sacrifice, then this book has done its work.

Thank you for reading.

TABLE OF CONTENTS

Epigraph iii

Dedication v

Acknowledgement vii

Preface ix

Chapter 1   Chicago At Dusk 1

Chapter 2   The Old Neighbor 16

Chapter 3   Duty Calls 24

Chapter 4   Breaking Point 35

Chapter 5   The Long Ride 47

Chapter 6   Chicago PD 59

Chapter 7   An Old Friend 67

Chapter 8   FBI 77

Chapter 9   Iron Sharpens Iron 89

Chapter 10   Ghosts In The Room 95

Chapter 11   The Assignment 101

Chapter 12   Love And Legacy 109

Chapter 13   The Long Ride In 117

Chapter 14   Fresh Meat 123

Chapter 15   In The Shadows 130

Chapter 16   Oligarch 140

Chapter 17   Fractures 150

Chapter 18   Fight Club 158

Chapter 19   Guns, Murder And Sirens 168

Chapter 20   Sticks And Balls 177

Chapter 21   Friends And Foes 183

Chapter 22   Breaking Cover 195

Chapter 23   Debrief 201

Chapter 24   Road To Vegas 206

Chapter 25   Vegas 211

Chapter 26   The Green Light 218

Chapter 27   It's Show Time 227

Chapter 28   The G-Suit 236

Chapter 29   All Is Lost 242

Chapter 30   Checkmate 248

Chapter 31   Denoument 260

Chapter 32   Badge Of Honor 266

Chapter 33   The Final Move 273

CHAPTER 1

CHICAGO AT DUSK

C hicago city had a way of stealing breath, especially when the sun leaned low against the horizon. The evening light bathed the skyline in fire, each tower gleaming with the last embers of the day. The city was restless, alive, buzzing with its endless appetite. Horns blared, tires screeched, and pedestrians hurried across intersections in a rhythm only Chicagoans seemed to understand. Vehicles clogged the arteries of Highway 90, a constant stream of metal and motion pushing toward every direction at once.

Cutting through the chaos, a GSX-1300R Hayabusa, the flagship of the Suzuki brand, darted like a needle threading between giants. The black and chrome accented crotch rocket's engine snarled as it weaved recklessly through thick traffic with a guttural roar with a blur of chrome against the muted concrete. Its rider balanced between danger and mastery, a sleek extension of the machine, leans into every turn. A helmeted head dipped low, mirroring the bike's aggressive posture and leaving streaks of taillights a vibrant red against the darkened asphalt. At the off-ramp, the bike slowed, screeching into place beside a red convertible stuffed with jeering gang members. Their laughter spilled out into the humid air, sharp and mocking.

The rider didn't so much as glance at them. His focus had locked onto something else entirely-a newly unveiled billboard towering above the city streets. Two workers descended the scaffolding, their job complete. Across the giant board stretched bold letters that glowed beneath spotlights:

"MUSCLEMANIA, COMING OCTOBER."

The image on display was no less commanding-men and women sculpted from iron and sweat, captured in mid-pose, bodies built into monuments of discipline. Parked at the base of the billboard was a black Escalade with tinted windows, sleek and menacing. The plate read simply B.O. In the corner of its rear window, a rectangle of red, white, and blue stripes hinted at authority, or perhaps a different kind of power altogether.

Three men stood nearby, their attention fixed on the billboard as though it were a coronation. One figure commanded immediate notice-a tall man dressed in a tailored suit that seemed to fit him like it was stitched to his very ambition. His wrist glittered with a gold watch, the kind that wasn't just expensive but carried weight and prestige. He gestured casually, yet with the air of someone used to being obeyed.

The gang in the convertible lost interest, their engine growling as they tore off east. The biker answered with his own reply-he revved his machine, the sound fierce, alive. Then he twisted the throttle and launched in the opposite direction, swallowed by the neon glow of the city.

South Canal Street

Night fell heavy., the bike screeched to a halt along South Canal Street, suspension jerking under the strain. The rider stood up then swung one leg over to regain his balance before removing his helmet and jacket, revealing a man who didn't just take up space but seemed to own it.

DEVIN CREWS

Late thirties, a haircut fresh enough to smell of the barbershop. A jaw that could cut glass. Shoulders carved broad, chest thick with power. He was the sort of man who turned heads without effort, a figure of equal parts discipline and raw presence.

Crews slipped into the shadows of a narrow path, the kind most people would ignore after dark. His boots fell silently against the cracked pavement as he cut between buildings, his eyes trained on the back staircase of an aging apartment complex. He moved like someone who'd done this before, quiet, deliberate, calculated. The iron steps groaned under his weight as he ascended.

Home

The back door opened with a soft creak, Devin easing it closed behind him. He paused, holding his breath, listening. The sound reached him instantly-loud, relentless, a bass-heavy throb bleeding through the ceiling. The floor above seemed alive with it, the rhythm pounding into his chest even here in the still darkness of his kitchen. Devin stood there for a long moment, his brow furrowed. The kind of night he'd walked into wasn't going to be quiet.

The noise grew louder as Devin moved through the dim apartment, the throb of bass rolling down through the ceiling like a heartbeat. He didn't need to wonder what it was, he could tell by the rhythm, the occasional chorus of female voices, the faint echo of laughter, A party. A women's party. By the time he reached the living room, the scene had already announced itself.

The space had been transformed. Red and white balloons clung to the ceiling in clusters, their ribbons dangling like loose vines. Streamers curled along the edges of picture frames and the light fixtures, catching the glow of lamps and throwing streaks of color across the walls.

On the dining table sat a cake decorated in careful frosting, the single word "BIRTHDAY" sprawled across it in cheerful letters. Bowls of cupcakes, their icing piled high with swirls of red sugar, and glasses of fizzy, fruit-colored drinks formed the centerpiece. It was unapologetically girlish, celebratory, an island of sweetness in the middle of Devin's usually plain apartment. But it wasn't the decorations that gave the room its pulse, it was the people.

Everywhere he looked, women filled the living room. They were dressed alike, as though someone had dictated the uniform: blue jeans and red t-shirts, their casual outfits forming a kind of collective banner of friendship. They moved in clusters, laughing, chatting, sipping colorful drinks. The music blared so loud it was impossible for anyone to speak without leaning close, but no one seemed to mind. Devin paused at the doorway, taking it all in. He wasn't expected yet, certainly not in the way he planned to appear. This was Tanya's night.

The Honoree

In the middle of the room, the woman of the hour sat like a star at the center of her orbit. Tanya, in her early thirties, radiated an easy beauty that didn't need embellishment but had been crowned with it anyway. A sparkling tiara perched above her hair, the light catching the rhinestones whenever she moved. Across her shoulder lay a bright red sash that marked her as the birthday queen.

Her dress was a white evening piece, elegant but playful, its shimmer accented with dustings of glitter across her cheeks. She was glowing, though not from the makeup, her laughter was warm, her smile constant, her presence magnetic.

She leaned in close to her friend April, who sat beside her holding a phone in her hand. Tanya's voice rose above the music, though not by much. "Is that him?" Tanya asked, nodding toward the screen April held clutched in her hand. April didn't hear at first, her eyes fixed on the glowing device. "What?" she shouted, pretending she hadn't caught the question. Tanya nodded again, pointing with more insistence at the phone. "Is that him?" April brushed her off, flashing a dismissive smile as if the subject didn't matter. "Oh, that? Never mind." Her tone shifted deliberately, her grin widening as she asked, "Where is the stripper?" At that, Tanya rolled her eyes and shook her head, though her smile betrayed her amusement. April's mood brightened immediately, her disappointment disappearing like a cloud split by the sun. She fanned herself dramatically with a fistful of one-dollar bills, already eager for what was to come.

The party around them only grew louder. Balloons wavered against the ceiling as if the music itself pushed at them. The thumping bass rattled cups and shook through the walls, a noise so heavy it seemed impossible that the neighbors wouldn't hear.

Devin remained unseen, just out of sight for the moment. Upstairs, the anticipation built as Tanya's friends laughed and sipped their beverages, unaware of what was about to walk into the center of their night. The decorations, the cake, the drinks-none of it mattered nearly as much as the surprise about to unfold. The party was just beginning.

The Surprise

April had been sulking only moments before, a cloud hovering over her otherwise bright demeanor. Something on her phone had stirred that shift-Tanya had noticed it, though she'd said nothing, deciding it wasn't her battle to fight. But now, in a blink, April's mood transformed, sadness dissolving into a wide, giddy smile. "Now this," she announced loudly, raising her glass with a sparkle in her eyes, "this is the part I've been waiting for." Her words, carried above the pulse of the music, were enough to rally the other women. They turned expectantly, laughter mixing with shrieks of excitement. The air thickened with anticipation, the kind that comes just before the curtain pulls back, when everyone knows something is about to happen. Then-darkness. The music cut with it, swallowed in an instant.

The only sound that remained was the collective gasp of women caught in the sudden void. For a heartbeat, the room was a black canvas, silent but for the muffled squeals of surprise and the shuffle of bodies trying to orient themselves. And then-light. Not the steady glow of lamps or the overhead fixtures that had been deliberately switched off, but a shimmering cascade of colors as a disco ball came alive. It dropped its first wave of glittering beams across the room, spinning lazily at first, then faster, scattering reds, blues, greens, and purples in dizzying swirls along the walls. Ribbons caught the light and shimmered like streams of fire. Balloons flashed like planets suspended in orbit.

The women squealed again, this time with delight. "Woooo!" one shouted, clapping her hands. Another whistled, the sound sharp and playful. The atmosphere shifted instantly, darkness giving way to a carnival of color, the air buzzing with expectation. And in the middle of it all stood a figure.

At first he was nothing more than a silhouette, broad-shouldered and immovable, like a statue rooted to the center of the room. The spinning lights caressed him, revealing the sharp outline of his chest, the brim of a hat tilted just enough to shade his eyes, the gleam of polished shoes that glinted like mirrors under the disco glow. Then the room caught its collective breath. The figure stepped forward, and the details sharpened under the spinning lights. It was a cop.

At least, that's what it looked like. The uniform was perfect, dark and pressed, with a duty belt strapped snugly around the waist. The women screamed and clapped, some already reaching into their pockets or purses for bills. They didn't notice, or maybe they did, but the duty belt was missing certain essentials. The holster was empty. The spot where a taser should have hung was bare. There was no badge gleaming from the chest. But none of that mattered. Because the face beneath the tilted hat was familiar.

Tanya's heart lurched as the man lifted his chin ever so slightly, the light spilling across his jawline, catching the mischievous curve of his mouth. Devin, her Devin. Her eyes widened, and for a split second she was torn between horror and laughter. Around her, her friends erupted into catcalls, whistles, and screams. April, practically bouncing in her seat, fanned herself with the bills she'd been holding all along. "Oh my God!" someone shouted. "He's hot!" Another voice cut in, shrill and gleeful, "Take it off, Officer!" Devin stood perfectly still, arms crossed, his expression unreadable under the slant of his cap. The disco ball spun faster, its colorful lights splashing across his chest like waves. He hadn't moved yet, but his stillness was its own performance, deliberate and commanding, as though the entire room existed only to wait for his signal.

The women leaned forward, caught between laughter and awe, their glasses half-forgotten in their hands. The atmosphere was electric. And Tanya-well, Tanya's mouth hung slightly open as she tried to process what she was seeing. Her man. Her brick house of a man. In a patrolman's uniform, In her living room. Ready to strip.

Devin stood perfectly still, his frame lit in fragments by the spinning disco lights. His police hat remains tilted just enough to shadow his eyes, concealing the playful glint he knew was there. The effect was deliberate-mystery was half the show. Around him, the room quivered with female laughter, squeals, and catcalling. Voices overlapped, some daring, some coy, all drunk on the thrill of spectacle. The music throbbed through the floorboards, not just sound but a pulse, syncing the women's excitement to a beat that promised more. He let them take him in.

The broad chest under the snug, but half-unbuttoned uniform shirt. The duty belt slanted lazily across his waist, conspicuously missing a gun or taser but weighted with the suggestion of authority. The stillness that read less like hesitation and more like command. Devin wasn't nervous. Quite the opposite, he basked in it.

The corners of his mouth curved, unseen beneath the shadow of his cap. He liked this. The catcalling swelled. "Come on, Officer!" "Shake it, baby!"-a chorus of voices egging him on. He soaked it all in, standing like a statue at the center of chaos, letting the anticipation stretch until it was unbearable. Then, without warning, he moved.

The gyrating began with hips rolling in a slow, deliberate rhythm, shoulders shifting with practiced grace. The women screamed, their hands shooting into the air as if they were at a concert. The disco lights washed him in reds and greens, spinning color into every flex of muscle, every glide of his body.

He let the rhythm build, each move more confident, more intense, until the air itself seemed to vibrate with it. And then-he stopped. The sudden stillness sent a shock through the room. Gasps echoed, followed by shouts. The music carried on but Devin froze in place, teasing them, daring them to beg.

Tanya, sitting amidst the chaos, her earlier statuesque elegance evaporating like a mist in a sudden sunbeam. Her eyes, wide and disbelieving, swept across the room as she held four fingers across her lips as if to physically contain the tidal wave of astonishment. A small, choked sound escaped her throat. Tanya glanced at April and caught sight of her best friend fanning herself with a fistful of crisp one-dollar bills. April's grin stretched wide, eyes glued to Devin as if she'd forgotten everything else in the world. "No!" April shouted, waving the bills like a flag. "Don't stop!" Another woman jumped in, her voice shrill with excitement. "Yes! Keep going!" The room erupted in laughter and shrieks.

Tanya's eyes narrowed. Her lips pressed into a line as she shot them both a look sharp enough to cut glass. She had expected some cheering, of course-this was a birthday party, after all. But there was a line, and her friends were dancing right up to it. "Easy, ladies," Tanya barked above the music, her tone carrying authority even in the chaos. "This one's taken." The women howled in response, some booing playfully, others throwing their heads back in laughter. But Devin-oh, Devin loved it.

He whipped around in a sudden, dramatic motion, the spin so swift that the air seemed to shift with it. His head tilted just enough to allow the women a glimpse beneath the brim of his cap. His gaze, sharp and magnetic, swept across the room. He studied them one by one, as though choosing his next victim. And then he moved again, this time slower, smoother. He glided across the floor, each step feline, every shift of his body dripping with calculated seduction. His movements weren't clumsy or rushed; they were deliberate, like a predator toying with prey.

His voice cut through the roar of the crowd, low and teasing, the kind of tone that made women lean in even when they already heard the words. "Ladies," he purred, dragging out the syllables as though savoring them, "back in the day, they called me Mr. D.C." The women screamed, some clapping, some whistling. A chant even began to form, voices bouncing off one another, echoing his name. He paused, his grin widening. "The 'C'," he added with a sly glance, "stands for-" "Whoa!" Tanya's voice cracked like a whip across the noise, sharp and commanding enough to halt the thought midair.

Every head turned toward her. She was on her feet now, arms crossed, her tiara shimmering under the disco lights. Her expression was firm, but her eyes betrayed a spark of amusement, a glimmer that revealed she wasn't entirely immune to the ridiculousness of it all. "Easy there, cowboy," she called out, her words cutting through the laughter and music. "They don't need to know all that," she instructed as she sat back down.

The women groaned, some booing, others laughing. April rolled her eyes dramatically, still fanning herself with her bills. Devin, unshaken, only smirked. He let Tanya's interruption hang in the air a moment longer, as if weighing her command against the demands of the crowd. Then, with a flick of his wrist, he broke the tension. Slowly, seductively, he peeled the gloves from his hands. He stretched it out, pulling the leather finger by finger, making a performance of the simplest motion. The women screamed louder, some nearly leaping from their seats. And then, with a sudden snap of motion, he flung the gloves into the crowd.

Two women caught them mid-air, squealing with triumph as if they'd won a prize. Another reached desperately, fingertips brushing the glove but missing. She groaned in frustration, and the winners waved their trophies with mock arrogance. Devin didn't pause. He reached up, fingers brushing the brim of his cap. He tilted it higher, letting his eyes meet Tanya's for the first time in the performance. The contact was electric, a silent acknowledgment, a private moment in the middle of chaos. Then, with a flick of his wrist, he sent the cap flying.

The room gasped as it spun once, twice, before landing squarely in Tanya's lap. The women exploded with laughter and shrieks. Tanya, caught off guard, looked down at the cap sitting in her hands. The brim pointed toward her, as though daring her to put it on, as though reminding her that this spectacle, this man, belonged to her. She looked back up, her cheeks flushed with heat. Devin stood there, chest heaving, the ghost of a grin tugging at his lips.

Center Stage

Devin stepped back to the center of the room. The disco ball spun above, scattering restless colors across his frame. Every woman's gaze clung to him, the laughter and squeals fading into a tense hush. He had the room entirely in his grip. For a moment he stood completely still, his presence filling the space with command. Then, with sudden precision, he snapped into a rigid stance. His legs spread wide, heels tapping the floor with his arms lifted high over his head. It was the pose of a man being frisked, but in Devin's hands it became something else-dominant, deliberate, sensual. The crowd screamed, voices rising in unison.

He held the position, chest rising and falling as the music pounded around him. Each second he lingered stretched the tension further. When he finally moved, it was slow, deliberate, designed to unravel them. His hands slid down his torso, teasing at the remaining buttons of his shirt. Gasps and laughter rippled across the room. April nearly bounced out of her chair, waving her bills in the air. "Yes! Don't you dare stop now!" she shouted.

Devin smirked, though his eyes sought only Tanya. She sat in the midst of the noise, tiara sparkling, the cap he had tossed earlier still in her lap. She tried to remain composed, lips pressed tight, but when he winked at her, her resolve faltered. A smile broke through, followed by a laugh she could not contain. Heat flushed her cheeks. "Boy, you better behave," she muttered under her breath, though no one heard her over the roar.

One by one, the buttons came undone. The shirt fell open, revealing the sculpted lines of his abs, the shimmer of sweat catching the lights. He peeled it away slowly, timing each move to the throb of the music. The women screamed louder, tossing bills into the air, hands reaching desperately for the shirt when he finally spun it overhead and flung it into the crowd. A frenzy erupted as they fought to claim it. Then the dancing began in earnest. His hips rolled in perfect rhythm, his steps sharp and precise, a performance that blended control with abandoned inhibition. The teasing was gone, now the show was on full display. Every move drew louder shouts, wilder laughter, higher energy. Women clapped, stomped, and circled closer, unable to resist the pull of his performance.

Tanya tried to look away, to regain control of the room, but her eyes betrayed her. She could not help but watch him, her other half, her man owning the moment so completely. Embarrassment and pride twisted together inside her, equal parts possessive and amused. The bass thumped harder, vibrating through the floor, shaking the glasses on the table, rattling the balloons overhead. The walls themselves seemed to hum with the rhythm. It was the kind of noise that bled through drywall and brick, loud enough to stir the neighbors from sleep. But inside the apartment, no one cared. The party was alive, hotter than ever, and Devin stood at the center of it all.

CHAPTER 2

THE OLD NEIGHBOR

The music rattled the walls of the old apartment building, creeping into every crevice like an invasive pulse. Bass lines throbbed through plaster, vibrated against pipes, and slipped beneath doorways, dragging laughter and shrieks of delight with them. Devin's performance inside the living room had turned the place into something wild, something electric, but not everyone in the building shared the thrill. Just beyond the wall, in the neighboring unit, Mrs. Eleanor Whitaker sat in her armchair with her calico cat pressed tightly to her chest. Eleanor was seventy-two, a woman whose sharp tongue had gotten her into more quarrels with neighbors than she cared to count. She lived alone, except for the cat, and she liked it that way. Quiet, order, predictability, these were the things she demanded. Tonight, though, quiet had been stolen from her and this was the final straw.

The thumping music had begun as a nuisance, just loud enough to force her to turn up the volume on her evening news broadcast. She had grumbled, reaching for the remote, mumbling to the cat that people these days had no respect for peace. The noise from across the way grew until it drowned out the newscaster's voice. Soon, the sound wasn't just in her ears, it rattled her bones.

The cat twitched uneasily against her, ears flattening at each pulse of bass. "Now you see, Clementine," Eleanor muttered, her lips pressed tight, "this is exactly what I've been telling the manager. Too many parties. Too many hooligans who don't give a damn about anyone else." She pushed herself up from the armchair with a grunt, slipping her feet into a pair of worn slippers. As she moved, her knees protested with a soft pop, before propelling her gently towards the front door. With her free hand, she grabbed her knitted shawl from the hook by the door and wrapped it tightly around her shoulders, careful to avoid unraveling her silver hair that was pinned up in a not-so-tight bun. She hated being forced out of her home, especially at night, but she was not about to let "the circus next door" run unchecked.

Pulling the door open, she stepped out into the hallway. The air out there seemed to vibrate with the same rhythm that had taken over her living room. Lights flickered faintly overhead, the old wiring struggling under the strain. She clutched Clementine closer and muttered, "Oh, it's worse than I thought." The hallway led to the narrow balcony that connected the units, a place where neighbors sometimes smoked or gossiped during the day. Now it felt like a theater balcony for the chaos erupting next door.

Eleanor shuffled to the outside railing and peered toward the source of the commotion. She didn't need to look far. Tanya's windows blazed with colored lights-greens, reds, purples-all leaking from the relentless spin of a disco ball. Shadows of women flickered across the curtains, their bodies swaying, arms raised, the occasional silhouette throwing dollar bills into the air. And there, in the middle, she caught sight of him: a half-naked man, broad and muscled, spinning in rhythm with the music, his body a machine of showmanship. Her mouth fell open in disbelief. "Of all the…" she sputtered, shaking her head. She looked down at Clementine, who only blinked lazily, tail flicking against Eleanor's forearm. "You don't want to see this filth, sweetheart. It'll poison your little mind." She turned the cat's head gently away from the window, though she kept her gaze on the man's silhouette. Intrigued.

A scream of laughter erupted from inside, followed by applause, the kind usually reserved for concerts or theaters. Eleanor's jaw tightened. She could feel her blood pressure rising with each second she stood there. Her mind raced with indignation-what if children were still awake on this floor? What if fire alarms went unheard because of the racket? What if-God forbid-the ceiling gave way under all that stomping and dancing?

The thought of calling the building manager crossed her mind. But she knew from experience that late-night calls rarely produced immediate results. The last time she had complained about the couple down the hall blasting salsa music until two in the morning, management hadn't sent anyone until the next day. By then, the music had stopped, and she'd been left looking like the cranky old woman everyone already suspected she was. No, she decided, she would handle this herself. But as she stood there, gripping her cat tighter, another roar of female voices broke out, followed by the unmistakable sound of furniture scraping against the floor. Something about it made her hesitate. She wasn't brave enough to confront an entire room of half-drunk women and a man stripping out of a police uniform. The idea of walking into that den of chaos, announcing herself with a sharp "Excuse me!"-no, that wasn't practical.

Eleanor sighed, her indignation thick in her chest. She shook her head slowly, muttering under her breath. "Disgraceful. Absolutely disgraceful. They should be ashamed of themselves." With a final glance at the glowing window, she turned back toward her apartment door. Each step was sharp, her slippers slapping against the concrete as though punctuating her anger. When she reached her unit, she yanked the door open, stepped inside, and slammed it shut behind her. Inside, she pressed her back to the door and exhaled heavily. The music still throbbed through the walls, as if mocking her, daring her to do something about it.

Clementine squirmed slightly, and Eleanor set her down gently on the armchair. The cat leapt onto the cushion and immediately curled into a ball, unfazed by the chaos. Eleanor, on the other hand, stood stiffly in the middle of the room, her face flushed with rage. She shook her head once more, this time at herself as much as at the party next door. "This is what the world has come to," she whispered. "Noise, sin, and shamelessness right on the other side of my wall."

She tugged the shawl tighter around her shoulders, sat down heavily beside her cat, and glared at the vibrating wall as though sheer willpower might silence it. But the music roared on, and Eleanor Whitaker seethed in her solitude

The Pec Show

The living room was no longer a living room. It had transformed into something else entirely. It was part nightclub, part stage, part private fantasy brought to life. The ceiling shimmered with the colors of the disco ball, the walls trembled under the pounding music, and every inch of the air felt thick with heat and adrenaline.

Devin owned it all. His duty belt, once strapped loosely across his hips, now dangled from the back of Tanya's chair, the handcuffs and empty holster gleaming faintly under the lights. It was as though he had shed not just the belt but the authority it represented. What remained was something raw and unfiltered; a man in complete command of his body, but willing to surrender it to the gaze of the blaring women. He was deep into his routine now, his movements sharper, faster, more daring. Sweat slicked his chest, catching the light in a sheen that emphasized the taut ridges of muscle beneath. Each roll of his hips, each twist of his torso, seemed to test the very limits of human endurance. Yet he made it look effortless, his body gliding with the precision of a dancer and the power of an athlete.

The women could hardly contain themselves. They screamed until their throats burned, clapped until their palms stung, stomped their feet like a stampede of wild horses. Some stood on chairs to get a better view, their faces lit with a mixture of awe and mischief. But Devin's expression remained intense, almost fierce, his eyes locked in concentration. Then, without warning, his face softened. The sternness broke apart, giving way to a boyish grin, playful and mischievous. It was a signal.

The crowd didn't know it yet, but Tanya did. She had seen that grin before, in the privacy of their bedroom, in front of the bathroom mirror, in the silly moments when he couldn't resist showing off. She knew exactly what was coming. The Pec Show, his favorite.

Devin stopped dancing for a moment and planted his feet wide, striking a stance that seemed borrowed straight from a bodybuilding stage. His chest swelled, his abs tight as steel, his arms flexed at perfect angles. He looked like a man carved out of marble, alive only because the gods had breathed motion into stone. And then it began. Boom! His left pec jerked upward, hard and fast, before descending slowly like a wave pulling back into the ocean.

Boom! His right pec shot up, answering its twin, a rhythm beginning to take shape. The women erupted, their voices rising in shrill harmony. Laughter mixed with shrieks, and applause rattled the windows. "Lord have mercy!" one woman cried "Somebody call 911, I can't take this!" shouted another.

Devin grinned wider, feeding on the frenzy. His chest muscles moved in perfect synchronization now, bouncing up and down in rapid succession, a hypnotic dance of flesh and control. The disco ball painted streaks of gold and violet across his body, each light shimmering with every ripple of his muscles.

The women were spellbound. They couldn't look away. Some doubled over in laughter, others clutched their hearts as if the spectacle might undo them. April, in particular, was losing her mind. Her phone lit up in her hand, the screen flashing insistently, but she barely gave it a glance. When she finally did, her smile faltered. The glow from the screen cast a brief shadow across her face, and Tanya caught it.

For a moment, the laughter and noise seemed to blur around them. Tanya's eyes narrowed as she watched her friend's expression twist with unease. Whatever April had seen, it wasn't good. But April, unwilling to spoil the party, slid the phone face down on the table and forced a grin. Tanya said nothing. The music swelled again, and Devin took the pause as his cue. He leaned into the performance, exaggerating the bounce of his pecs, flexing harder, faster, until the crowd dissolved into pure chaos. April was on her feet now, her earlier distraction forgotten. She cupped her hands around her mouth and shouted above the noise, "Take it off! Take it off!" Her voice cracked like a spark, and the crowd caught fire. "Take it off!" the others echoed, a chorus of women demanding more. Their chants grew louder, bolder, until the words became a rhythm of their own, blending with the beat of the music. "Take it off! Take it off! Take it off!"

Tanya's heart skipped. She had expected cheering, maybe even some chanting, but the boldness of her friends left her breathless. These were women she had shared wine nights and whispered secrets with, women who had comforted her through rough times, who had laughed with her through better ones. Now they were catcalling her man as if he were a prize on display. Her jaw tightened, but her body betrayed her. Heat spread across her face again, her lips curving in an involuntary smile. She wanted to hush them, to remind them who he was, but a part of her thrilled at the sight of him being adored. It was complicated-pride and jealousy, love and embarrassment all tangled in a knot she couldn't undo. Devin, meanwhile, basked in it. His grin widened, his movements grew even more deliberate. He thrived on the attention, not only from the crowd but from Tanya. Every time his eyes darted to her, his performance sharpened, as if he wanted her to know he was still hers even as the others begged for more.

The chants grew louder still, shaking the very air of the room. Bills fluttered through the air like confetti. The disco lights spun faster, reflecting off sweat-slick skin, filling the space with dizzying color. And Tanya, caught between her embarrassment and her thrill, realized the night was spiraling into something she hadn't expected.

Meanwhile across the way, Eleanor was a still landscape of warm, deep slumber, nestled into her faux leather cushion. She had fought sleep long enough and sleep was victorious. Her floral housecoat had slipped open, revealing a faded pink nightgown. A slipper dangles off a foot that now rested on a foot stool, mouth agape. The only sound that mattered in the room was the rhythmic, gentle snoring that puffed lightly from her lips. The cat watched her sleep, dividing its attention between her snoring and the muffled sound still pulsating through the walls. Her silver hair is no longer in its original place, cascading in soft wisps around her wrinkled face. She looked peaceful.

CHAPTER 3

DUTY CALLS

Devin lived for the spotlight. Even in a crowded room full of catcalls, he knew how to command silence, how to bend anticipation until it nearly snapped, and how to turn the most ordinary gesture into theater. A natural showman, he didn't need encouragement, but tonight the women gave him more than enough. Their chants of "Take it off!" still reverberated in the room, urging him further, daring him to push the boundary. With a grin that balanced on the edge of mischief, Devin reached down with both hands, grabbing the waistband of his pants in the front. His thumbs hooked under the belt loops, pulling taut, his posture telegraphing what everyone thought was coming. Gasps filled the air, followed by an eruption of cheers so loud it nearly drowned the bass.

The women went wild. Hands slapped the table. Bills waved in the air like flags at a parade. April, laughing uncontrollably, stomped her foot and shouted louder than the rest, "Do it, Officer, do it!" But Tanya saw it differently. Her stomach twisted at the sight of him teasing the edge of indecency, his hands poised to strip away the final layer between performance and exposure. It wasn't just the women egging him on-it was the look in their eyes, the hunger, the way their shouts carried more than simple fun. For the first time that night, Tanya felt something that cut deeper than embarrassment.

Possessiveness

Her hand shot up before she could think, palm outward in a sharp, commanding gesture. Her eyes locked onto Devin's, the message clear: Don't you dare.

He saw her, and for a moment their gazes clashed in silence across the storm of noise. His grin faltered ever so slightly, his hands still gripping his pants, caught between the thrill of the show and the plea of the woman he loves. Before Tanya could shout his name, before she could push through the crowd and grab his wrist, salvation arrived in the form of a crackling noise.

The police radio

The device, forgotten until now, sputtered to life with static, the sudden intrusion slicing through music and laughter alike. Devin froze mid-movement, his head snapping toward the sound. Tanya's heart leapt with relief. She lunged for the radio hanging from his discarded belt and yanked it free. The disco lights painted streaks across her face as she pressed the heavy device into his hand, as though returning a weapon to a soldier.

The music softened as if the party itself understood the shift. Then the dispatcher's voice spilled out, flat and urgent. "All units, be advised of a shooting at the Dearborn Housing Units. AMR is in route. I repeat, we have an active shooting at Dearborn. Units, respond." The room fell silent. Devin's expression changed instantly, the playful showman gone, replaced by the steel-eyed officer who wore the badge with pride. He straightened his posture, the weight of responsibility settling over his shoulders like armor. His jaw tightened. "Sorry, ladies," he said, voice steady but edged with urgency. "Duty calls." The reaction was instant and unanimous: groans, protests, and laughter all tangled into one sound. The women booed playfully, stomping their feet in disapproval. April fanned herself with mock despair, shouting, "Come on, just one more minute!" Another woman cried, "We paid good money for this!" though she had thrown only crumpled bills onto the floor.

Devin offered them a half-smile, the faintest apology, but he was already reaching for his belt. Tanya could see it in his face-there was no room for delay, no compromise between performance and duty. April, never one to let an opportunity pass, leaned across Tanya with a grin so wide it almost split her face. "Girl," she whispered loudly enough for everyone to hear, "I need to get me one of those."

The women laughed, their frustration dissolving into amusement. Tanya, however, did not laugh. "Be careful what you wish for," she replied flatly, her eyes never leaving Devin as he gathered his things. "Cops work long hours. Too many lonely nights to count." Her words silenced April for once. She leaned back, chewing the inside of her cheek as if she had just been reminded that fantasy often carried consequences.

Devin buckled the belt around his waist with swift precision. The room, which moments ago had been filled with whistles and shrieks, now watched him in awed silence as he transformed into something else. No longer the stripper in the moonlight, no longer the charismatic sport playing stripper games for his fiancé and her thirsty friends, but the real thing.

The belt was fully loaded now: flashlight, handcuffs, pepper spray, extra magazines. And at the end, dangling from its loop, the set of car keys that would take him away from Tanya and back into the city's chaos. Tanya's chest tightened. The shift from fantasy to reality was too abrupt, too raw. She wanted to pull him back, to tell him to let someone else handle it, to remind him that tonight was supposed to be hers. But she knew better. She had always known better. Devin didn't just wear the uniform. He lived it.

Shadows at The Door

Devin buckled the last clip on his duty belt, leaving three glaringly empty slots; one for the taser, another for his service pistol, and the third for the radio still clutched in his hand. It was the unmistakable picture of a man called to duty before he was ready, half-armed yet already halfway gone. Before Tanya could protest, before she could remind him once more that tonight was supposed to belong to them, he leaned down and pressed his lips firmly against hers. It was not the quick peck of a distracted partner but the heavy, grounding kiss of a man trying to reassure her in the only way he could.

She clung to him longer than she intended, her fingers curled against his uniform shirt, memorizing the warmth of him through the fabric. She knew the feel of his body better than anyone else, yet in that moment it seemed fleeting, like trying to hold smoke in her hands.

When he finally pulled back, he smiled faintly, that mixture of charm and determination that had first drawn her to him. "Happy birthday, honey," he murmured, his voice low but steady. "Gotta run." Her heart sank at the words. She searched his eyes, desperate to hold him for just a few minutes longer. "But you're not on the clock yet," she said quickly, trying to anchor him in place with logic, with anything she could. "You still got like…" "I know," he interrupted gently. She hated the way he said it—calm, resigned, as though duty always outranked time, always outranked her. "…Thirty minutes," she finished dryly, her voice small now, stripped of its earlier fight. But by then, he was already moving, his boots echoing against the hardwood as he disappeared down the hallway toward their bedroom. The sight of his broad back vanishing into the dim corridor left her both proud and hollow.

Tanya exhaled heavily, her chest tight, but before she could gather her thoughts, movement on the couch caught her attention. April. April's face had lost its earlier shine, her laughter and teasing replaced with something brittle, something tight. Her fingers trembled slightly as she lifted her phone, the glow of the screen washing her features in pale blue. Tanya saw it immediately, the fear etched in her friend's eyes, the way her lips pressed together as though holding back words that wanted to spill out. "What is it?" Tanya asked, stepping closer. April didn't answer right away. She stared at the phone as though it had delivered a sentence she'd been dreading. Her hand shook, then dropped the phone into her lap as if it were suddenly too heavy to hold.

When she finally looked up, her voice was barely a whisper. "He's here. He found me." The blood drained from Tanya's face. "What?" April didn't wait for her to process. She shot up from the couch so suddenly the cushions groaned in protest. Her movements were frantic, driven by panic rather than reason. Without so much as a glance behind her, she headed for the front door.

Tanya's instincts kicked in. She rushed after her, heels clicking against the floor, her heart hammering. "April, wait!" But April didn't stop. By the time Tanya reached her, April had already flung the deadbolt back, her hand on the handle of the heavy wooden door. The music, still pulsing faintly in the background, seemed out of place now, like laughter at a funeral. Tanya's breath caught in her throat as April pulled the door open just wide enough to reveal the thin mesh of the screen door. And beyond it-the silhouette of a man. Even through the flimsy barrier, his presence was like a storm pressing against glass. His face was twisted in fury, his mouth moving rapidly, spitting words they couldn't hear through the music and the walls. His arms flailed with wild energy, fingers stabbing the air as if each gesture could pierce through the door itself.

Tanya's stomach dropped. April's hand lingered on the handle, trembling. For one terrifying second, Tanya thought she would unlock the screen door, let him in, let the chaos inside swallow them all. Not on her watch. With a burst of adrenaline, Tanya threw herself in front of her friend, slamming her body against the door frame and blocking the path. She grabbed the handle from the inside, yanking it back with such force the screen rattled in its frame. "Stop!" she barked, her voice sharp, commanding, louder than she thought she was capable of. "Don't open it."

April's eyes went wide, darting between Tanya and the man outside. Her chest rose and fell in shallow gasps, tears threatening to spill but refusing to fall. "What does he want?" Tanya demanded, her voice cutting through the muffled shouts from beyond the screen. April swallowed hard, her lips trembling as though every word was both truth and confession. "He's crazy." "Then why," Tanya shot back, her grip tightening on the door handle, "would you even think about letting him in?" April said nothing, her silence louder than any excuse.

The man outside pounded his fist against the door, rattling it in its frame. His mouth moved faster now, his words fierce, but the barrier between them muffled everything. Tanya and April could only watch the anger take shape in the violent thrust of his hands, the veins standing out in his neck, the fire in his eyes. Tanya's pulse thundered in her ears. The tattooed man at the door wasn't just angry, he was furious and dangerous.

Crossroads

Tanya's eyes burned with frustration as she turned back to April, her voice sharp enough to slice through the tension hanging in the apartment. "I told you a long time ago to leave him," she said, the words trembling with equal parts anger and care. "What do you even see in him, April? Haven't you had enough?" April's lips parted, but no words came. Her silence was a confession. She couldn't answer, or maybe she didn't want to. Tanya could see it written across her friend's face—the shame, the fear, the endless cycle she had witnessed before. It was the same story she had warned April about countless times, and still here they were.

Beyond the screen door, the man continued to rage, his shadow flickering in the porch light as he hurled words they couldn't quite hear. Tanya didn't need to hear them. His tone alone carried everything she needed to know: hostility, threat, possession. Tanya drew in a breath, then shifted her gaze to the man outside. She squared her shoulders, standing taller, letting her voice rise so he could hear her through the thin mesh of the door. "What do you want?" she demanded, her tone steady, controlled, laced with the authority she didn't know she had until this moment.

For a beat, the man stilled, his mouth snapping shut, his glare sharpening into something colder. His hands, which had been flailing with every word, dropped to his sides, then curled into fists. The silence between them was heavier than his shouting had been. Tanya's pulse quickened, but she refused to step back.

In the garage, Devin was a world away from the confrontation. The night air was cool against his skin as he popped the trunk of the black-and-white parked neatly inside. The cruiser gleamed under the dim light, every polished curve a reflection of the years he had spent inside it. It wasn't just a car—it was his second partner, his shield, his silent witness to nights of chaos and mornings of calm. He moved methodically, muscle memory guiding his hands as he loaded his backpack, tucked his bulletproof vest inside, and checked the secure fit of each strap. The familiar weight settled onto him, grounding him in routine. He was dressed in a tan Five Eleven tactical trousers paired with a coordinating long-sleeved top and a pair of olive-green combat boots.

With practiced precision, Devin set his duty belt on the front seat. He reached for the radio, the taser, the service pistol-each piece clicking into its rightful place. The motions should have been mechanical, but tonight, something about them felt heavier. Maybe it was the way Tanya had looked at him when he left the living room, or maybe it was the simple truth that every time he strapped on the belt, he carried the risk of not coming home.

He stared at the cruiser for a long moment. The silence of the garage wrapped around him, the muffled beat of the party upstairs faint but still lingering. "Buddy," he whispered, leaning down to kiss the cool metal of the hood. His lips brushed against the paint with reverence, almost like a prayer. His hand followed, stroking gently over the car's curve, his voice low and heavy with unspoken things. "I'm gonna miss you." The words lingered in the air, fragile but final.

At the front door, Tanya stood her ground as the man outside inched closer to the screen, his face twisted in frustration.

She felt April shifting nervously behind her, tugging at her arm. "Tanya," April whispered urgently, "let me go out and talk to him." Tanya turned on her, eyes flashing. "You sure about this? After everything he's done? After everything you've told me?" April bit her lip, her eyes darting between Tanya's fierce stare and the shadowed figure beyond the door. She nodded faintly, though her body betrayed her-her hands trembled, her voice wavered, her shoulders hunched as if expecting a blow that hadn't yet come.

Tanya shook her head in disbelief. Her friend was about to walk willingly back into the storm she had just been rescued from. And yet, there was a part of Tanya that understood. Toxic love had a gravity stronger than logic, and April was caught in its orbit.

The man outside slammed his palm against the screen again, making both women flinch. His mouth moved in exaggerated shapes, but the words were drowned by the pounding of Tanya's heart in her ears. She didn't need to hear them. She knew threats when she saw them. "You should leave," Tanya said loudly, her voice firm, addressing him directly now. She leaned into the door as if sheer willpower could reinforce the flimsy mesh. "Before you get yourself into trouble." The man sneered, the kind of sneer that told her he wasn't used to being challenged-least of all by a woman. His hands curled into fists again, his shoulders rising like a predator ready to pounce. Tanya's throat went dry, but she refused to step back. Behind her, April whispered again, "Please, Tanya… let me just talk to him. I can calm him down." Tanya turned sharply, gripping April's shoulders. "Or you'll make it worse." April's eyes welled with tears. Her silence was the answer Tanya dreaded. Meanwhile, in the garage, Devin lingered at the hood of the cruiser, lost in a moment of quiet reverence. To anyone else, the car was nothing but steel and paint, a tool of the job. To him, it was memory itself—a thousand rides through siren-lit nights, conversations with partners who'd moved on, moments of triumph and tragedy.

He pressed his palm to the metal, feeling the cold bite of it against his skin. In the reflection of the hood, he saw his own eyes staring back, shadowed, serious, full of weight he rarely allowed himself to acknowledge. Duty called, but tonight, for the first time in a long while, Devin wondered what it cost.

CHAPTER 4

BREAKING POINT

The night had shifted from laughter and music to a sharp-edged tension that pressed against every wall of the apartment. At the front door, the figure was no longer just a shadow beyond the screen. He was fully visible now.

Hector

In his early thirties, with heavily tattooed arms coiled with inked stories of violence and survival. His stance was loose, unsteady, as though his body couldn't quite remember how to balance itself. His eyes were bloodshot, his lips slick with the lazy smirk of a man who had already lost control but refused to admit it. To a stranger, he could have been mistaken for any gang member prowling Chicago's streets after dark. But April knew him too well-or, perhaps, not at all anymore. "What do you want?" April demanded, her voice cracking despite her effort to sound steady. Hector's lips curled into a crooked grin. His words slurred, his Spanish accent heavier than usual. "Open the door, fool!" April's breath caught. She shook her head, clutching the edge of the frame as if it were the only thing keeping her standing. "You're drunk." "I'm not drunk," Hector shot back quickly, his body swaying even as he said it. His tone carried the wounded pride of a man desperate to maintain power. "You know me better than that." April's chest tightened. She thought of the man she once knew with warm smiles, promises whispered in the dark, the kind of charm that had once pulled her in so easily. That man was gone, replaced by the stranger swaying outside her best friend's door. "No," she whispered fiercely, her voice breaking under the weight of her own truth. "That's the problem. I don't know who you are anymore. Leave me alone!" For a split second, there was silence. The kind of silence that tricked you into thinking maybe he would listen. Maybe he would turn and stumble away into the night. But Hector was not a man who walked away.

With sudden violence, his right fist slammed forward. The brittle crack of wood giving way echoed through the apartment as his hand punched straight through the screen door. Splinters flew. April and Tanya screamed, their voices colliding with the sound of shattering wood. Before April could move, Hector's tattooed arm snaked through the hole, his hand snapping around her wrist like a vise. His grip was rough, bruising, pulling her toward him. "Come here!" he growled, dragging her closer, his breath hot with liquor and rage. April cried out, her body jerking against his pull, trying to wrench free. Tanya lunged forward, clawing at Hector's arm, desperate to break his hold. The thin frame of the door shook under the struggle, the mesh tearing wider.

In the garage, Devin paused mid-motion. The sharp BANG from upstairs reached him through the concrete and steel, faint but unmistakable. He froze, his body tense, eyes snapping upward as though he could see straight through the ceiling. For a moment, he waited-listened. The night air pressed in, heavy with stillness. Then, slowly, he exhaled. A smile crept across his face, the kind that showed every pearly white tooth, casual, unbothered. He shook his head, chalking it up to nothing more than the echoes of a rowdy birthday party. After all, the women had been drinking, laughing, dancing-noise was part of the night.

He turned back to the police cruiser, continuing his ritual, the weight of his gear clinking as he adjusted it. The car purred faintly as he checked the systems, unaware of the storm raging just a few feet above his head.

At the front door, chaos had erupted. April screamed as Hector's grip tightened, her body yanked forward so forcefully she crashed against the frame. The sharp snap of breaking glass rang out as her arm collided with the pane in the door. "April!" Tanya shouted, grabbing at her friend with both hands, trying to pull her back. But it was too late. A jagged edge sliced across April's skin, leaving a crimson trail down her forearm. She gasped in pain, her voice strangled as blood welled from the fresh cut. "Let her go!" Tanya shrieked, pounding against Hector's tattooed arm. "You're hurting her!" Hector only snarled, his grip unrelenting. His eyes burned with a feral intensity, the kind of look that promised destruction no matter what words were spoken. Behind them, the music had died completely, silenced by the violence unfolding at the door. But outside, the noise was growing.

The commotion had drawn attention. Neighbors stirred from their quiet routines. Doors opened. Lights flickered on in nearby apartments. Within moments, a small crowd had gathered, drawn to the mayhem spilling out onto the street. Murmurs spread among them-half in shock, half in gossip. Some pulled out their phones, recording. Others shouted warnings or encouragement, though none dared step too close. April's breath came in short gasps, her body trembling as she fought against Hector's pull. Blood dripped down her arm, staining the floor in bright, urgent drops. Tanya's fury surged, her voice rising above the chaos. "Let her go before someone calls the police!" But Hector only tightened his grip, his smile darkening.

COLLISION

The night air inside the garage was calm until it fractured with a sound that cut through Devin's world. "Devin!" The yell was sharp, panicked, feminine. It wasn't just noise-it was a plea. Tanya's voice carried urgency, desperation, and the kind of fear that made Devin's chest tighten. In that instant, his body moved before his mind could catch up.

He bolted from the cruiser, his boots slamming against the concrete. The echoes of his steps ricocheted through the garage as he lunged toward the stairwell. His muscles coiled and released like springs, each stride devouring the distance. He didn't bother with careful pacing. He skipped steps, taking the staircase in violent bursts-three at a time, shoulders brushing the narrow walls as he propelled himself upward. At the top, he burst through the door, lungs burning, eyes scanning in a split second. And then he saw it. The world slowed.

The intruder was inside now, his heavily tattooed arms locked around April in a vicious arm-twisting grip. April's face contorted in agony, her mouth open in a scream that barely left her throat. Blood still trickled from the cut on her arm, staining Hector's hand, slickening his grip as she fought uselessly against him. Her body arched under the pressure, her wrist bent at an angle it was never meant to endure. Hector's smirk was gone. His face was hard, animalistic. He was winning. "What the …" Devin's voice thundered, his chest heaving with rage.

Tanya's eyes snapped to him, wide with relief and fury all at once. She pointed a trembling finger toward Hector, her voice cracking as she cried, "He hit me!" That was all Devin needed to hear. Something in him snapped. He moved with the suddenness of a storm breaking free. One moment, Hector had the upper hand, and the next, Devin was on him with a force so violent it ripped April out of his grip. Devin's palm slammed into Hector's chest with such brutal precision that the man's body lifted off balance and crashed backward. The impact rattled the wall, a framed picture tumbling to the floor with a sharp crack of glass.

Hector's eyes went wide as he hit the wall, the air exploding from his lungs in a strangled gasp. For a fleeting moment, fear registered there. He hadn't expected this. He hadn't expected anyone bigger and stronger than him. And now, he panicked. Scrambling to regain control, Hector's hand darted to the nearest object within reach—a long, thin umbrella leaning against the corner by the door. His fingers curled around the handle, knuckles white as he yanked it free.

He brandished it like a weapon, his tattoos stretching as he tightened his grip. His lips curled back, revealing teeth gritted in desperation. With a guttural growl, he swung it wildly, the motion fast and fueled by adrenaline. But Devin was already reading him. He ducked, his body fluid, his instincts honed from years of training and discipline. The umbrella whooshed past his head, slicing the air with wasted fury. Devin's hand shot upward, faster than Hector expected. His fingers clamped around the umbrella's shaft, arresting its movement mid-swing. In one seamless motion, Devin yanked.

The force ripped the umbrella from Hector's hands effortlessly; it was as if the object itself had betrayed him. It clattered across the floor, useless now. For a heartbeat, the room went still again. Hector's chest rose and fell in rapid bursts, his eyes darting between the lost weapon and the towering figure in front of him. Then, with a roar born of humiliation, Hector lunged. His fist flew forward in a desperate punch. The knuckles connected-square against Devin's jaw. The sound of flesh against flesh echoed. Tanya gasped, April let out a strangled cry. The crowd gathering at the door pressed in closer, murmurs rippling through them. But Devin didn't flinch.

The punch landed, but it was like hitting a stone. Devin's head barely moved, his body unmoved, his eyes never leaving Hector's. The impact that should have staggered another man barely registered on him. Slowly, almost deliberately, Devin turned his gaze back to Hector. His eyes were cold now, stripped of humor, stripped of hesitation. They burned with a warning that made the air in the room thicken. Hector swallowed hard. For the first time, he realized just how much danger he was in.

The Grip of Control

Devin moved like a machine tuned for precision, his every motion clean, efficient, unrelenting. The room barely had time to catch its breath before he clamped down on Hector's wrist, twisting it with such speed and authority that the smaller man's defiance dissolved into panic. The crackle of bones shifting under strain echoed faintly, followed by Hector's grunt of pain. He jerked, flailed, tried to resist, but resistance against Devin was like pushing against a brick wall-unyielding and immovable.

In one smooth transition, Devin shifted his stance, his torso rotating, legs grounding him like rooted steel. The motion dragged Hector off balance, and within a blink, Devin's other hand was clamped firmly around the intruder's throat. The change was immediate. The bravado drained from Hector's face. The cocky grin, the violent slur of his words, the manic energy-all of it evaporated under the crushing power of Devin's grip. His menacing tattoos, his bad boy swagger, his alcohol-fueled rage meant nothing in the iron palm wrapped around his windpipe.

The room went silent except for the muffled gasps of April and Tanya, and the faint murmur of the neighbors who had gathered outside. All eyes locked on the sight of one man raising another as though he were weightless.

Hector's feet left the ground. It wasn't quick; it was deliberate. Devin lifted him slowly, controlled, with the calm strength of someone who knew exactly how much power he wielded. Hector's legs kicked wildly, a blur of denim and inked skin, his sneakers scraping uselessly against air. But it did nothing. The harder he fought, the tighter Devin's hand seemed to press into his throat. The veins in Hector's temples bulged as he gasped for breath, the sound ugly and broken. "What's your problem?" Devin asked, his voice low, almost conversational. The man in his grasp reeked of alcohol, but Devin remained in control. It wasn't a scream or a roar; it was worse than that. Calm. Cold. The kind of tone that unnerved everyone in the room because it made the violence feel controlled, clinical, inevitable.

Hector tried to answer, but his words came out as half-choked syllables. His kicks weakened, his arms flailed with less conviction. Still, he fought, but it was clear the fight was leaving him. Devin's eyes narrowed. He tilted his head slightly, studying the man he held suspended like a misbehaving child. "Are you done here?" The question wasn't rhetorical-it demanded an answer.

Hector coughed, his throat rasping under the pressure. Finally, words squeezed out, broken and choked. "Who da fuck are you? Put me down, homes!" Devin's lips pressed into a thin line. Then, slowly, he repeated the words back, his tone mocking but steady, his gaze locked into Hector's panicked eyes. "Who da fuck am I?" He leaned in closer, his voice dropping into a dangerous whisper. "I'm the one who's taking you to jail. That's who." The declaration landed heavier than the chokehold itself. It wasn't just a statement of fact-it was a promise.

Hector thrashed again, his fear shifting back into anger. "Man, fuck you!" he spat, though the words were hoarse, weak, stripped of their usual bravado. Devin's eyes flared with something darker, and for a moment the room felt smaller, the air thicker. He tightened his grip just slightly, enough to make Hector's eyes bulge. "Fuck me?" Devin echoed softly, dangerously. Then his voice sharpened into a blade. "No. Fuck you! You picked the wrong one." The room hung on the words. Tanya, clutching her chest, didn't breathe. April, her wrist still throbbing from Hector's earlier grip, didn't dare move.

Devin's gaze slid briefly toward April. She was trembling, her wide eyes shining under the glow of the still-turning disco ball above. Without breaking his hold on Hector, Devin reached over her head with one massive hand. There, on a side table cluttered with party favors and playful decorations, lay a ridiculous object—one of Tanya's gag gifts, a penis-shaped decorative hairpiece, cheap plastic and designed for laughter, not violence. But in Devin's hand, even something absurd became a weapon. "Open wide," he muttered. WHAM! The motion was swift, startling. He shoved the novelty hairpiece straight into Hector's mouth, headfirst. The intruder gagged instantly, his words smothered, his curses strangled into muffled nonsense. His eyes flared with shock, humiliation, fury-but he couldn't speak, couldn't spit the object free under Devin's crushing hold.

The room erupted with gasps and nervous laughs from the women who had been watching in shock. The absurdity of the act cut through the violence for only a heartbeat, but Devin's cold stare reminded everyone this wasn't a game. Slowly, deliberately, Devin lowered Hector back down, his feet finding the ground again. But the grip on his throat never loosened. Devin's palm stayed clamped, his authority absolute. Hector's sneakers squeaked as they touched the floor, his legs trembling, his pride shredded along with his voice.

He stood there, panting through his nose, muffled by the crude gag, caught between humiliation and the suffocating knowledge that he had no control left. Devin's grip remained steady, unshaken. The message was clear: Hector's fight was over.

Checkmate

The room still vibrated with tension, every woman frozen where she stood, eyes locked on the violent choreography playing out in the hallway. Devin's grip was unyielding, Hector's body still trembling under the pressure of the chokehold and the gag humiliation. But Devin wasn't done. With a sudden surge of motion, he spun Hector around, twisting his arm behind his back in one fluid movement. The crack of bones and sinew straining echoed, and Hector yelped, his body folding against the wall. His cheek pressed into the plaster, tattoos smeared against white paint.

The crude gag—Tanya's ridiculous novelty-slipped free from Hector's mouth. He spat it out with fury, sending the plastic projectile flying. It struck Devin across the cheek, WHAM!

The impact wasn't painful, not really, but it was insulting. The absurdity of it—the mocking toy hitting him square in the face-ignited something primal. Devin's eyes darkened. His jaw clenched. A guttural growl tore from his chest, not the kind of sound born from pain, but from fury.

In one violent motion, he snatched Hector away from the wall as though the man weighed nothing, spinning him like a rag doll. Before Hector could regain his footing, Devin slammed him back into the wall with bone-rattling force. The drywall groaned under the collision, a small crack splintering out from the point of impact. Hector's breath exploded from his lungs, a strangled cough echoing through the room. His defiance drained. His body sagged against the wall, but Devin didn't give him room to fall.

The women gasped again, some clutching their mouths, others exchanging glances that wavered between fear and awe. Tanya's heart thundered in her chest. She had seen Devin angry before, but never like this. This wasn't just anger—it was authority, control, a reminder of who he was when the badge was strapped to his chest. Devin's hand moved to his belt, the leather creaking under the shift. His fingers found the steel. A sharp click broke through the silence as he whipped out a pair of shiny handcuffs, their polished surface catching the dim light of the room. The sight alone made Hector's eyes widen. "Don't…" Hector croaked, his voice hoarse, cracking under fear.

Devin didn't hesitate. With a practiced flick of his wrist, he slapped one cuff around Hector's wrist, the steel snapping shut with finality. He jerked Hector's arm behind him, forcing the other wrist into place. The second cuff clicked shut with the same metallic bite. The sound was victory. The sound was final. Devin leaned in close, his chest heaving, his face inches from Hector's ear. His voice came out in ragged breaths, low but thunderous in its authority.

"Checkmate, asshole." The words landed heavier than fists. Hector groaned, his body sagging against the wall, the fight completely drained from him. His tattoos no longer made him look dangerous; they made him look foolish, reduced to inked warnings that no longer held weight against the man restraining him.

The crowd outside murmured louder, phones raised higher. This was no longer just a fight—it was a spectacle. Devin, still holding Hector firmly with one massive hand, turned his head slightly. The absurdity of the night had not gone unnoticed, and in a move that felt both casual and deliberate, he reached out toward the nearby table with his free hand.

The table was littered with remnants of the party-half-empty glasses, scattered decorations, and a large bowl filled with Planters peanuts. Without breaking his hold on Hector, Devin plunged his hand into the bowl, scooping out a generous handful.

He tossed a few into his mouth, crunching down loudly. The salt and crunch seemed almost comically out of place against the backdrop of violence and restraint, but somehow, in Devin's hands, it worked. The women stared, some in disbelief, some in admiration. Even Tanya, though still tense, couldn't suppress the flicker of a smirk tugging at her lips.

Devin chewed, swallowed, and then glanced toward the door as though daring anyone else to step forward. With Hector cuffed, peanuts in hand, and authority radiating from every line of his body, Devin began moving toward the exit. The intruder stumbled at his side, his dignity shattered, dragged like a captured animal before the audience that had watched his downfall. Devin didn't look back. The message was clear; Hector's party was over before it even began.

CHAPTER 5

THE LONG RIDE

The night had a strange way of resetting itself. Only minutes earlier, the apartment had been alive with screaming voices, a clash of rage and fear that shook the walls. Now, the outside world was still, as though the violence had been swallowed whole by the night air.

The streets lay deserted, the quiet broken only by the occasional hum of a distant car or the faint flicker of a streetlamp fighting to stay lit. Litter tumbled lazily across the pavement, pushed along by a wandering breeze.

From the driveway of the apartment building, a lone police cruiser rolled forward, headlights carving twin tunnels through the darkness. The black-and-white looked almost regal in its solitude, its polished frame reflecting every fragment of light it caught. Behind the wheel sat Officer Devin Crews. POLICE written across his chest, etched in his tactical ballistic vest. His jaw was tight, though his posture had relaxed into something that suggested complete control. He didn't need to check the rear seat to know Hector was there-slumped, cuffed, and humiliated. Still, Devin's eyes flicked up to the rearview mirror, his expression calm but sharp, the kind of look that reminded any man sitting in the backseat of a cruiser, who was in charge. The city lights blurred into streaks of color outside the squad car as officer Crews drove the perp towards the county lockup. Hector's gaze fixated on the thick glass and metal mesh separating the two men, representing the boundaries of different worlds. The radio crackled with an unintelligible dispatcher's voice, the sound swallowed by the low, insistent hum of the engine and the damp, cool air seeping in through the vents. It was a long dark drive, and one Devin had made countless times. "So…" Devin finally said, his voice smooth, almost conversational, like they were on nothing more than a late-night drive. "How should we do this?" Hector didn't respond. His body sagged against the seat, wrists bound, eyes glassy from the mix of adrenaline, alcohol, and defeat. He stared upward at the cruiser's ceiling, refusing to meet Devin's gaze in the mirror. His chest rose and fell unevenly, each breath a reminder of just how quickly power had slipped from his hands. The perp's mind was racing now. *"Damn, stupid. God, I'm so stupid. I know I should leave that girl alone.* He thought to himself. The drinking, the altercation, the panic—all rushing through his mind like a broken film reel. Each streetlight felt like judgement, and he could smell the stench of regret clinging to the vinyl seat. He focused on the reflection of city lights streaking across the glass, trying to iron out the frantic knot of fear in his gut. Another assault charge lingering. Whether it'd be simple assault or assault on law enforcement which carries a much severe punishment, was yet to be determined.

Devin smirked faintly, shaking his head as though amused by the silence. He tapped the steering wheel with one hand, his other hand resting easily by the gear shift. The street stretched out before them, long and empty, like a road that could lead anywhere. "Lights and sirens to county…" Devin mused aloud, his tone playful. "Or a quick stop on Dearborn for some action?" He asked the perp. The suggestion hung in the air like bait. Still, nothing from the backseat. Hector didn't even twitch. He just blinked, slow and heavy, his eyes glossy with defeat. His earlier bravado had drained completely, leaving behind a hollow shell of a man who had finally run out of words.

Devin studied him in the mirror for a beat longer. The silence didn't frustrate him. If anything, it gave him a strange satisfaction. He thrived in moments like this- where his authority was so absolute that no response was necessary. "Dearborn it is," he declared finally, his voice carrying the weight of finality. He adjusted his grip on the wheel, leaning back into the seat like a man who had just made an important decision.

His lips curled into a smile, faint but genuine, the kind of smile that spoke more of control than amusement. "I don't like going to county either," he continued, his tone almost conversational, like he was talking to an old friend instead of a cuffed intruder. "It's crowded with criminals. Can't stand 'em." The irony wasn't lost on him. From the backseat came a faint shift, Hector adjusting his shoulders against the leather, but he still refused to answer.

Devin's gaze lingered in the mirror a moment longer. For a fleeting second, their eyes almost met—Hector's dull and defeated, Devin's sharp and steady. It was a quiet standoff, one where words weren't needed.

Outside, the cruiser rolled smoothly through the empty street, its engine a steady hum against the silence of the neighborhood. Street after street slipped past them, each one darker and quieter than the last, as though the city itself had given way to their private journey. And in that solitude, Devin's words seemed to fill the night itself.

Dearborn Street

The projects at 122 Dearborn had always carried an edge of menace, but tonight it was transformed into something else entirely. The streets were alive with flashing lights and the restless buzz of radios. Squad cars were everywhere, angled across the road like jagged teeth, their red and blue beams slicing through the night. Barricades had gone up hastily, cutting off entry points and forcing onlookers back into shadows. Residents of the neighborhood stood in clusters just beyond the tape, their voices low but anxious, their faces reflecting the chaos they could only glimpse. Whatever had started here earlier had escalated into something bigger, darker. It wasn't just another night in the projects. This was something that would leave marks, long after the lights faded.

Devin's cruiser rolled in slowly, its engine humming low, headlights sweeping across the fractured scene. His hands tightened around the wheel as his eyes took everything in-the tension in the officers' stances, the urgency in their movements, the unmistakable sense that control had slipped from their grasp. "Holy shit," Devin muttered under his breath. "What'd I miss?" His words weren't loud, but the weight of them filled the space inside the car. He shifted in his seat, one hand drumming against the steering wheel, the other resting lightly near the gear shift. His eyes flicked up to the rearview mirror, finding Hector's reflection slouched in the backseat.

The man hadn't moved much since the ride began. His glossy eyes stared blankly, but Devin wasn't going to let him sit there without carrying the weight of what they were driving into. "You see what you've done, here?" Devin asked, his voice sharp but edged with a bitter humor. His gaze lingered in the mirror a beat longer, watching for any reaction. Hector blinked, but said nothing, his silence the only rebellion he had left. "Lighten up, dude, I'm just messing with you." Devin exhaled, shaking his head as he brought the cruiser to a controlled stop. From his vantage point, he could see officers crouching behind their cars, weapons drawn and pointed toward the looming silhouette of one of the high-rises.

Shouts echoed faintly in the distance—orders barked, replies shouted back-but the details blurred into the tense hum of a city holding its breath. He reached for the radio clipped at his shoulder. His thumb pressed down, the familiar click punctuating the moment. "Hey Rob," he said into the rover, his voice casual but carrying the weight of curiosity. "What'd I miss?" For a second, only static filled the cabin. Then the radio crackled to life, Rob's voice spilling through in bursts of static-laced urgency. "Started as a robbery," Rob said, his tone clipped, professional. "Now it's a hostage situation. You staying?" Devin snorted softly, shaking his head as though Rob could see him. "Nope. Not staying for that," he replied firmly. His eyes drifted back to the building, noting the tension radiating from every figure in uniform. "I'm getting outta here." The radio hissed before Rob's voice came again, lighter this time, almost teasing. "Good. We don't want you getting your hands dirty on your last day."

Devin's lips curved into a smirk. A chuckle slipped out, low and genuine, echoing faintly in the cruiser's confined space. "Damn right," he murmured, half to himself, half into the mic. For a moment, the air between them across the radio waves felt less like an exchange of duty and more like the easy banter of men who'd shared countless nights on the job. "We're gonna miss you, buddy," Rob added after a pause, his voice carrying the weight of camaraderie and something unspoken.

Devin's smirk softened. His eyes lingered on the flashing lights ahead, the barricades, the neighbors whispering in the shadows. His last day with this unit. It had come faster than he thought it would. He let the silence stretch for a beat longer, letting the words settle. Then the calm was broken. "Goddamnit," Rob's voice snapped over the channel, laced with frustration. "The letter boys just arrived. I guess they'll be taking over from here." Devin's brows lifted slightly as he leaned back in his seat. The phrase carried weight, even unspoken. Everyone in law enforcement knew who "the letter boys" were.

The feds.

When they showed up, the game changed. Local cops stepped back. Control shifted. Devin exhaled slowly, his hand tightening briefly around the wheel before relaxing. His reflection in the windshield was calm, composed, but his mind was already racing.

Letter Boys

The black SUV rolled in with the kind of presence that turned heads. Its tinted windows reflected the swarm of flashing lights, the chaos of police cruisers, and the restless crowd pressed behind barricades. The vehicle glided to a stop as though it owned the street, and when the doors swung open, silence rippled briefly through the scene.

Four figures emerged. They were cut from a different cloth than the local patrol officers standing guard. Windbreakers hugged their frames, dark and sleek, the unmistakable white letters stretched boldly across their backs: FBI. Their walk was casual but purposeful, shoulders squared, jaws set. They had that particular air-hip, cool, but serious-men who knew they didn't need to prove their authority. It followed them like a shadow, and even the beat cops shifted instinctively as they passed, creating a subtle gap in the field without a word exchanged. Local police officers who had been anxiously guarding the entry way to the apartment complex, instinctively stepped back as an Emergency

Response Team (ERT) van eased to a stop. The rear door swung open, revealing more federal agents in riot gears. The lead agent, a grizzly bearded man took command of the scene and began giving instructions. His voice was low but carried authority. In an instant, the air had changed, until a gunshot rang out from the fifth floor.

Officers huddle behind the barricade of police cars, their blue and white lights strobing against the drab brick of the apartment buildings. A thick tense silence ensued that was only broken by clipped, urgent chatter from police radios and the occasional muffled shout from a fifth-floor window. Snipers, nearly invisible in their positions on neighboring rooftops, scan the surroundings through high-powered scopes, their presence a silent promise of swift, decisive action should negotiations fail. The stood prepare to eliminate all imminent threats. The mobile command center, a large, unmarked van, sat idling away from view of the apartment windows.

Devin observed from behind the wheel of his cruiser, one hand draped lazily over the steering wheel, the other tapping rhythmically against the console. His lips curved faintly at the sight. Over the radio, Rob's voice broke in again, filled with a kind of admiration laced with envy. "I want one of those jackets," Rob drawled. "That's gonna be you someday, Devin. What took you so long anyway?" Devin let the words hang a moment before twisting slightly in his seat. His gaze drifted to the rearview mirror, then to the backseat itself. Hector was slumped there, motionless at first glance, the faint rise and fall of his chest the only sign he wasn't entirely gone. His head lolled against the seat, eyes shut, lips parted slightly in drunken slumber. Devin arched a brow. The corner of his mouth twitched. "Had a dance recital," he said into the radio, his tone bone-dry, cutting through the tension with humor only he could deliver. "My partner's in the backseat. Sleeping." A burst of static laughter came through, Rob's voice first to respond. "You still shakin' your ass for cash, D?" Devin hummed thoughtfully, dragging out the pause just long enough to make it sting. "Umm …" He let the syllable drawl, leaning into the tease.

That was all it took. Another officer chimed in from a nearby patrol car, his voice cutting in over the open channel, full of excitement and mischief. "Hey, Devin," the officer called, his laughter audible even through the crackle. "Can you teach me to shake my ass like that? I need something to fall back on after retirement!"

A ripple of chuckles carried faintly across the barricade line, even from officers close enough to overhear without the radio. The tension of the hostage situation was momentarily punctured by the humor-a relief valve they all needed, if only for a heartbeat. Then came the static again, sharper this time, followed by a voice that brooked no nonsense. "Hey! Hey!" The tone was firm, the authority behind it unmistakable. The nightshift supervisor. "Fellas, keep this channel clear for official police business. Save the gigolo talk for the breakroom." Silence reigned for a moment after, the reprimand sinking in. A few officers smirked quietly to themselves, the kind of rebellious grins that thrived on being chastised, but no one dared key up the mic again-at least not right away.

Inside Devin's cruiser, the momentary levity faded into stillness once more. He leaned back into his seat, his eyes flicking between an active crime scene and the FBI agents. He observed their every move. Their presence was undeniable, their movements sharp and efficient. A rustle from the backseat pulled his attention. Hector stirred. His head lifted sluggishly, eyes squinting against the assault of red and blue light streaming through the cruiser's windows. He blinked, confusion etched into every line of his face as he tried to piece together where he was, what had happened, and how the night had slipped from his control so completely.

Devin's gaze caught him in the rearview mirror. Their eyes met for a fraction of a second. Hector's hazy, clouded with defeat, Devin's sharp, steady, and utterly unmoved. A cruiser hummed softly around them, the outside world alive with chaos, but in that small capsule of steel and silence, the balance of power was crystal clear.

County or Station

The hum of the cruiser deepened as Devin dropped the gear into drive. A sudden surge pushed the vehicle forward, tires screeching faintly against the pavement as he peeled away from the barricaded street. The momentum jolted Hector violently against the backseat. His cuffed wrists clattered against the vinyl, his head snapping to the side before colliding with the frame of the door. "Ouch!" Hector groaned, his accent thick as he twisted against the restraints. "That hurts, homie. Take it easy. Don't be a dick."

Devin's grip on the wheel tightened just slightly, but his expression didn't change. His eyes flicked to the rearview mirror, catching the reflection of Hector's pained scowl. "That's it," Devin said flatly, his voice carrying the weight of finality. "I'm taking you to County Jail." The words landed like a hammer. Hector's face changed instantly. His earlier bravado slipped further, replaced with a twitch of unease. County. Everybody knew what County meant—crowded cells, hostile inmates, endless nights of noise and danger. It wasn't the kind of place you wanted to spend a weekend, even for someone like him who lived too close to chaos on the outside. "Wait, wait," Hector said quickly, his tone softening as his head lifted toward the front seat. His voice carried a hint of desperation. "I'm sorry, bro."

Devin raised an eyebrow but said nothing immediately. The silence stretched, filled only by the steady hum of the engine and the rhythm of tires rolling across cracked asphalt. The city around them blurred into streaks of neon and shadow, but inside the cruiser, the tension lingered.

Finally, Devin exhaled slowly through his nose, shaking his head as if considering something far heavier than the choice at hand. He glanced again into the mirror, meeting Hector's wide, uncertain eyes. "You know what, man," Devin said at last, his tone shifting. It was no longer the cold, clipped bark of authority, but something lighter, almost conversational. "I'm in a very good mood tonight, so I'll do you a solid." Hector's brows lifted. His lips parted slightly, hope flickering in his expression like a candle struggling against the wind. "It's Friday," Devin continued, letting the words hang as he slowed the cruiser just enough to emphasize the weight of what he was about to say. "And if I book you into County right now, they won't let you out until Monday. That's three days you don't want to live through. Trust me."

The truth of it settled over the backseat like a stone. Hector knew it. He'd heard the stories, lived parts of them himself. County jail was its own kind of hell, and Devin had just painted the picture clearly enough to make him swallow hard. "I'll take you to the station instead," Devin went on, his tone almost casual now. "You can cool off tonight, sober up, maybe get some sleep. Then they'll cut you loose in the morning." He let the promise linger, watching Hector carefully in the mirror. For a moment, Hector was silent. His eyes darted from the window to the floor, his lips working as though he wanted to argue but knew better.

Finally, Devin tilted his head, his eyes locking with Hector's reflection. "Deal?" The single word was a challenge. Not a request. Hector swallowed, his throat bobbing. His shoulders slumped slightly, the fight gone out of him. When he spoke, his voice was quiet but resigned. "Thanks, man." "Okay, we've got a deal," Devin responded.

"One last thing, make sure I never see your face again, got it?"

"I got it, homes."

Devin gave a single nod, satisfied. His hands tightened on the wheel, steering the cruiser smoothly down the dim-lit avenue. The city stretched out before them, its lights glowing against the night sky, but inside the car, the weight of the exchange lingered. For Hector, it was a reprieve. For Devin, it was another reminder of the thin line he walked every night-between law and mercy, between duty and humanity. Tonight, Hector was receiving mercy.

CHAPTER 6

CHICAGO PD

Chicago Streets gave way to silence as the cruiser turned into the long driveway of the police headquarters. The building loomed like a fortress, steel and stone washed in the glow of floodlights. To the public, it was a symbol of order; to those brought here in the back seat of a squad car, it was the beginning of a long, uncertain night. Devin eased the black-and-white toward the gate. He reached for his keycard, slid it across the sensor. A faint beep followed, then the heavy mechanical groan of the gate as it began to swing open. Metal shifted against metal, slow and deliberate, as though reminding everyone entering that nothing moved quickly here.

The cruiser slipped into the sally-port. The moment the rear bumper cleared, the gate rumbled shut behind them, sealing the space with an air of finality. Hector shifted uneasily in the back seat, his eyes darting to the walls that enclosed them. There was no way out now.

Devin killed the engine, climbed out, and rounded the rear of the vehicle with measured steps. He popped the trunk, the sound echoing off the concrete walls. From inside, he retrieved his service pistol, the metal gleaming faintly under the harsh fluorescent lights. With care born of ritual, he placed it into the secured compartment inside the trunk. The slam of the lid was sharp, decisive. Only then did he turn back to the cruiser's rear door. He opened it, reached in, and pulled Hector out. The man stumbled slightly, his wrists raw from the cuffs, his head ducked in resignation. The two men entered through a steel-plated door that buzzed open at Devin's swipe of his card. The door shut behind them with a final metallic thud.

The holding room was cold, sterile, and unforgiving. The faint hum of fluorescent lights filled the silence, punctuated only by the whir of a computer resting on a steel desk. Mounted to the wall was a camera, its black lens unblinking, waiting. Devin guided Hector inside, his hand firm but not cruel on the man's arm. He positioned him near the far wall where tape markings outlined footprints on the linoleum floor. "Stand on the wall and face the camera," Devin instructed, his voice calm, steady.

Hector glanced around, eyes darting from the desk to the camera, then to the door that had sealed shut behind them. His throat bobbed as he swallowed, then he obeyed. He stepped onto the footprints and lifted his chin toward the lens. Devin slid into the chair at the desk. His fingers moved swiftly across the keyboard, the clatter filling the sterile air. The mounted camera flickered to life, its red light glowing like a watchful eye. "Okay, here we go…" Devin said, his tone light but professional. His gaze flicked up briefly to the man in front of him. "How are the cuffs—too tight?" Hector's lips parted. His voice was lower now, stripped of earlier swagger, softened by fatigue. "Not really," he admitted, the accent in his words rough but clear. Then, with a surprising edge of sincerity, he added, "Thank you for not being too rough with me. The last guy that arrested me was a major asshole."

Devin arched a brow, his fingers pausing for a second on the keyboard. His expression didn't change much, but in his eyes there was the faintest flicker of amusement. Before he could reply, the camera flashed. The burst of light was sharp, sudden, catching Hector off guard. He blinked, grimaced, his head jerking slightly as though he'd been struck. "Turn to the right," Devin instructed smoothly. Hector complied, shoulders tense, his profile now square to the lens. Another flash. "Turn around and face the glass." Hector turned, exhaling through his nose, his eyes fixed on the two-way glass that gave nothing back but his own reflection. The camera clicked one last time, capturing his image—the mugshot that would follow him longer than the bruises fading on his wrists.

Devin typed a few more keystrokes, then rose from his chair. His movements were efficient, practiced, stripped of any wasted energy. "Alright," he said, his voice clipped but not unkind. "We're done here." The corridor beyond was narrow, its walls lined with peeling paint and the faint smell of disinfectant. Devin walked ahead, his hand guiding Hector, who shuffled quietly, his eyes downcast. Every step echoed, the sound bouncing between steel doors and concrete floors.

They stopped before a heavy cell door. Devin swiped his card again, the lock clicking open with a mechanical groan. He swung it wide, the hinges shrieking faintly. The cell was small, barely more than a box of cinderblock walls and a steel bench bolted to the floor. The fluorescent light above buzzed faintly, casting the space in a flat, unforgiving glow.

Devin turned Hector around. The man stood still as the officer removed the cuffs, the click of metal releasing loud in the confined space. Hector rubbed his wrists, relief washing briefly across his face as he flexed his hands. The skin was red, slightly swollen, but free. For a moment, their eyes met—Hector's searching, Devin's steady and unreadable. Then the door swung shut with a heavy clang. The sound reverberated through the concrete like a verdict. Hector turned slowly, staring at the steel that now separated him from the world outside. His chest rose and fell with shallow breaths. His fingers traced the faint marks left by the cuffs, as though the pressure of them lingered long after they were gone.

It was then, as silence wrapped around him, that the severity of his situation fully sank in. The swagger, the taunts, the bravado—none of it mattered here. Inside these walls, stripped of his weapons and his audience, Hector was just another man in a cell. And he knew it.

The break room at Chicago PD Headquarters wasn't much to look at, but for the men and women who filed through its doors every night, it was a sanctuary. The walls were painted in an unconvincing shade of beige, somewhere between dull coffee and tired plaster, and the air always smelled faintly of burnt coffee and reheated leftovers. A television mounted in the corner played a local news channel on mute, its subtitles crawling across the screen.

The long table in the middle bore the scars of years of use-scratches, faint gouges, coffee rings that no cleaning solution could erase. Still, it was here that friendships were forged, jokes traded, and the silent stress of the job momentarily set aside. Officer White, lean and tired-looking, brushed past Devin as the door swung shut behind him. White nodded once in acknowledgment but didn't say a word. That was White's way-quiet, efficient, never lingering longer than necessary. Inside, several officers were already settled in. Sergeant Bloom occupied the largest chair at the head of the table. He was a man of the streets and of his own appetites—forties, stocky, his uniform stretched just slightly around his midsection. Fifteen years on the force had left him with both a sharp wit and a body softened by too many late-night meals. Tonight, he had brought a home-cooked dish, the rich smell of seasoned meat and potatoes wafting through the room. Beside him sat Officer Brown. Young, sharp-eyed, still wearing the freshness of someone in their twenties who hadn't yet been weathered by the grind of the job. Brown idolized men like Bloom but carried himself with the restless energy of someone eager to prove his worth.

The door closed softly behind Devin as he stepped into the room, a soft drink in one hand and a crunch bar in the other. His presence drew attention almost instantly, though he didn't carry himself like someone demanding it. Brown was the first to break the silence. His palms smacked against the tabletop, beating out a rhythm that sounded like a drumline, each strike echoing through the small room. The sound, a boisterous backdrop to his bellowing announcement. His grin was wide, mischievous, the kind of grin that made Devin shake his head before the words even came. "Oh, oh! The fed is here," Brown announced, his voice full of mock ceremony, but the words were in synch with every beat of the table.

Devin's eyes narrowed slightly, his mouth tugging into a dry half-smile. "Oh stop it," he said, his tone flat, unamused but not truly offended. "I'm not the fed. I'm just gonna be working for them." That was enough to earn a low chuckle from Bloom, who paused mid-bite to waggle his fork in Devin's direction. "But isn't that the goal though?" Bloom asked, his mouth still full, his eyes twinkling with good-natured ribbing. Devin shrugged, setting his drink on the table. "Yeah. Once I get my foot in the door, then I'm gonna apply." The response was matter-of-fact, but underneath it lay something heavier—a quiet ambition, one tied not just to personal pride but to legacy. Devin didn't need to say it aloud; they all knew what drove him.

Bloom leaned back in his chair, the wood creaking under his weight. He studied Devin for a long moment before smirking. "Like father, like son, huh?" The words landed with a familiarity that made Devin glance briefly at the floor before lifting his gaze again. His father's shadow loomed long, even here in the laughter and the stale smell of reheated food. "Sure thing," Devin replied finally, his voice steady, controlled. "But until then, my detail is to whip those new recruits into shape." There was a pause as Devin cracked open his soft drink. The fizz erupted in a sudden rush, foam rising to the lip of the can until it threatened to spill over. Devin lifted it quickly, sipping off the excess with practiced ease. He tore into the crunch bar next, unwrapping the foil slowly before snapping off a piece. "Gotta have my protein," he added dryly, his tone intentionally flat, as though making a joke only he fully appreciated. The others chuckled quietly, shaking their heads. Bloom, however, set down his fork with deliberate slowness. His face softened for just a moment, sincerity slipping through the banter. "It's your last night with us," he said. "So take it easy out there."

The room grew still. The gravity of the words lingered longer than the laughter had. Everyone knew what "last night" meant. It wasn't just the end of a shift. It was the end of an era. Devin was moving on, stepping toward something bigger, and whether they admitted it aloud or not, the others felt the weight of that departure. Brown was the one to break the silence, his grin returning, though softer this time. "Too late," he said, leaning back in his chair. "He already busted a perp tonight." The words set off a ripple of chuckles across the room. A few officers shook their heads, others muttered under their breath, but all of them glanced toward Devin, waiting for his reaction.

Devin, for his part, remained unfazed. He didn't bother to smile, didn't bask in the acknowledgment. He simply took another sip of his drink, his face unreadable. That was Devin's way-steady, composed, never giving more than was necessary. Sergeant Bloom, unwilling to let the room slip into silence again, suddenly pushed back his chair with a scrape. He rose to his feet, grabbing his duty belt with both hands as though preparing for a performance. His chest puffed out, his face contorted, and then it came-a loud, obnoxious belch that rattled the air and drew groans and laughter from everyone present. "Okay, heroes," Bloom announced loudly, his voice booming with mock authority. "Let's go out there and fight crime. Last I checked, it ain't gonna fight itself."

The room erupted with laughter, the tension shattered in an instant. Even Devin allowed himself the faintest of smirks, though his eyes carried a weight the others didn't notice. Because while they laughed and joked, while they filled the room with camaraderie and the small comforts of routine, Devin knew this was his farewell tour. Every sound, every face, every exchange-it was all part of a chapter he was closing. And tomorrow, the world would look different.

CHAPTER 7

AN OLD FRIEND

The kitchen smelled faintly of coffee and dog food, an odd but familiar blend that Tanya had grown used to over the years. Morning light spilled in through the half-open blinds, painting warm stripes across the counter and the refrigerator. The hum of the old appliance filled the otherwise quiet apartment. Tanya bent low to refill Baxter's water bowl, her ponytail swinging forward over her shoulder. The German shepherd circled impatiently at her feet, nails clicking against the tile floor, his soft whimpering the kind of sound only a dog could make-half plea, half anticipation. "There you go," Tanya murmured, her voice gentle but firm. She topped the bowl, set it down, and added a biscuit beside it for good measure. Baxter dove in immediately, lapping noisily at the cool water before crunching into his treat. Tanya smiled despite herself. "Enjoy. We'll go for a walk later."

The refrigerator door bore the reminders of a shared life: a magnet holding up Devin's dental appointment slip, a couple of faded photographs-one of the two of them at the beach, another of Baxter as a puppy-and a child's crayon drawing given to Devin by the neighbor's kid. It was simple, modest, lived-in.

She wiped her hands on her tights and started toward the garage, following a muffled, rhythmic noise that had been tugging at her attention for the past few minutes. The closer she got, the louder it became—a steady thump punctuated by grunts of exertion. When she pushed the door open, the scene revealed itself.

The garage, stripped of its vehicle, had become a shrine to discipline. Dumbbells lined the far wall, neatly stacked. A heavy punching bag swung slightly from the rafters, vibrating from the impact of recent blows. The walls were plastered with posters of bodybuilders in impossible poses, frozen mid-flex, their physiques both inspiration and intimidation. The air smelled of iron and sweat. In the center of it all was Devin. His gray shirt clung to him, soaked with perspiration, his arms and shoulders glistening as he struck the bag with fierce precision. Each punch was sharp, controlled, as though he were exercising something more than just energy. He hadn't noticed Tanya yet; his focus was too deep, his breathing ragged but purposeful. "I told you to wait for me," Tanya called out, leaning against the doorway, her tone somewhere between reproach and affection.

Devin turned, chest heaving, his face lit with the kind of half-grin that came only when he was caught red-handed. "Jump in," he said, still out of breath. Tanya didn't hesitate. She grabbed a pair of gloves from the shelf, slid them on with a practiced tug, and moved toward the bag. Her movements were fluid, automatic—her body remembering what her mind didn't need to command.

WHAM! The first kick echoed like a drumbeat.

WHAM! The second shook the bag, chains rattling overhead.

WHAM! The third landed solid, clean, powerful.

Then came the punches-quick, sharp, unrelenting. Her fists became a blur, striking with the confidence of someone who had done this a hundred times before. Devin watched her with the faintest smirk as he dropped to the floor for pushups, his muscles tightening with every press. They switched places seamlessly, a rhythm between them, unspoken but strong. Devin hammered the bag, his fists like pistons, while Tanya dropped for sit-ups, her breathing steady, her gaze fixed on the ceiling. It was more than a workout; it was ritual, bonding, a language only they spoke.

By the time they collapsed side by side on the floor, backs pressed against the cool wall, both were drenched in sweat. Their chests rose and fell in tandem, the silence between them filled only by the faint hum of the overhead light and the sound of Baxter's occasional bark from the kitchen. Tanya tilted her head toward him. "Baxter is waiting for us." Devin let out a low chuckle. "Yeah, I heard you two talking in there." Without warning, he sprang up, crossing the room with renewed energy. Tanya frowned in confusion until she saw where he was headed.

In the far corner stood an object that had once made her laugh out loud when Devin first installed it: a stripper pole, gleaming from floor to ceiling, polished as though it belonged in some neon-lit club. At first, she thought it was a joke. But Devin had insisted it was for "core strength training." Now, he wrapped one hand around it, spun himself gracefully, and broke into a mock-sexy number. His hips swayed with exaggerated flair, his shirtless body twisting in ways that were both ridiculous and undeniably impressive. Tanya laughed, clapping her hands, shaking her head as she watched him perform. "You're crazy," she said through her laughter, her eyes shining.

He slid down the pole with a final flourish, hopped over, and flopped onto the ground beside her again. They slapped a high-five, the sound sharp in the otherwise quiet garage. For a moment, everything was light. Then Tanya's tone shifted. "You start Monday, right?" Devin didn't answer right away. He just nodded once, his eyes fixed straight ahead. His jaw tightened, the weight of the question pulling him into silence. Tanya studied him carefully. "You're getting closer," she said softly. "Your dad would be very proud."

The air thickened instantly. The room now seemed heavier, quieter. Devin's face betrayed what he usually tried to hide-sadness creeping through the cracks, the shadow of grief that never fully went away. "Yeah," Tanya continued, her voice quieter now, almost a whisper. "I miss him too." Devin's lips pressed into a thin line. He exhaled slowly before speaking. "I know. But…he was ready. He told me that during his final days."

He shifted, turning to face her, his eyes glistening under the dim light. Tanya waited, patient, giving him space to say what needed to be said. Devin continued after mustering up the courage. "He said the pain was excruciating. It was … it was very hard watching him go out like that." Devin's voice cracked slightly as it often did when he spoke of his father. His hands curled into fists on his knees. "I can still see it. The way he tried to smile through it. The way he tried to protect me from the truth even at the very end." His throat tightened, words catching, but he forced them out. "He was ready to go. He'd made peace with it. Spent half his career taking down Russian mobsters, right up until the very end. He never quit." Tears welled in his eyes, spilling despite his efforts to hold them back. His voice softened, breaking. "It was just…so damn hard watching him go like that."

Tanya's heart ached at the sight. She reached across the space between them, her hand finding his. She squeezed lightly, grounding him, her gaze steady on his. "Hey," she said gently. "You don't have to carry all of that alone. I'm right here." Devin turned his head slightly, his eyes locking with hers. The redness around them betrayed the tears, his strength crumbling in the intimacy of her presence. For a long moment, neither spoke. Silence became their shared language, filled with understanding, with grief, with love.

Finally, Tanya broke it, her voice steady but warm. "Let's go enjoy our weekend." The simplicity of the words carried weight. A reminder that life, no matter how heavy the past, still stretched forward. Devin blinked, exhaled, and nodded slowly. His grip on her hand tightened, a silent acknowledgment, a promise. They sat there a while longer, leaning against the wall, sweat cooling on their skin, their breaths slowly returning to normal. Outside, the faint sound of the city hummed on, indifferent to the quiet war of grief and hope inside that garage. And for Devin, as much as for Tanya, the weekend ahead felt like a lifeline, one last chance to hold onto the simple things before the weight of Monday returned.

When Devin came upstairs, Tanya was already slipping her feet into her walking shoes, her hand instinctively reaching for the doggie bag hanging from the closet knob. "Give me a second," he told her before bolting into the bedroom. Tanya searched for keys, waste bags and treats as she waited for Devin. He reappeared a few minutes later with the dog's leash in hand. They moved in a silent, comfortable choreography of a long-established couple, each knowing the steps; both casting an expectant glance towards the door where a low, insistent whine was beginning to rise. "Okay, buddy," Devin murmured, clicking the heavy leather into the dog's collar, "time to go."

The air in the park smelled faintly of cut grass and damp earth, a reminder that spring was in full bloom. Children laughed in the distance, chasing each other around slides and swings, while joggers passed with earbuds tucked firmly in place, their strides measured and unbothered by the chatter of the world around them. The sky was a clear blue, interrupted only by the occasional drift of a cottony cloud. Devin and Tanya walked side by side along the path, Baxter's leash stretched loosely between Tanya's hand and the eager dog. The German shepherd's ears flicked at every sound, his body language shifting from alert to relaxed and back again with every passerby.

Baxter had grown into himself. What once was a clumsy, oversized pup now moved with strength and purpose. His paws thudded against the gravel in quick succession, muscles beneath his coat flexing with unrestrained energy. Tanya often joked that he was the only "child" they could handle together without arguments. Devin never said it out loud, but there was something grounding about the dog—something loyal and uncomplicated. The wind picked up, carrying the soft rustle of leaves, sending a cascade of pollen drifting lazily across their path. Tanya adjusted her grip on the leash, tightening slightly as Baxter sniffed the ground. Then it happened-suddenly, violently, like a coiled spring released. Baxter bolted.

The leash yanked forward so abruptly that Tanya almost lost her balance. She squealed, half-laughing, half-panicked as she stumbled forward, her sneakers skidding across the path. Her arms flailed for a moment before she caught herself, knees bent, trying not to fall. "Baxter!" she shouted, but the dog was already focused on something else—a Labrador across the grass, tail wagging, inviting mischief. "Help me!" Tanya laughed, shooting Devin a desperate glance.

Devin reached instinctively toward the leash but stopped halfway. His pocket buzzed, and a shrill ringtone cut through the moment. He frowned, patting his jeans until he pulled his phone free. "Sorry," he muttered, distracted. "My phone's ringing." Tanya gave him a sharp look, but he was already fumbling with the device. By the time he raised it to his ear, the ringing had stopped. A voicemail notification blinked across the screen. Devin tapped it, curiosity pulling him out of the moment. A man's voice filled his ear, grainy with static but unmistakably familiar. "Hey, 'DC,' it's Mike. I'm in town for the weekend. I'm doing the Muscle-mania show at the Grand Hotel. Come through and show support. It would be like old times. Okay, see you, buddy." Devin froze for a moment, staring out across the park without really seeing it. Mike. It had been years since he'd heard that voice outside of memory. Years since he'd stepped foot in the world of bodybuilding competitions, stage lights, and cheering crowds. A part of him-buried but not dead-stirred at the mention of Muscle-mania. He looked up just in time to see Tanya, now sitting on the ground, her rear planted firmly in the grass, defeated. Baxter had dragged her to the Labrador and was happily sniffing away, oblivious to her frustration. Her expression, when she looked at Devin, was half-exasperated, half-amused. A sheepish grin tugged at her lips as if to say, Don't you dare laugh at me. Devin slipped his phone back into his pocket and crossed his arms. "This ain't break time," he said, his tone deliberately flat. Tanya narrowed her eyes at him, her glare sharp enough to cut through steel.

Devin relented with a small chuckle, extending his hand. "You need help?" She took it, and he pulled her to her feet with one smooth motion. Tanya dusted the grass from her tights, shaking her head. "He's getting too big," she said, glancing at Baxter, who was now wagging his tail triumphantly, oblivious to the chaos he'd caused. "Are you hurt?" Devin asked, scanning her quickly, eyes lingering on her knees and elbows. "Just a little scratch," Tanya replied, lifting her arm to show a faint red mark. It wasn't serious, but the sting was fresh. "You're a nurse," Devin teased, his lips quirking into a grin. "You got this." Tanya rolled her eyes, though the corners of her mouth betrayed her amusement. "Being a nurse doesn't mean I want to play patient on my days off." They stood there for a moment, watching Baxter, who had now rolled halfway onto his back, pawing at the Labrador in clumsy affection. Other dog owners chuckled as they walked by, their smiles carrying the universal recognition of shared chaos.

Devin bent down, shortening the leash with a firm tug. "You need to get this under control," he muttered. Tanya arched a brow. "Me? He listens to you better than me. Why don't you try?" Devin crouched lower, snapping his fingers at Baxter. The shepherd's ears perked immediately, his playful distraction cut short. Within seconds, he padded back toward Devin, obedient as ever, tongue lolling, chest heaving with happy pants. Tanya crossed her arms. "Of course. Just like that. You're the favorite." Devin smirked, scratching behind Baxter's ear. "Nah, he's just smart enough to know who's boss." She bumped him with her shoulder as they resumed walking. "Oh please. You spoil him more than I do. Don't act tough." Devin didn't answer. His thoughts were drifting back to the voicemail, to Mike, to the mention of Muscle-mania. He felt Tanya's gaze linger on him, curious, questioning, though she didn't ask. Not yet. She knew him well enough to let him decide when to share.

The path curved around a grove of trees, and the wind picked up again, rustling the leaves like whispered secrets. Devin squeezed the leash tighter in his hand, his other brushing against his phone in his pocket, the weight of the message heavy despite its simplicity.

Old times.

It echoed in his head, stirring memories of sweat, lights, and applause. A version of himself that still lived beneath the uniform, waiting. Beside him, Tanya reached for his hand, lacing her fingers through his. He glanced at her, saw the slight smile on her lips, and let out a breath he hadn't realized he was holding. For now, the walk continued. But the seed had been planted, and Devin knew-whether he wanted it or not-something was stirring back to life.

CHAPTER 8

FBI

The sedan rolled to a slow stop at the curb, its paint dulled by years of city weather but still carrying a sheen when caught by the morning sun. The hum of the engine died as Devin leaned slightly out of the open window, his eyes lifting to take in the building that towered above him. The FBI Chicago Field Office wasn't flashy. Its architecture was all glass and concrete, sharp lines and no-nonsense design. But to Devin, it was majestic. The symbol of something bigger than himself. A place where the whispers of his father's legacy seemed to echo. He squinted against the light, letting his gaze linger on the broad façade, the emblem etched near the entrance. His chest rose with a measured breath, that subtle mix of nerves and excitement only moments like this could bring. "Damn," he muttered softly, mostly to himself. The driver, a fellow officer doing him a favor, smirked without looking. "You gonna get out or just drool at it all day?" Devin chuckled, shaking his head. "Nah. Just taking it in. You only get one first time seeing this up close."

The car pulled forward, circling the perimeter, slipping into the shadows of the parking structure. The building loomed above as though watching them, its mirrored windows catching slivers of the city skyline. Devin sat back, but his eyes never left the sight until concrete swallowed the view whole. He couldn't help it. This was more than a building— it was the next step. A doorway into a future his father had wanted for him, one he'd promised himself he'd earn. Back across the city, Devin stepped out of the sedan and into the cool shadow of the parking structure. He adjusted his jacket, squared his shoulders, and walked toward the elevator that would bring him closer to his future. For him, today was about possibilities. Dressed in a tailored suit, he navigated a sidewalk and stepped into an archway leading into the building. A revolving door greeted him, as he felt a cool rush of recycled air that hung in the lobby. The polished marble floor reflected the weak morning light filtering through the high, arched windows. He flashed his badge to the armed security guard who returned a satisfying nod and pointed him in the right direction. Devin looked like a man ready to trade the chaotic energy of policing for the structured intensity of the Bureau.

Across town, life pulsed at a very different rhythm. The emergency ward at Memorial Hospital was its usual mix of ordered chaos. Monitors beeped in staccato rhythms, the low murmur of voices rose and fell like waves, and the occasional cry or laugh punctured the steady hum. Nurses moved briskly between stations, their hands practiced, their eyes sharp.

Tanya sat hunched over a terminal, typing in patient data with rapid precision. Her ponytail swayed as she leaned forward, biting her lip in concentration. The fluorescent lights above buzzed faintly, casting her skin in a pale glow. She'd grown used to this pace—the endless charts, the constant ringing phones, the unpredictable flow of emergencies that shaped her every shift. But even so, no amount of routine could dull the instinctive tension that came whenever the ward shifted suddenly. The phone on the desk rang, sharp and urgent. Tanya glanced up just as her co-worker grabbed the receiver. A clipped exchange, a widening of eyes, and then the call ended abruptly. "Gunshot victim! Lobby!" The announcement rippled through the room like a bolt of electricity. Chairs scraped. A stretcher screeched as it was pulled into motion. Nurses who'd been calm one moment were suddenly all fire and focus. A doctor barked orders. "AED, stretcher, let's move.

Go, go!" Tanya pushed back from her chair, already on her feet. Her heartbeat quickened, not with fear but with clarity. This was what she'd trained for, what she thrived on.

The team clustered at the elevator, pressing the button repeatedly as if urgency could bend machinery to their will. The light above remained stubborn, unmoving. Seconds dragged, each one heavier than the last. "This is taking too long," Tanya muttered under her breath. Without hesitation, she snatched the AED from the nurse beside her. "I'll go!" Before anyone could object, she bolted toward the stairwell. The heavy door clanged shut behind her as she pounded down the stairs two at a time, the weight of the device clutched to her chest. Her lungs burned, but she didn't slow. By the time she burst into the lobby, the sight before her was chaos incarnate.

A man lay on the cold tile floor, body jerking violently as convulsions wracked him. Blood pooled beneath his shirt, staining the white fabric crimson. His face was pale, twisted in agony. A small crowd of bystanders hovered, their fear palpable, their inaction louder than their presence.

Tanya dropped to her knees beside him, the AED already sliding from her arms. Her voice cut through the panic like a scalpel. "You!" she snapped, pointing at a young man crouched nearby, his hands trembling. "Open it!" His eyes widened, but he obeyed, fumbling with the case until the device sprang to life with mechanical chirps. Tanya didn't wait. She ripped open the victim's shirt, her hands slick with blood before she even realized it. Her stomach twisted at the warmth against her skin, but she forced herself steady. "Stay with me," she muttered to the man, though his eyes rolled back, his body betraying him. She grabbed the sticky pads, pressed one to his chest, but the adhesion faltered against coarse hair. Frustration flared hot in her chest. She scraped, pressed harder, adjusted, her hands working faster than thought. Finally-connection.

The machine beeped its readiness. Tanya's pulse raced with it. "Clear!" she shouted. The jolt hit the man's body like a thunderclap, arching him upward before slamming him back to the ground. Gasps erupted from the onlookers. For a moment, nothing. Then-a breath. Shallow, uneven, but there. His chest rose, fell. Stabilization, fragile but present. Relief flooded Tanya's veins, but there was no time to savor it. The rest of the team arrived in a rush—doctor, nurses, the elevator finally releasing its captives.

The doctor knelt, eyes scanning quickly. "Great job," he said, genuine respect in his tone before barking to the team, "Get him to the OR. Now!" The stretcher clattered into place, lifting the man from the floor. They wheeled him away, blood trailing faintly on the tiles. Tanya sat back on her heels, her hands trembling, her palms sticky with red. Her breath came heavy, ragged, but her eyes stayed locked on the retreating team until the doors swung shut.

A moment of silence settled over the lobby. The crowd, still frozen, slowly dispersed, their whispers hushed. Tanya's co-worker touched her shoulder. "You saved him," she said softly. Tanya exhaled, her shoulders sagging as the adrenaline began to ebb. She wasn't sure if the words comforted or haunted her. In her line of work, "saved" was only temporary-until the next moment, the next crisis, the next fragile life hanging by a thread. Still, she pushed herself to her feet, blood staining her scrubs, determination already hardening again. There was no time to linger. There never was. For Devin, today was about possibilities, for Tanya, it was survival. And though they didn't yet know it, the paths they were on-different but intertwined-would soon collide in ways neither could have imagined.

Baptism by Bureau

The air inside the FBI Chicago Field Office carried a weight all its own—part history, part pressure. The walls seemed to vibrate with the collective echoes of briefings past, strategies plotted, and decisions made that would never find their way into the public eye. Devin Crews stepped into the briefing room, shoulders squared, attire crisp, a hint of cologne clinging faintly to him. He looked sharp—he had made sure of that. His shoes were polished, his tie straightened, his hair freshly lined. It wasn't just vanity; it was respect. This room was not the place to arrive sloppy.

Rows of agents filled the room, their jackets draped across the backs of chairs, their notepads already scribbled with lines of shorthand that only they could decipher. The low murmur of conversation died down as Supervisor Harold Benson's gaze lifted to the doorway. "There he goes," Benson said, his voice warm but commanding, the kind that naturally carried to every corner of the room without needing a microphone. "Agents, you all remember Officer-" He corrected himself with a deliberate pause, his smile widening. "I mean Detective Crews." The applause that followed surprised Devin. It wasn't thunderous, but it was genuine. The kind of polite, professional acknowledgment reserved for someone who had earned at least a little respect before ever stepping into this room. Devin's throat tightened, though he managed a nod. Benson gestured broadly toward him. "Congratulations, and welcome on board."

There was an ease to Benson's presence, a confidence born of decades navigating rooms like this. His suit fit well, his graying hair trimmed neat, but what stood out most was the twinkle of humor in his eyes. "The people at Chicago PD were gracious enough to let us borrow their detective," Benson continued, "to revamp our physical training program. We've got him for sixty days. I hope that's enough time to whip us all into shape." He rubbed his belly with exaggerated flair, and laughter scattered across the room. Devin smiled faintly, though his eyes wandered toward the portraits mounted along the walls-black-and-white photographs of past agents, their stern faces a gallery of sacrifice and achievement. He wondered how many had lived to retire, how many had died with unfinished work still gnawing at them. "That goes for me too," Benson added, patting his midsection. From the back of the room, a voice rang out. "You've gained a few pounds, sir!" The room erupted in laughter, louder this time, the kind that carried relief.

Benson's head snapped toward the sound with mock indignation. "Who said that?" More laughter followed, though no one owned up to it. Devin chuckled along but kept scanning the room, cataloging faces, mannerisms, posture. Old habits from the street—observe first, talk later. Benson let the room settle before turning back toward Devin. "How does that sound, Crews?" The question cut through Devin's thoughts, snapping him back. He stood a little straighter, voice firm. "I'm here to serve, sir-in any way, shape, or form." The response earned a ripple of murmurs, a few chuckles. He knew how it sounded-half formal, half eager-but he didn't regret it. Better earnest than flippant.

From the third row, a whisper carried just far enough. Agent Christopher Mack, early forties with sharp features and an expression that seemed permanently skeptical, leaned toward a colleague. "He's just a meathead with muscles." Devin didn't flinch. He'd heard worse, on the streets, in locker rooms, even from fellow officers who thought his size and dedication to the gym made him more brawn than brain. He let it slide, though he caught the faint smirk of the agent Mack had whispered to. Benson, oblivious or simply choosing to ignore the comment, pressed on. "Agent Mack will be your liaison. Get with him later to discuss your details." The room shifted, and this time it was Mack's turn to look unsettled. His jaw tightened, and the faint smile vanished. Benson clapped his hands together. "Okay! If you're Alpha Team, remain in your seats. Everyone else, you're dismissed." Chairs scraped against the tile as agents rose. Conversations resumed in low tones as bodies funneled toward the exits. Within a minute, the room had thinned, leaving only seven agents scattered among the front rows.

One of them walked to the projector, flicked a switch, and the whir of the machine filled the quiet. The screen lit up, first with static, then with an image that sharpened into focus: a man's face. Hard features. A hint of scars around the eyes. Possibly Russian, judging by the name scrawled in block letters beneath the photo.

Benson waited until the door clicked shut before resuming, his tone shifting. The humor faded, replaced by something heavier. Devin's eyes locked on the image. Whoever this man was, he was no small-time street thug. The posture, the gaze, the way the photo itself seemed to carry menace, meant he was someone dangerous. The room settled into silence, all attention now drawn toward the screen. And for Devin, it was the first taste of the world he'd been chasing— not just the discipline of the gym, not just the chaos of the beat, but something sharper, deadlier, and infinitely more complex. And as Benson began to speak again, Devin knew: this wasn't just another briefing. This was the doorway his father had once walked through, and now, it was his turn.

Shadows on the Wall

The hallway stretched long and quiet, its walls lined with framed photographs and plaques. The air smelled faintly of polished wood and the sharp tang of cleaning agents—sterile, professional, yet reverent. Every step echoed softly beneath the fluorescent glow, a rhythm almost too loud for a place that seemed designed for whispers. Agent Christopher Mack led the way, his stride clipped and confident. He didn't look back often, but when he did, his eyes carried that same trace of skepticism he had shown in the briefing room. Trailing him were two other agents, Kyle Lowrey and Rudy Dodson. Lowrey was tall, lean, his skin dark and smooth, his presence quietly commanding. Dodson, by contrast, was broader, stockier, a perpetual smirk tugging at his lips as though he always knew the punchline to a joke no one else had heard.

Devin walked behind them, his pace slower, deliberate. His eyes were drawn not to the men around him but to the portraits mounted on the walls. They marched along in silent rows, passing the faces of men and women, some stern, some smiling, all frozen in time. Each bore a nameplate beneath, dates etched in brass, a story condensed into two bookends: birth and death. It wasn't casual curiosity that slowed him. It was searching.

Mack noticed, of course. He slowed his own stride until he was shoulder to shoulder with Devin. "Looking for your pops?" he asked, his voice carrying an edge-not cruel, but pointed. Devin's lips tugged into the faintest smile, though it was tight, restrained. "Something like that." Mack's brow arched, reading more than Devin wanted to give away. But he didn't press. Instead, he motioned ahead with a tilt of his head. "Follow me." They turned into a side corridor, narrower, the lights softer here. At the end of it loomed a doorway with bold letters etched into the frosted glass: Memorial Room. Mack pushed the door open without hesitation. "Gotta be one of these since he's recently deceased," he said, stepping aside to let Devin enter first.

The room was hushed, the kind of silence that carried weight. It wasn't empty—Lowrey and Dodson lingered near the doorway, respectful but watchful. Rows of photographs lined the walls here too, but these were different. Larger. Framed in dark wood. The inscription above them read in solemn capitals:

The Heroes Wall

Devin's breath caught. His eyes scanned face after face, the familiar rhythm of features he didn't know but recognized all the same for bravery and courage—the set of a jaw hardened by duty, the eyes that held both pride and fatigue. He walked slowly, each step dragging a little more than the last, until finally…There he was. "Thomas P. Crews, Special Agent. 1982 – 2016." The name glinted beneath the portrait, and Devin felt the floor tilt beneath him. The photograph was painfully familiar. His father's hair neatly combed, his suit pressed, his tie just slightly askew the way he had always worn it. The eyes were the same as Devin's— sharp, unflinching, but with a warmth hidden beneath. The resemblance was stunning, almost eerie, as though the photograph itself were a mirror into the future.

Devin's chest tightened. He hadn't expected it to hit this hard. A deep sigh escaped him, slow and shaky. His throat constricted as though words wanted to form but couldn't find their way out. Memories flickered of late nights watching his father polish his badge, mornings when he'd leave before dawn, the proud but weary smile when he'd return home. And finally, the hospital bed, the voice rasping through pain, "Be better than me, son. Be ready." Mack stood back, his arms folded, his expression unreadable. But his eyes-keen and calculating, lingered on Devin longer than necessary.

For once, Devin didn't notice. His hand lifted, almost instinctively, and his fingers brushed lightly against the glass of the frame, tracing the outline of his father's face. The cool surface shocked him back into the present, grounding him. Lowrey cleared his throat softly, as though breaking a silence too heavy to let linger. "That your old man?" Devin nodded, his voice low. "Yeah. That's him." Dodson stepped closer, tilting his head toward the photograph. "Looks just like you." Devin's lips pressed into a thin line. "That's what people say." Mack shifted, his tone carefully neutral. "He was a good agent. Stories about him still circle around." Devin glanced at him then, finally tearing his eyes from the portrait. "Stories, huh?"

Mack gave a small shrug. "You know how it is. The Bureau holds onto its legends. Especially the ones who burned bright before they burned out." The words stung, though Devin couldn't tell if Mack had meant them that way. He inhaled deeply, letting it wash over him, then exhaled slowly. "My father didn't burn out," Devin said quietly. "He gave everything he had. Right up until the end."

The silence that followed was thick. Lowrey's gaze softened, Dodson's smirk faded. Even Mack's jaw shifted, a muscle ticking as if he hadn't expected Devin to push back so firmly. Devin turned back to the wall, his eyes still locked on the face that would forever be both a reminder and a weight. He whispered, almost too softly for the others to hear, "I'll make you proud." No one responded. They didn't need to. The room itself seemed to hold the echo of the vow.

The air outside the Memorial Room felt lighter, but only slightly. As they stepped back into the hallway, the silence stretched between them. Mack finally broke it, his tone less sharp this time. "Your old man left a mark here," he said. "Big shoes to fill." Devin glanced at him, then straight ahead. "I'm not trying to fill his shoes. I'm trying to make my own." It wasn't boastful. It wasn't defensive. It was just truth, plain and steady.

Mack studied him for a moment, his eyes narrowing slightly, then he gave a faint nod. No smile, no approval-but maybe, just maybe, a sliver of respect. Lowrey let out a low whistle, shaking his head. "Well, damn. Guess this just got a little more interesting." Dodson chuckled under his breath. "Yeah. Welcome to the Bureau, Crews." Devin didn't answer. His mind was still back in that room, his father's eyes watching him from the wall. And in that moment, more than ever, he knew: this wasn't just a job. It was a legacy. And legacies, he thought grimly, came with a cost.

CHAPTER 9

IRON SHARPENS IRON

The Bureau's Prep Building loomed like a cathedral to physical excellence, its sheer size enough to draw a hushed whistle from Devin as soon as he stepped inside. Sunlight spilled through tall panes of glass, bathing the floor in warm light. The air smelled faintly of disinfectant and rubber mats, a mix every athlete recognized instantly, but here it carried something more-a promise, an edge.

Devin paused at the threshold, his eyes roaming upward to the vaulted ceiling where steel beams stretched like the ribs of a giant. His gaze swept left to right, cataloging every piece of state-of-the-art equipment: rows of treadmills gleaming like fresh recruits, racks of dumbbells polished to near mirror shine, ellipticals and bikes aligned with military precision. And it wasn't just machines—this place had everything. To the right, an indoor running track circled above, its red surface inviting and smooth. Beyond that, he glimpsed the glossy shine of a full basketball court, hoops lowered for drills, lines marked out crisp and clean. The faint sound of a bouncing ball echoed, carried by some unseen players. To the far end stretched a pristine pool, its surface undisturbed, the smell of chlorine faint but distinct. Signs pointed toward saunas and steam rooms, tucked away like private sanctuaries for sore muscles. "This place…" Devin muttered, his voice almost reverent. "It's like heaven for athletes." Mack, walking a half step ahead, gave a dismissive wave. "Come, let's go check out the weight room." Devin's grin widened. "Now you're talking." The two men strode past the machines and mirrored walls until they reached a double door labeled Weight & Aerobics Room. Mack pushed it open with one hand, stepping aside as though presenting a prize. Devin's breath caught.

This wasn't just a gymnasium—it was a temple. Rows upon rows of gleaming barbells stretched in both directions, neatly organized by weight. Squat racks, deadlift platforms, and bench presses lined the walls like sentries. In the center, specialized machines stood ready for every imaginable movement—lat pulldowns, cable crossovers, leg presses. The floor was laid with thick mats to absorb the sound of clanging plates. Even the air felt different, heavier, charged with effort.

Devin's home gym suddenly seemed laughably tiny by comparison. "I love it," he said, almost under his breath, though loud enough for Mack to hear. Mack smirked knowingly. "I knew you would." Devin walked deeper into the room, running his hand along a rack of dumbbells, the cold steel grounding him. He could almost see himself here for hours already—hours lost in the grind, sweat soaking his shirt, muscles burning in a way only athletes understood.

Mack leaned against a nearby bench, arms folded, watching him with mild amusement. "Hey, listen! What're you doing Sunday?" Devin turned, still half-distracted by the equipment. "Sunday?" "Yeah. The boys are going fishing. You should join us. Good way to relax, get to know the team outside all this." The offer was genuine enough, but Devin shook his head. "Sorry. Already made plans. Going to a Muscle-mania show at the Grand." The words landed like a weight between them. Mack blinked, his expression shifting from casual to something closer to disgust. "Ewww," he drawled, dragging the sound as though tasting something sour. "Men walking around in their underwear? Won't catch me at one of those. Never!" Devin chuckled, but there was an edge to it. "You never know. What'd you do if you met a girl who was into bodybuilding and competing?" Mack tilted his head, his smirk turning sharp. "I'd check the Adam's apple."

Lowrey, who had followed them quietly, snorted out a laugh. Dodson muffled his with a cough. Devin only smiled, letting the jab roll past him. He'd heard every variation of mockery aimed at bodybuilding before; too vain, too flamboyant, too close to vanity shows. But he knew what it meant to him: discipline, art, control. And no sneer could erase that. He turned away, running his hand across the cold bar of a squat rack. The steel felt alive under his touch, humming with the promise of strength, of identity.

Mack clapped his hands once, the sound echoing in the vast room. "Alright, let's stop screwing around. Time to go meet Sherry for in-processing. She's got some forms for you to fill out." Devin gave the bar one last lingering look before straightening. "Lead the way."

As they walked back toward the administrative wing of the campus, Devin's mind lingered on the exchange. He wasn't necessarily rattled; Mack's verbal jabs were nothing compared to what he'd faced on the streets, but it was telling. Some men wore their contempt openly, while others hid it under jokes. Mack was the kind who straddled both. But Devin had bigger things to focus on. Sunday wasn't just another day-it was a return. The show at the Grand wasn't only about friends or old memories. It was about reconnecting with a part of himself he hadn't touched in years. A part that was as much a part of him as the badge now clipped to his belt.

The Bureau wanted his strength for training, but bodybuilding-that was his language. His father had never fully understood it, but he'd respected it. And now, standing on the cusp of two worlds-the Bureau and the stage-Devin felt the weight of both identities pressing down, demanding space. "Devin," Mack's voice cut in, dragging him back to the present. "You spacing out already?" Devin blinked, then grinned faintly. "Just thinking. Big place. Lot to take in."

Dodson clapped him on the shoulder. "You'll get used to it. Just don't let Mack's charming personality scare you off." Mack shot him a look, but Lowrey laughed openly, the sound rolling down the hallway.

They reached a set of glass doors marked Administration. Inside, the air was cooler, quieter, the bustle of fitness equipment replaced by the low buzz of computers and printers. Desks stretched across the room, manned by clerks and staff in suits. Mack gestured toward an office tucked in the corner, blinds half-open. "That's Sherry. She'll get you squared away." Through the slats, Devin caught sight of a woman in her late thirties, sharp-eyed, her hair pulled into a tight bun. She shuffled papers with brisk efficiency, her phone cradled between shoulder and ear. Even from a distance, Devin could tell she was the kind who missed nothing. As they approached, Mack leaned closer, his voice low enough for only Devin to hear. "Word of advice—don't try to charm Sherry. She eats rookies like you for breakfast." Devin smirked. "Good thing I'm not a rookie, then." Mack shook his head, a grin tugging at his lips despite himself. For a brief moment, the tension eased. But beneath it, Devin could still feel the currents pulling-duty, identity, and the looming shadow of Sunday's show.

The Prep Building's doors closed behind them with a soft hiss, but the impression lingered. For Devin, the place wasn't just an office or a training ground. It was a test. A test of strength, yes-but also of balance. Between the man who carried his father's name on the Heroes Wall and the man who once thrived under the stage lights, flexing under spotlights while strangers cheered. Though his bodybuilding days felt like a distant memory, he didn't know how long he could walk both paths. But for now, he would try.

And as Mack's words replayed in his mind, *men walking around in their underwear*, Devin smiled to himself. Let them scoff. He knew the truth. Discipline, sacrifice, and the iron never lied.

CHAPTER 10

GHOSTS IN THE ROOM

The personnel office smelled faintly of old paper and stale coffee, the kind of scent that clung to bureaucratic corners where forms outlived people. Files were stacked haphazardly on a desk that seemed perpetually on the verge of collapse, folders tilting like drunks at last call. Behind the desk, a civilian clerk sat with her back to the door, rhythmically sliding documents into a cabinet. Devin followed Mack in, both men wearing easy smiles after their tour of the prep building. But the moment the clerk turned, Devin froze mid-step. Her eyes widened. For the briefest second, her hand slipped, and a file nearly toppled from her grip.

It was Sherry, Sherry Aikman—he recognized her. Late thirties now, her hair pulled back in a no-nonsense bun, a crisp blouse tucked into charcoal color slacks. But her face-those sharp cheekbones, the steady green eyes-was unmistakable. The air thickened, heavy and unbreathable. "Hey Sherry," Mack said, oblivious at first. "I've got another newbie for you." He stopped short, eyes darting between them, quickly sensing the tension. The silence carried weight, too sharp, too familiar to ignore. "You two know each other?" Mack asked, tone curious, almost teasing. Sherry's gaze didn't waver from Devin. Her lips parted as though to answer, but instead she spoke directly to Mack. "Hey, Chris … can you excuse us for a minute? I got it from here." Mack looked between them once more, eyebrows raised in suspicion. Then he chuckled under his breath, backing toward the door. "Sure. Just, uh, dial nine-one-one if you need help." The door clicked shut behind him.

Sherry folded her arms, still watching Devin. The years hadn't softened her. If anything, she looked sharper now, like steel polished by fire. "Are you gonna offer me a seat?" Devin asked, trying for levity though his voice came out rough. "I would," Sherry replied coolly, "but I don't want you to feel trapped." He swallowed hard, throat dry. The words stung more than they should have. An awkward silence lingered, thick with things unsaid. Sherry could feel a knot of old tension instantly cinching in her chest, a physical reaction she hadn't anticipated.

Finally, Devin broke it. "Look. I wasn't ready, okay? The past is the past. We're professionals now." "Okay," she said flatly, turning back to her monitor. The clatter of her keyboard filled the void between them, sharp and efficient. She didn't look up as she asked, "What's your first and last name?" Devin blinked. The formality cut deeper than it should have. He craned his neck to look into a back office with the door half open. "Is there anyone else back there that can help me?" he muttered. "No," Sherry politely said, still typing. "It looks like you're stuck with me, again." Her fingers hovered over the keys, waiting. The implication in her tone was clear: either give the name or stay in limbo. Detective Crews realized he would have to suspend all disbelief if he wanted to get past this unfortunate reunion. He exhaled hard through his nose. "Devin… Devin Crews." Her fingers resumed their dance across the keyboard. "That wasn't so hard, was it?" He clenched his jaw, eyes wandering around the room to distract himself. That's when he saw it-a picture on the wall, framed in dusty wood.

It was a class photo. Nine cadets standing shoulder to shoulder, fresh-faced and eager, dressed in Illinois Police Academy uniforms. And there they were—him and Sherry, side by side, a decade younger, smiling like they had the world ahead of them. The inscription on the bottom read: Illinois Police Academy—Class Photo. A reluctant smile tugged at his lips. "I see you kept that," he said softly, pointing toward it. Sherry's eyes flicked up to the frame, then back to him, unamused. "That's Crews with an 'S,' right?" She asked rhetorically. The warmth drained from his smile. He could see where this was going. "It's gonna be a long few weeks here, I see," he muttered under his breath. "Longer for me," she replied dryly, striking the "S" key.

Their eyes locked for the briefest moment, both filled with equal measures of contempt, regret, and something far more complicated. She claims to have moved on and hated his guts for breaking up with her, but her eyes betrayed her. They told a different story. It's funny how a person can look the same—The same familiar frame, the same familiar smile. Even the way he talked hadn't changed much and yet he felt like a stranger separated by a decade of silence. She watched him turn, and when their eyes met again, the low murmur of the shop seemed to have dropped out completely, replaced with the echo of their shared history. For a sharp, aching moment, the only thing that seemed to matter were the unasked questions hanging between them. *Are we going to pretend that the intense, confusing disaster that we were, never happened?* She thought to herself, scanning him from head to toes. She took a deep breath, a small gesture pulling her back to present and she knew instantly that her world was about to get a bit more complicated. That night, Devin trudged into his apartment, shoulders heavy from more than just fatigue. The instant the door opened, Baxter came barreling toward him, tail wagging furiously. The dog launched himself into Devin's arms, tongue out, yipping with uncontainable joy. "Whoa! Buddy, you're getting heavy," Devin laughed, though the weight in his arms was comforting. He ruffled Baxter's fur before lowering him to the ground.

Tanya looked up from the couch where she sat curled in her scrubs, hair pulled back loosely after a long shift. "Hey, hun." "Hey, babe," Devin replied, collapsing beside her with a sigh that seemed to deflate his whole body. "How was your day? Anything exciting?" she asked, half teasing, half genuinely curious. "I am spent," he admitted, leaning his head back against the couch. "But also…" He hesitated, stroking Baxter absently as the dog curled into his lap. "I ran into something. Someone, actually." Tanya tilted her head. "Oh?" "An old face. From way back." His voice trailed off, unwilling to dive deeper. He shifted instead. "But…hey I saw Pop's dedication today at the Bureau. They spoke very highly of him." His lips curved faintly. "It meant a lot."

The subject change was smooth, but Tanya noticed the deflection. Still, she let it slide. "And what about you?" he asked quickly. "How was your day?" "Same old," she said dryly. "Sick people. Trauma center. You know how it is." Devin reached over, squeezing her hand gently. In her tired smile, he found some anchor against the storm inside him.

The next day, the prep building was alive with energy. A large group of federal agents sweated through their grey shirts and blue shorts, grunting, straining, drenched in exertion. Their movements were rough, uncoordinated, but earnest. Devin's own shirt bore a bold word across the back: INSTRUCTOR. He walked among them, voice carrying. "Hydrate! Thirty seconds!" Bottles tipped back, water spilling over faces and down throats. At that moment, Agent Mack strolled in, as effortlessly cool as ever. Dark shades perched on his face, a lazy grin stretched wide. He looked like he'd stepped out of a catalog, not a federal office. He sauntered up to Devin, surveying the organized chaos. "You really tidied up around here. Looks good." Devin smirked. "Thanks." Mack removed his shades, eyes glinting. "I see you survived Sherry." "She's tough," Devin admitted, understatement thick in his tone. "You're telling me!" Mack laughed, clapping him lightly on the shoulder. "Sorry I didn't make your class. Duty calls, you know. Hey, meeting at one sharp. Boss wants you there. Don't be late."

He waved to a few agents on his way out, the kind of man who seemed to collect camaraderie like loose change. Devin turned back to his recruits. "Time's up! Grab a partner and some gloves!" The clang of wall lockers opening and closing, the squeak of sneakers, and the muffled groans of exhausted agents filled the room as they paired up. Devin stood at the center, voice rising above the din, but his mind kept flickering back to the personnel office.

To Sherry.

To that class photo.

To all the words left unsaid.

The past wasn't past. It was sitting at a desk down the hall, staring at him with brown eyes that still had the power to undo him.

CHAPTER 11

THE ASSIGNMENT

FBI Chicago Field Office briefing room buzzed with low voices, clinking mugs, and the scraping of chairs. A dozen men and women in various shades of gray and blue clustered around the oval table, some standing, some leaning against the wall, most trying to look more awake than they felt. Devin slipped in just as the last available chair was free, sliding down into it with an exhale. Only when he looked to his left did his stomach knot.

Sherry! of all the people in the room, fate had to seat him beside her. She didn't turn her head, but Devin felt the cold awareness radiating from her. He shifted in his seat, trying to focus on the scattered papers in front of him instead of the faint smell of her perfume—something crisp and clean, the same kind she'd worn ten years ago. The fragrance was a bright, effervescent burst of Italian bergamot, green apple and jasmine. Devin recalled how captivating the scent was.

Across the room, Mack caught sight of the two of them sitting together. He grinned like a cat who'd just found cream, mouthing something Devin couldn't quite make out before giving him a thumbs-up. Devin rolled his eyes. By now he was getting very familiar with Mack's playfulness.

The hum of voices died the moment Special Agent Harold Benson entered. In his fifties now, Benson carried the authority of experience, a man who'd seen enough to never raise his voice yet command a room all the same. His dark suit looked tailored but practical, a tie knotted neatly at the throat. He held a thick manila folder in one hand, a steaming mug in the other.

The room straightened in unison. Benson set his mug down, opened the folder, and without preamble said, "Yesterday, we got calls from NSA and Homeland. They picked up chatter on Russian operatives trying to interfere with our upcoming election." A collective shift rippled through the agents. Chairs creaked, pens stilled.

Benson reached for the clicker and pointed it toward the projection screen on the far wall. With a soft hum, the screen flickered to life, and a black-and-white image filled it. A man's face. Wrinkled, tired, but dangerous. Aleksei Lebedev. "Sixties and stands about five feet nine inches." Benson continued, his tone flat but weighted. "Russian national. Currently serving time at MCC. Frail on the outside, yes-but don't underestimate him. He's old-school KGB, and his reach runs deep. Even from inside a cell." The image froze on Aleksei's gaunt expression. His pale eyes stared out across the room, as though he were surveying every agent there. "We need somebody to get close to him," Benson said. "Somebody inside. Someone who can infiltrate his organization from the ground up." He paused deliberately, letting the weight of the words settle before lifting his mug and taking a slow sip. He lowered it gently back onto the table. "So," Benson asked evenly, "who wants to go to prison?" The kind that rang louder than any noise. No one moved. No one volunteered, this was unusual.

Devin glanced around. Agents avoided eye contact, suddenly fascinated with their notes or coffee mugs. Beside him, Sherry's expression remained perfectly neutral, though her crossed arms spoke volumes. The silence stretched. It was as if the very air tightened, waiting. Then the door swung open.

A man entered, sharp suit, sharp stride, sharper presence. His badge, clipped neatly to his breast pocket, carried weight: His badge said DIRECTOR. "Benson," The Director projected into the room, his voice brisk. Benson excused himself and stepped into the hallway, the door swinging shut behind him.

Mack wasted no time. He straightened his tie, smoothed his suit jacket, and bounded up to the podium like it was a stage. "So," he said with mock seriousness, surveying the room, "who wants pizza?" Laughter broke out instantly. Hands shot into the air. Even the tension in Devin's chest loosened for a moment as the room chuckled. Mack gave a smug nod, enjoying his moment as the would-be clown prince of the Bureau. Devin leaned back, shaking his head. Sherry's lips twitched—was that the ghost of a smile? He couldn't be sure.

Out in the hallway, the tone was far different. The Director's jaw was set like stone as he delivers the bad news. "Aleksei was just diagnosed with stage two cancer. Whatever you're planning, Harold, you need to do it fast." Benson's brows furrowed. "How long do we have?" The Director's eyes were cold. "Weeks. Months if we're lucky. But he's still pulling strings. Still dangerous. We need preliminaries on my desk ASAP."

He turned sharply, already walking away, his polished shoes echoing against the tiled floor. As he disappeared down the hall, an assistant emerged from a nearby office, tablet in hand. Her tailored skirt and neat bun made her look like efficiency personified. "Sir, do you have a minute?" she asked. "Of course," Benson replied, regaining composure. He followed her briskly into the office, already running scenarios in his mind as they disappeared behind double doors.

An early Saturday morning sunlight streamed through the garage windows of the couple's apartment. The floor was dripping wet with sweat and a punching bag swung wildly under Tanya's strikes.

WHAM! BAM! WHAM!

She landed three kicks in quick succession before following up with a flurry of punches. Sweat glistened on her forehead, strands of hair slipping from her ponytail. Devin stood nearby, arms crossed, watching with an approving smirk. "You've been practicing without me." "Someone has to keep up with you," Tanya shot back, grinning as she delivered one last kick before stepping aside.

They switched. Devin stepped forward, muscles flexing under his tank top, his strikes heavier, sharper, each thud reverberating through the garage. It seemed more than a workout—it was released. Every punch seemed aimed at ghosts only he could see.

They alternated, pushups and sit-ups in between, their bodies moving in rhythm until exhaustion forced them to collapse side by side against the wall. Their breathing was heavy, ragged. Tanya's head tilted toward him. "Baxter's waiting for us," she said, half-laughing, half-serious. "I heard you two talking in there earlier," Devin replied, smirking as he wiped sweat from his brow.

The doorbell rang. Both froze, still catching their breath. Tanya raised an eyebrow. "Are you expecting someone?" Devin shook his head slowly, muscles still taut with the afterburn of exertion. "No," he said, pushing himself to his feet. "I'll go check it out." The doorbell rang again. This time, longer.

The doorbell rang again, sharp and insistent, echoing through the modest apartment. Devin wiped his palms against his sweat-damp shirt and pulled the door open. What he saw on the other side made his chest tighten instantly. "Sherry." Her name slipped out before he could stop it, more exhale than voice.

There she was, standing on his doorstep in broad daylight, the city sun casting sharp angles across her face. Her dark hair pinned neatly, her stance professional, her eyes sharp as glass. But seeing her here, outside his home, struck a nerve he hadn't prepared to feel. His jaw tensed, teeth grinding as he instinctively glanced back into the apartment. Without a word, he stepped outside, pulling the door shut behind him as though to shield what was inside. "What!" His voice came out sharper than he intended. "How did you even get my-" And then he stopped himself. The memory clicked. Of course she would know. Of course she has access to personnel files. The Bureau had its ways, and Sherry always had hers. "Never mind," he muttered, exhaling. "What are you doing here?" Sherry didn't flinch. Her voice was calm, even deliberate, as if she had rehearsed this on the way over. "We got off on the wrong foot the other day. But I have something you might want to hear." Despite himself, Devin felt his guard shift. His posture stiffened, his curiosity betraying the irritation in his tone. "I'm listening."

Sherry took a measured step closer, her eyes narrowing slightly. "You still dream of being a special agent?" He hesitated. The question was loaded, personal. But his answer was simple. "I've applied," he said carefully, "if that's what you're asking." Her lips curled-not into a smile, but something more like acknowledgment. "And what if I told you there's a way to increase your chances of being selected?" That caught him. Devin's pulse quickened. He tried to mask the sudden interest in his eyes, but Sherry saw it immediately. She always had been able to read him. "I'm listening," he repeated, softer this time.

Sherry folded her arms. Her voice lowered, words clipped with intent. "The Board is looking for someone to go undercover into MCC. Our target-Aleksei Lebedev. You've heard the name. He's sick, and we don't know how much time he has. If you want to make an impression, this is your chance. Step into the fire. Prove yourself." Devin stared at her. The weight of what she was saying pressed down on him. MCC. Undercover. Aleksei. This wasn't simply a routine task; it felt like stepping right into the heart of imminent danger. "That sounds like deep cover, and I don't believe I qualify." Sherry's gaze hardened, sharp enough to slice through the silence between them. "I know how badly you want to be like your—" The front door swung open. "Devin?" Tanya's voice cut the air as she stepped outside. She stopped dead in her tracks.

For a moment, time stilled. Tanya's eyes locked onto Sherry's. Sherry met her gaze without hesitation. The stare between them was immediate and unflinching, two worlds colliding without words. Tanya's hand tightened on the doorframe. "What's going on?" Devin's chest tightened again. He turned slightly, caught between them, caught in a trap that had nothing to do with criminals or the Bureau. "This is Sherry," he said quickly, his tone clipped. "She's … from The Bureau." He forced a short exhale. "She was just leaving."

The silence that followed was heavy, thicker than the humid air of the street. Tanya's eyes flicked from Sherry to Devin, searching, measuring. Sherry, for her part, didn't blink. Her expression was unreadable—professional mask perfectly intact, though something in her eyes glinted, perhaps amusement, perhaps something colder. "Sorry for the disturbance," Sherry said finally, her tone crisp and formal. "That's all I had." She turned without another word, her heels clicking against the pavement as she walked back toward the car parked on the curb. Her movements were precise, deliberate, as though she knew exactly the impression she was leaving behind.

Devin stood frozen on the porch, watching her retreat. Tanya, still by the door, kept her eyes fixed on him, her silence louder than any question she could ask. The air felt heavy with unspoken things, things Devin wasn't sure he was ready to face. And then the sound of Sherry's car door closing broke the stillness, the engine starting up, and with it came the knowledge that nothing about this moment would be left behind.

CHAPTER 12

LOVE AND LEGACY

Sunlight spilled through the blinds, striping the living room floor with warm, uneven bands. Devin stood there, still damp with the sweat of the morning's workout, his shoulders stiff, his eyes fixed on the ground as if he could anchor himself against the storm brewing inside.

Across from him, Tanya leaned against the wall, arms folded tightly across her chest. She looked at him not as a nurse, not as his partner in late-night workouts and shared laughter, but as the woman who had tethered her future to his. The look she gave him only meant one thing, *speak now.* His voice was controlled when he broke the silence. "The Bureau needs an agent to go undercover," Devin said finally, his voice low, cautious. He wasn't sure if saying the words aloud would make them feel more real or more impossible. "Sherry thought I might be interested and that explains the visit." Tanya tilted her head slightly, her ponytail brushing her shoulder. Her eyes narrowed in disbelief. "But you're not even an FBI agent." She cried out. "I know." He exhaled, rubbing the back of his neck. "That's not even the problem. The assignment is in prison." Her lips parted, but the sound that came out wasn't words-it was a gasp, a hollow "oh" that echoed in the space between them. Devin nodded, answering her silence. "I know."

For a moment, Tanya didn't speak. She shifted her weight against the wall, her gaze sliding past him as if she were trying to process the enormity of what he had just confessed. She pressed her palms flat against the cool paint behind her, grounding herself, then finally said, "Don't tell me you're actually considering this." Her tone sharpened, urgency spilling into the room. "There's gotta be another way, Devin. This sounds…dangerous doesn't even cover it. It's madness." "I know it's risky, but let's just think about-" "No," she cut in, her voice firm, rising with the edge of desperation. "I don't like it. We just talked about starting a family, D. We just talked about building something real, something stable. What happens to that if something happens to you in there?" Her words hung in the air like shards of glass, each one sharp enough to cut him.

He opened his mouth, but no words came. Tanya's face softened only slightly before she turned away, but not before her eyes caught with his one final, piercing question. "What's more important to you?" She let the question hang unanswered. Then, with a slow shake of her head, she walked away, leaving Devin rooted in place, his silence louder than any response.

The door to the bedroom closed softly behind her. Devin remained standing in the living room, his thoughts churning. Family. Legacy. Love. Duty. They crashed against one another like waves in a storm, refusing to give him peace.

The next day, Devin found himself standing alone in the Memorial Room at the FBI field office. The silence here was different—thick, reverent. The walls were lined with photographs of fallen agents, each framed in somber wood, each inscription etched in gold.

His eyes searched until they landed on the face he knew better than his own reflection. "Thomas P. Crews, Special Agent, 1982 – 2016." His father's gaze, frozen in time, continues to stare back at him. The resemblance was striking-the same jawline, the same steady eyes, though Thomas's were locked in the unyielding stillness of memory.

Devin swallowed hard, the weight of unspoken words pressing at his throat. He leaned closer, almost whispering, his breath fogging the glass. "Dad, what would you have me do?" The question wasn't new. He had asked it in the quiet of sleepless nights, in the silence after workouts, in the pauses between calls. But here, in front of the portrait, it carried more weight. *"You spent half your career taking down mobsters," he murmured. "You risked everything for the job. And when it was your time, you were ready to go. You said it yourself. But me? I'm not ready. Not to leave her. Not to leave…"* His words faltered. His hands curled into fists at his sides. He searched the portrait as though the face of his father could speak, and could give him the clarity he craved. But the only response was silence. Silence, and the faint echo of his own doubt. "Maybe this is it," he said softly. "Maybe this is how I prove myself. To you. To them. To me." A knock at the door pulled him back to the present. "Crews?" It was Benson. Devin straightened, his jaw setting, his heart still pounding. "Yeah?" "Director wants to see us."

Benson's office was neat, the kind of order that came from years of repetition. Files stacked with military precision, pens aligned, a faint scent of aftershave lingering in the air. But Devin barely noticed. His decision was already burning in his chest. "I'll do it," Devin blurted as he entered. His voice was steady, but beneath it was an urgency, a defiance. "I'll go undercover." Benson's brows lifted, but his expression remained neutral. "Are you sure?" Devin nodded. But before he could elaborate, Benson lifted a hand. "Hold that thought. Follow me."

The older man led him out into the hall. They walked side by side, silent, until they reached the elevator. The ride up felt endless, the hum of the cables echoing in Devin's ears like a drumbeat. When the doors opened, they stepped into a much larger office—sleek, imposing, the kind of space where decisions carried the weight of nations.

Behind the desk sat the Director. A man whose presence filled the room before he even spoke. His eyes lifted, sharp and assessing, as Benson ushered Devin in. "Sir," Benson began quickly, "we've got our guy. Wait-" he raised a hand, preempting the response he expected. "I know what you're going to say. But before you do, I want to mention that technically, he's one of us. For the next forty-eight days, at least." Benson glanced at Devin, then back at the Director. "Besides, nobody else wants to do it."

The Director leaned back in his chair, fingers steepled. His gaze moved from Benson to Devin, studying him with a silence that seemed to stretch forever. Finally, he asked, his voice even but firm, "Have you run this by CPD?" Benson hesitated. "No, sir." "I'll run it by them," the Director said at last, his tone clipped. "But I can't promise you they'll be on board." The words landed heavy, but Devin didn't flinch. He had already made his choice. For better or worse, the path was set. And somewhere in the quiet corners of his mind, Tanya's voice echoed still: What's more important to you?

Into the Fire

The screening room had the feel of a vault-sealed, suffocating, and whirring with the kind of tension that only came when secrets too dangerous for the world were being unspooled within its walls. The lights were dim, the air cool enough to raise goosebumps. The thick metal door had closed behind them with a hiss, leaving Devin acutely aware that once again he had crossed into territory from which there was no easy way out.

He sat among them now, Benson with his tired yet authoritative air, Mack with his easy swagger and irreverent grin, and two senior agents who looked as though they had been carved from granite. Devin shifted in his seat, trying to make himself smaller, though his broad shoulders and brick-like frame refused to cooperate. On the screen before them, frozen in midstride, was a man Devin already felt he knew and dreaded in equal measure. A grainy still from surveillance footage captured Aleksei Lebedev, a slight, pale figure stepping toward a sleek Gulfstream G150 jet. Even in the still, there was something calculated about his posture—an old man, yes, but not one to underestimate.

Benson's voice cut through the silence, measured, deliberate. "That's him. Aleksei Lebedev. Got popped two years ago. Arms, money laundering, election interference—you name it, he had his hand in it. Right now, he's serving time at MCC. Your job, Crews…" He turned his head, fixing Devin with the weight of his stare. "Your job is to get close to him. Do whatever it takes to get him talking." The words landed like stones. Whatever it takes. Mack leaned back in his chair, smirking. "Just don't sleep with him." A chuckle rippled around the table, thin and uneasy, but Devin didn't move. He frowned, jaw tightening. This wasn't a joke. "Agent Mack," Benson snapped, his tone sharp enough to slice through the humor. "Sorry, sir," Mack said, raising his hands in mock surrender, though the grin never fully left his face. "Go on." Benson sighed, pinching the bridge of his nose before continuing. "We need Lebedev to give us the names of his accomplices. Quietly. Cleanly. We can't afford another screw-up in November."

The unspoken words hung in the air like smoke: Another election, another disaster, another failure on our watch. Devin leaned forward, his voice steady but carrying an edge. "And my safety?" Mack was quicker to respond than Benson. "The Warden will be in on it. He'll make sure you're safe…

ish." He leaned across the table, eyes glinting with mischief. "Just don't drop the soap, Crews. The Warden can't save you then." The other agents laughed, but Devin didn't. His frown deepened, the words grating against the storm inside him. "Look," Benson interrupted, his patience thinning. "This won't be easy. They're going to test you, whether you like it or not. That's the nature of going undercover in a place like MCC. If you want out, say it now." To say he never thought about backing out would be untrue, He had been doubting his ability to pull this off ever since the words escaped his lips. Devin's gaze was still on the screen, on the frail figure of Aleksei paused midstride. But his mind was drifting-back to Tanya's voice, trembling with fear, her eyes sharp when she asked him what mattered more. Back to his father's portrait, eyes steady, silent, expectant.

He didn't hear Benson's last words. He barely registered Mack shifting beside him. His thoughts were a tangled knot, pulling him further away. "Hey." The snap of Mack's voice jolted him. "Focus, Crews." Devin blinked, realizing his fingers had been drumming absently on the table. He straightened. "Sorry. I just… I gotta make a phone call." Benson's brows rose. The two senior agents exchanged a look. Mack leaned back in his chair, smirking again. "Really? Now?" But Devin was already pushing his chair back. The legs scraped against the floor, loud in the quiet room. Without another word, he stepped out into the hallway, his phone already in his hand.

The fluorescent lights overhead buzzed faintly. He tapped his screen, the familiar contact flashing up at him. "Hey, Mikey!" His voice softened, lighter than it had been in days. On the other end, the warmth of an old friend's laugh. Devin closed his eyes for a second, just listening. "Something came up, brother," he said after a beat, the words heavy. "I'm gonna have to pass. Maybe I'll catch the next show."

There was disappointment on the line, though Mikey tried to mask it. Devin could picture him-backstage somewhere, tanned, oiled, flexing, getting ready to step into a spotlight that once might have been Devin's. For a moment, Devin felt the pang of that lost life. A life of iron and stage lights, applause and medals. A life that had always seemed simpler, even if it never truly was. "Stay strong out there, brother," Mikey said at last. "You too," Devin replied, his throat tight. He hung up before the weight of nostalgia could crush him. For a long moment, he stood in the empty hallway, staring at the screen gone dark in his hand. Then, with a deep breath, he squared his shoulders and walked back into the secured room.

The laughter had died down. The agents were waiting, eyes curious. Devin sat down in his seat. "So," he said, clearing his throat. "Where were we?" Benson studied him carefully. "Crews… are you sure about this?" Benson could see that Devin had something on his mind. Devin's lips curled into the faintest shadow of a grin, though his eyes betrayed the storm beneath. "How's the food in there?" he asked lightly. "Gotta have my protein." A ripple of chuckles moved across the table, but Benson didn't smile. His gaze lingered on Devin as though he could see straight through the armor of humor. Devin met his stare and didn't look away. Inside, though, Tanya's voice still echoed: What's more important to you?

CHAPTER 13

THE LONG RIDE IN

Metal chains clinked with every jolt of the prison bus, a grim symphony of restraint and inevitability. The vehicle was hot, stuffy, and smelled of sweat, cigarettes, and fear. The interior was a muted gray with a metal gate separating guards from inmates. Shackled wrists and ankles rattled against steel as rows of men sat pressed together, some with hollow eyes staring at the floor, others flashing tattoos that told stories of past battles and bravery. The men caught glimpses of a distorted passing highway and greenery. The heavily barred windows were proof that any attempt at escape would be futile. Each mile, a reminder of what was to come, high razor-wired fences of the penitentiary.

Devin sat near the middle, his head freshly shaved to bald, his broad frame filling the narrow space beside a thin, trembling figure. The kid couldn't have been more than twenty-two, his skin pale, his eyes rimmed red from the tears he fought to hide. Devin kept his gaze forward, but his awareness was sharp, every detail burned into memory. This wasn't just survival. This was infiltration.

From two seats ahead, a man with tattoos wrapped around his neck, had one arm resting over the back of his seat. His grin was all menace as he stared towards the back. "Hey!" he called, locking onto the trembling kid. "Hey, I'm Big Perk, where you heading to?" The scared detainee shifted, shoulders curling inward. His voice came out hoarse. "MCC." The tattooed man smirked. "Why you crying, huh? You afraid to get raped?" A ripple of laughter came from the surrounding seats. The scared kid swallowed hard, his voice cracking. "Aren't you?" The man's grin widened. "I've been in before. They know me in there …" He looked around, inviting the others into his performance. "…ain't nobody touchin' me."

Devin leaned slightly toward the boy beside him, his voice steady, grounding. "No one is going to rape you." The tattooed man's eyes snapped to Devin. His grin faltered, then returned sharper, more pointed. "You sure about that, big guy?" Big Perk directed the question towards Devin. The boy whimpered, shoulders shaking now, and the tattooed man pressed on like a predator smelling blood. "You got money?" he asked, voice taunting. "N-no," the boy stammered. "You know people on the inside?" The boy shook his head. Big Perk continues peppering his prey with questions. "You know how to fight?" "No," came the whisper, so soft it barely carried. The tattooed man leaned back, clucking his tongue. "Yikes," he said, loud enough for the whole row to hear. "They sure gonna rape you." Big Perk let out a belly laugh. The laughter was cruel this time, sharper, bouncing around the metal cage of the bus. The boy broke then, his sobs echoing down the aisle, raw and uncontained.

At the front, the driver winced. He glanced at the guard riding shotgun—a heavy man in uniform whose head was bobbing against the window, fast asleep. "Hey," the driver barked. "Hey, wake up." The guard jerked upright, wiping drool from his cheek and blinking rapidly. "What? What's goin' on?" "We got another one crying in the back." The sleepy guard hauled himself up, turning toward the rows of shackled men. A wire gate separated him from the passengers, but his eyes scanned them with the weary disdain of someone who had long since stopped seeing them as men. "No crying on the bus," he barked. "Save that for your cellmate. Plenty of men with broad shoulders up in that joint." The laughter that followed was mean-spirited, but it gave the guard exactly what he wanted—control. He smirked and dropped back into his seat.

Devin stared forward, jaw tight, his expression unreadable. Inside, though, his thoughts burned deep. This was the world he was stepping into, a world where cruelty was currency, weakness was blood in the water, and survival meant more than fists. The boy beside him leaned closer, whispering through his sobs. "Is it…is it really like that in there?" Devin didn't answer right away. His cover demanded silence, toughness. But the flicker of humanity in him couldn't stay buried. "Keep your head down," he said finally, his voice low. "And remember you're not as alone as you think." The boy sniffled, nodding, clinging to the words as though they were a rope thrown into a storm.

By late afternoon, the bus rattled to a halt. Outside, razor wire curled along the tops of high concrete walls, glinting in the dull sun. Guard towers loomed, rifles slung casually across shoulders, eyes hidden behind mirrored sunglasses. The bus idled at the massive east gate. A mounted guard stood on a platform, shotgun in hand, his voice booming across the yard. "Open east gate!"

The massive iron doors groaned, sliding apart slowly. The bus rolled through, the sound of heavy metal grinding filling the air. The gate clanged shut behind them with finality. The detainees shifted uneasily, their chains rattling. For some, this was their first step into a nightmare. For others, a return to a place they knew too well.

The door of the bus hissed open. One by one, the new inmates shuffled down the steps, shackles clinking, shoes scraping against the concrete. They were lined up shoulder to shoulder in the yard, watched by guards with batons and cold stares. From across the yard, a figure approached. Short, compact, with a stride that radiated authority despite his stature. Gary Litchfield, the Warden of MCC, looked like a man who thrived on making others uncomfortable. His hands were clasped behind his back, his grin wide and unsettling, showing a slight cleft in his upper lip. "Well, well," he drawled, his voice cutting across the lineup. "Let me guess, you all didn't do it…right?" A few nervous chuckles broke out. Most men kept their eyes down.

"Damn," he continued, shaking his head. "I'm getting good at this. Every last one of you, innocent as lambs. Hmm hmm hmm…that DA must be a jerk." He paused, his grin widening. "So, here's the deal—if you just pay me off right now, you'll be out by morning." The inmates shifted, confusion rippling down the line. Could he be serious? Was this the kind of place where freedom could be bought at the gate? The guards chuckled, their laughter confirming what the men didn't want to believe—they were being toyed with.

The Warden laughed too, the sound sharp. "I'm just kidding. I don't take payments. That would be illegal, I hear." His chuckle echoed through the yard. He stopped directly in front of Devin, craning his neck to look up at the mountain of muscle before him. His grin faltered just slightly, but he masked it quickly with mockery. "And you must be Gabe," he said, savoring the name Devin had been given for this mission. "The tough guy. You're not gonna create problems for me, are ya'? I've seen guys tougher than you cry like a baby." Devin kept a blank stare, his eyes hard. He said nothing.

The Warden smirked, satisfied with the silence. He turned, taking a few steps before tossing one last barb over his shoulder. "Enjoy the stay, boys! Hope you leave a good Yelp review on your way out." The guards laughed again, the sound carrying like nails on a chalkboard. The inmates stood still, the weight of their shackles matched only by the weight of what awaited them inside. And Devin, beneath the shaved head and the hardened stare, felt the enormity of what he had just stepped into. This was no game. This was the fire he had agreed to walk through.

CHAPTER 14

FRESH MEAT

The clang of steel doors sliding open was unlike anything Devin had ever heard before. It wasn't just loud-it was final. It was the sound of freedom evaporating, the sound of walls closing in. He stepped out of his cell into a corridor that stretched like a tunnel of despair, lined with steel bars and concrete walls that had soaked in decades of rage, fear, and hopelessness. The air smelled faintly of bleach, sweat, and something sour that clung to his nostrils. The sound of dozens of feet shuffling in unison filled the narrow space as prisoners filed out of their cells, creating a river of orange jumpsuits that pressed forward under the watchful eyes of guards.

Devin kept his face impassive, head shaved, a blank stare. He blended in, but inside his chest, his heartbeat was a steady, controlled rhythm. He wasn't just another inmate. He was here for a reason. He couldn't forget that. The march toward the cafeteria was slow, punctuated by the crash of gates opening and closing behind them. At each checkpoint, bars clanged shut like a reminder that escape was nothing more than fantasy. Along the way, quick exchanges happened—a folded scrap of paper passed hand to hand, a tiny bag slipped into a pocket, a handshake that lasted just a moment too long. Transactions carried out in full view but never challenged. Devin was clocking all of this.

Devin watched, memorizing. Deals were happening in plain sight, and the guards didn't seem to bat an eye. When they did, it was haphazard at best. The cafeteria smelled of stale grease and disinfectant. Fluorescent lights buzzed overhead, casting a pallid glow on the rows of bolted-down tables. Inmates shuffled forward with their trays, side-stepping along the line while food servers slapped indistinguishable slop onto dented plastic trays.

The man next to Devin in line, leaned close, his voice low and conspiratorial. He was heavily tattooed like most of the other inmates. He nods at Devin. "Hey, big guy. I'm Terry. But in here?" He winked. "Call me Big T." Devin glanced sideways at him. He wasn't impressed. He tilted his head toward the man ladling food behind the counter…"but you're smaller than him," Devin said pointing to the worker. Big T burst out with a chuckle.

"Ha! You're funny. I like that."

Big T nudged Devin with an elbow. "Stick with me, big man. I know the whole system in here. I'll tell you who's who, who to steer clear of, and who'll stab you if you breathe wrong." Before Devin could answer, the food server stopped, glaring at them. His arms were thick as tree trunks, tattoos peeking from under his sleeves. His eyes locked on Devin, hard and unblinking.

"We got a problem?" The server asked with a sharp projection. Big T puffed out his chest, ready to bark something back, but Devin raised a hand and stopped him cold. "No, we don't," Devin said evenly. He leaned slightly forward, locking eyes with the server. "You got any protein back there? Chicken? Milk?" The server blinked, confused. "What?" "Protein," Devin repeated softly. "Something with meat. Chicken. Milk." Big T tugged at his sleeve. "Hey, you're holding up the line, big man." Devin exhaled, gave the server one last glance, then shook his head. "Nevermind." He slid his tray forward and moved on. "Do your job, kitchen boy," Big T shouted as he walked away.

Devin chose an empty table in the corner, away from the noise. Big T followed, plopping down beside him with his tray piled high. "You want someone to spit in your food, tough guy?" Devin asked, his tone dry. Big T waved him off with a laugh. "That's a myth, man. Nobody does that. And if they do, they gotta see me outside." "Be careful what you wish for," Devin muttered, stabbing at the pale lump on his tray that vaguely resembled potatoes.

Big T chewed noisily, then leaned forward, mouth still half full. "See that guy over there?" He gestured with his chin. "They call him Forty-Seven." Devin squinted. The man Big T was pointing at was lean, tattooed, and surrounded by a small circle of followers. "Why Forty-Seven?" Devin asked. Big T chuckled, then burst into a full laugh. "You'll find out. Ain't no one messing with him in this joint." Devin pushed his tray away, unimpressed. "I need to find someone in here. You're gonna help me." Before Big T could answer, a shadow fell over the table. Three men stood there—Skinheads, their heads shaved smooth, their arms inked with swastikas and hate. Their eyes burned with hostility. "This table's ours," one of them said flatly. Devin's gaze flicked instinctively to the guard across the room. The guard didn't move. Didn't even seem to care. It was clear: here, there would be no help.

Devin sized the trio up. He knew he could take all three if he wanted to. His muscle memory told him exactly how, but the mission he was on screamed at him to stay low. Drawing attention here was suicide to the mission. He rose slowly, his tray in hand, his face calm. Without a word, he stepped aside. Big T hesitated, glared at the Skinheads, then followed him. The eyes of other inmates tracked them, measuring, judging. Weakness, or wisdom? Devin didn't care. He'd chosen survival.

They ended up at another table where a thin man with sharp features and an accent waved them over. His skin was pale, his eyes bright with curiosity. "Don't worry," the man said as they sat down. "They do that to everybody. Right now, you are fresh meat." Devin studied him. "Where you from?" The man's lips curled into a faint smile. "Ukraine." Devin nodded slowly, filing the information away. Every connection mattered. He wanted to ask the Ukrainian for his name but thought that may be too suspicious. *Not yet*, he said to himself. He watched the room as hundreds of men sat hunched over plastic trays, eating and holding conversations. For a moment, it was peaceful when suddenly the low din was shattered like a glass. It started with a shout, a primal sound of rage over a spilled carton of milk. What followed next was a sickening thud of tray hitting skin. An inmate rose up, chair scraping back, to face his attacker. The two men collided and tumbled between tables. The immediate reaction was a shockwave across the room. Others scramble away from the fight while others leapt onto benches and tables to get a better view. The guards blew their sharp whistles and rushed to the scene, armed with OC spray canisters. The fight was quickly dissolved with the show of force.

The yard was its own kingdom. A vast space surrounded by towering fences and coiled razor wire that shimmered under the afternoon sun. A mixture of concrete and dirt baked by the indifferent afternoon heat. Inmates sprawled across the cracked pavement in groups defined by skin color, tattoos, and invisible lines of allegiance. Some played basketball, others pumped rusted weights, and some simply sat in clusters, heads bent close, voices low. Devin stepped out into the chaos and headed straight for a guard leaning on the fence, a mean—looking man with a toothpick between his teeth. "Hey," Devin said, steady. "I need to make a phone call. It's important." The guard smirked without even looking at him. "Gabe, right?" Devin nodded his head. For a moment he had forgotten his new name. The guard then turns towards Devin. "I need to see my son and get him away from that whore, but the judge won't let me. Looks like we're both fucked."

He flicked the toothpick away, eyes hardening. "Step the fuck off, inmate!" Devin froze. He hadn't expected that. He thought every guard in here would be on his side. Clearly, not all of them were. He paid close attention to the guard's name badge, OFFICER JOHANSEN, before walking away slowly, his mind racing.

He found Big T on a bench, watching handshakes that weren't just handshakes and deals that weren't just conversations. Devin sat down beside him. "So," Devin said, keeping his voice low, "why do they call him Forty-Seven?" Big T grinned. "That's one bad dude. Told a guard once to switch his cell to forty-seven 'cause it had a better view. Guard told him to fuck off. That guard doesn't work here any more. He's at home … hooked up to a ventilator, if he's even alive." Devin absorbed that, his jaw tightening. "So … tell me," he said, "who's who around here."

Big T pointed casually across the yard. "Over there-Skinheads. Nazis. They are everywhere, bro. Over there, that's Gage. He runs the Six-Nines, Black gang. Always beefin' with the Nazis. Over there, that's Julio—head of the Mexicans. They don't bother anybody, but don't think they are soft. And then …" He paused, searching for words. He gestured toward a small cluster of flamboyant men laughing loudly. "… the ladies." One of them waved at Devin with a playful gesture clearly meant to be flirtatious. Devin gave no reaction. He scanned the yard again-and froze.

Across the pavement, the young man from the bus still had the look of fear in his eyes and was being shoved around by a pack of gang members. One man, leaning against a pole, offered a slow, cruel smirk as another, larger inmate casually flicked tiny stones towards his prey, forcing the young man to keep his gaze pinned to the ground. The taunts weren't yelled, they were whispered, a soft venomous dictation of what would happen next, punctuated by mocking laughter that sounded dry and brittle in the air. His skinny frame crumpled under their jeers, their shoves, their laughter. Seeing this from afar, Devin half-rose from the bench, instincts screaming at him to intervene. But then his eyes locked on another figure. A man walking with authority, flanked by two heavyset henchmen. Older, frail-looking, but exuding power like it was stitched into his skin.

Aleksei Lebedev

The same face Devin had seen in the FBI briefing room, his target—the man whose organization he was here to infiltrate. Devin sat back down quickly, forcing his face into neutrality. Big T followed his gaze. "You know him?" Devin shook his head, too fast. "No." Big T smirked. "Well, don't ever get on his bad side. He runs this place." Out in the yard, the scared kid tore free of his tormentors and bolted across the pavement. Laughter followed him, bouncing off the walls, the sound of prey escaping the jaws for now. Devin watched, his stomach heavy. He wasn't here to save everyone. He couldn't afford to. But still, he felt the weight of it all.

CHAPTER 15

IN THE SHADOWS

The day had dragged like lead. Prison days had a way of stretching endlessly, each hour bleeding into the next. By the time chow was over and the inmates were herded back toward their cells, Devin could feel the weight of confinement pressing in tighter than the concrete walls around him. The corridor echoed with shuffling feet, some in chains, and muttered curses. Every step was a ritual, the same daily march from one cage to another. But for Devin, each step was a calculation on how to move without looking too strong, too weak, too eager, too detached. Everything in here meant something. Everything could be twisted against anyone at any time.

He spotted a guard up ahead, not officer Johansen from earlier but another with an indifferent facial expression. He was chewing his gum as if he hated the taste of it. Devin seized his chance. "Hey," he said, low and calm. "There's been a mistake. I've got a bunkie. Pretty sure the Warden wouldn't be happy about that." The gum-chewing guard barely glanced at him. Before he could answer, another voice cut sharp through the corridor.

It was him, officer Johansen. The same one who had dismissed Devin's plea for help earlier in the yard. "Hey, hotshot!" Johansen barked. His lips curled in something between a sneer and a grin. "Step da fuck off." His eyes burned with a challenge. He wanted a reaction, wanted to prove he could rattle the new guy. Devin stared back for a beat, jaw tight, he had so much to say but said nothing—he turned and walked away. The guard's laugh echoed down the corridor, loud and satisfied. His cell was worse than he imagined. The stench of unwashed clothes and rotting food hit him like a slap. Clothes were scattered across the floor. A half-empty ramen cup sat festering on the desk. His new cellmate, sprawled on the top bunk, didn't even look up from whatever crude magazine he was flipping through. "Don't mind the mess," the man muttered, his voice flat, as if daring Devin to complain.

Devin tossed his own small pile of belongings onto the bottom bunk and sat down heavily. His shoulders stiffened, his mind racing with every instinct, screaming to organize the living space, to clean, to control the chaos. But control here wasn't about neatness. It was about survival. So, he sat back, stared into the dim air above him, and forced himself to breathe. Minutes bled into silence until a voice broke through. "Hotshot! You got a visitor." Johansen shouted. His grin carried through the bars. Devin rose, his muscles coiled and walked past him. Their eyes locked and Devin saw toughness staring back at him. The guard gave him a hard shove on the shoulder. Devin stumbled slightly but didn't retaliate. Not here. Not now.

The guard wanted a reaction from the inmate, but Devin wasn't ready to give him the satisfaction. When he arrived in the visiting area, he heard muffled conversations and clinking of phones. Rows of thick plexiglass divided inmates from civilians, the air heavy with unspoken words, the ache of separation. Devin scanned the room, his gaze hard, until he saw him—Agent Mack. But Mack wasn't dressed like a law enforcement agent. He looked like another civilian in casual clothes and a relaxed posture. It was a disguise, but Devin knew better than to mistake his easy grin for comfort.

Devin slid into the seat across from him and picked up the receiver. His knuckles whitened as he pressed it to his ear. "What the heck is going on?" he hissed into the mouthpiece. His voice was low, controlled, but every word throbbed with anger. Mack raised a hand, palm down, urging calm. "Crews, try not to draw attention," "It's Gabe, damit! ... and don't call me that in here," Devin snapped. "You'll blow my cov.. . he caught himself before lowering his voice further. "Don't worry my friend, this is an attorney visit, so the line is clean." Mack reassured his colleague. Devin felt a bit at ease hearing that, but the fact still remains that he was very unhappy with the turn of events. "What the hell, Mack? I've got a damn cellmate. You told me the Warden had this covered."

Mack leaned forward, his eyes sharp now, the grin gone. "Yeah, about that. The Bureau decided to go dark on this one. They don't trust the Warden. He's corrupted, Dev-" He caught himself. "Gabe." Devin's stomach twisted. "You mean I'm here on my own?" Mack exhaled, his voice dropping to a near whisper. "Sorry, partner." The line went silent. Devin's jaw worked as he bit back the rage threatening to spill. Alone. They'd thrown him into the pit and snapped the rope. His cover was his only armor now. He couldn't afford to slip. He lowered the receiver slowly, staring through the glass at Mack. Suddenly, an alarm went off, and inmates were ushered out of the visiting area.

"This is how you do it?" He asked, raising his voice with rage. "This is the plan?" Mack didn't answer. He didn't need to. The silence was answer enough.

That night, the prison latrine reeked of bleach and sweat. The mirrors above the sinks were scratched so badly they reflected more ghosts than faces. The white tiles were stained and a long fluorescent tube burned overhead. Devin leaned over a sink and allowed water to drip from his hands. When he looked up at the mirror, he was staring at the blurred version of himself staring back. His face looked harder now, colder, the shadows cutting deeper lines into his jaw. Then he felt it. The shift in the room.

The three thugs from lunch. Skinheads. They slid in through the doorway, shutting out the murmur of the cellblock. Other inmates glanced in, saw what was coming, and cleared out. The silence that followed was heavy. Devin straightened slowly, gripping the edge of the sink. Their reflections loomed behind him. "You're the one they call Gabe, right? One of the skinheads blurted out but didn't wait for and answer before adding… "this is our house, we're just here to make sure you know not to fuck with us." They laughed as they caressed their knuckles.

Devin turned, calm, his eyes scanning them one by one. It was at this moment he knew he would have to drop the nice guy act and come to blows with the bullies. "I'll let you get one free hit," he said, his voice even, measured. He pointed at the smallest of the three. "Just you. The rest of you—nothing." The smallest guy snickered nervously, looking at his crew. "He's funny," he muttered. Devin's lips curled faintly. "Okay, no free hits," he said. "I've changed my mind." He gestured with his palm in one smooth motion calling on the first attacker.

The biggest thug lunged first, swinging wide. Devin's body reacted faster than thought. He caught the wrist mid-swing, yanked the man forward, and swept his leg clean. The thug hit the tiles hard, air rushing from his lungs as he wheezed in pain. The second came charging, teeth bared. Devin pivoted, drove a kick into his ribs so fast and sharp that the man flew back, slamming into the stalls with a crash. The last one froze. Fear cracked his tough exterior. He turned to bolt.

Devin was already there, hand locking around his collar. Devin dragged him back into the fray, clamping him in a headlock just as the first thug regained awareness and staggered to his feet, dazed and furious. Devin hurled the one in his grip straight into the torso of the other attacker. Both men stumbled into metal stall walls before tumbling down to the floor in a crashing heap. The third man jumped onto Devin's neck but was quickly flung onto his back. He cried in pain. Devin didn't stop, there was an unusual look in his eyes, like a man possessed. The confined space turned grappling into a desperate, slippery struggle, feet sliding on wet ceramic floor as they traded heavy blows. As the skinheads wailed, Devin hammered them with controlled blows, fast and brutal, until the three of them lay groaning on the floor, their bravado shattered. Devin stood up and picked up the smallest of the three men, bringing him to his feet, body slummed over. Devin thrusted the limp body into a porcelain sink, which gave way with a splintering crack and a rush of cold water. All three men laid motionless on the floor as the fight was over as quickly as it had started.

Devin straightened, chest heaving but face calm. He looked down at them, his eyes cold as ice. "Tell the rest of your crew," he said, his voice low, lethal. He spat on the tiles near their faces. "I'm not the one to fuck with! Checkmate!" He grabbed his towel from the rack, slung it casually over his shoulder, and walked out of the latrine without another glance.

Two inmates leaned against the wall outside, having watched the whole thing. Their eyes followed him with new calculation, a mix of respect and fear. Word would spread fast. In prison, it always did. And Devin knew he had just made his first real move.

The First Invitation

The cafeteria buzzed like a hive, packed with bodies, noise, and the smell of boiled starch and bleach. Trays clattered against metal tables, conversations overlapped in shouts, mutters, and the occasional bark of laughter. Devin walked in with his tray balanced on one hand, his shoulders squared, his eyes scanning every corner of the room. Today, he carried himself differently. A small change, but enough. His stride had a rhythm to it, not cocky, but deliberate-like a man who had survived his first test and lived to talk about it. And in prison, that was everything.

He spotted Aleksei. The Russian sat in a corner; his table marked like territory. Four men sat close, too close, their eyes scanning for threats even as they leaned-in to listen to him. Aleksei wasn't large, but power radiated from him. He ate with deliberate calm, his gestures small, precise. Around him was a silence, as if the chaos of the cafeteria simply knew to leave that corner untouched. Devin's gaze lingered, then shifted. He had other business first.

The Skinheads.

They were already seated at a table near the center of the cafeteria, three of them. Their shaved scalps were cross hatched with scars and fresh bandages. Their eyes tracked Devin the moment he entered, their jaws tightening in recognition. Big T followed close behind, his grin wider than usual. Confidence rolled off him now, borrowed from Devin's shadow. Devin walked straight to the Skinheads' table and stopped. He didn't speak. He didn't ask. He simply stood there, tray in hand, his height casting a shadow across their food.

The room seemed to pause. Conversations thinned, whispers replacing them and people began to stare. Everyone knew what this was—a test of pride, of survival. One by one, the Skinheads pushed back, their chairs scraping the floor as they stood up, food trays in hand. Their glares promised revenge, but their bodies told another truth: defeat still lingered in their bones. They stepped aside, moving toward another table with muttered curses. Devin set his tray down and sat. Big T slid in next to him, his grin unshaken. "Damn," he muttered, spearing a lump of gray meat with his fork. "You really know how to pick your enemies." Devin said nothing. He grabbed a bite and shoved it into his mouth and ate slowly, methodically, his eyes occasionally flicking toward Aleksei's corner. And sure enough, Aleksei was watching.

The Russian's gaze was cool, calculating. He didn't smile, but his nod was perceptible and said everything. Later, in the yard, the air was sharp with the smell of sweat and cut grass. The expanse of concrete and chain-link wire seemed to pulse with tension. Men clustered in groups, some around weight benches, others circling handball courts. Every group was a flag, a boundary, a declaration of allegiance.

Devin sat on a bench with Big T and another inmate, their small talk a cover for constant observation. But his focus was fixed across the yard. Aleksei again. This time, the Russian was outside, a book in hand, though Devin doubted he was reading. He glanced up, their eyes met, and Aleksei raised a hand in a subtle beckon. Devin rose without hesitation. That was when tension in the yard shifted elsewhere.

The shouting started with a spark of verbal attacks—one voice, then two, then an eruption. The Six-Nines, their tattoos a mosaic of black ink and defiance, squared off against the Nazis. Insults flew, sharp and venomous. A bottle clattered against the ground, and the crowd tensed, waiting for the first blow. Devin froze, caught between instinct and mission. He scanned quickly: the guards were on edge, rifles aimed, but hesitation ruled. Then a loud POP! POP! The warning shots split the air. Silence fell, heavy and sudden. The echo rang against steel and concrete. Slowly, reluctantly, the inmates began to back away keeping their eyes on the opponents. For now, the fight aborted but the anger simmering just below the surface, remained palpable. Devin exhaled.

Timing was everything. He moved quickly, weaving through dispersing bodies until he reached Aleksei's table. Four men surrounded Aleksei like an orbit, their eyes narrow as Devin approached. They shifted, protective, as though ready to intercept him. But Aleksei raised a hand and his men slowly backed down. "Come," he said, his accent thick, every word very deliberate. Devin stepped closer. "What's your name?" Aleksei asked, his pale eyes fixed on him. "Gabe." Aleksei's lips curled in a thin smile. "I heard what you did. The bathroom. The cafeteria. You made strong men with battle scars to walk around like whipped dogs with tails tucked between their legs. I like that." I can use a man like you. Devin shrugged. "I'm not Russian." Aleksei chuckled, leaning back. His crew bristled, their faces tightening with disapproval. "I can wave that," he said. "Because I like you. Devin studied him. It was too soon, too easy. No one handed out invitations without a test hidden inside. But this was the crack in the wall he needed. Before he could answer, shadows loomed. Three guards approached. One of them was Johansen. "Hey, hotshot," he sneered, his voice carrying. "The Warden wants to see you." The goons shifted, their hostility now aimed at the guards. Devin stood slowly and nodded. "I'll be back," he said simply. Aleksei's smile deepened, just slightly. His men didn't share it.

The walk to the administrative wing was done under watchful eyes from the guard tower. The only sound Devin could hear were the hollow, rhythmic echo of four pairs of boots. Flanked by two officers, Devin kept his eyes fixed on officer Johansen ahead. The air in the admin building was cleaner, colder, a stark contrast to the cell blocks. Polished wooden doors lined the corridor. Devin mind began racing of the possibilities of the visit. *Maybe the bureau has come to its senses and let the warden in on the mission*, he thought to himself. The Warden's office was brighter and more modernized than the rest of the prison. The blinds were drawn halfway, stripes of light cutting across the desk. Papers were stacked neatly, a crystal decanter of water glinting in the corner.

The Warden stood near the desk, his posture casual but his eyes sharp. Beside him sat an older man in a tailored suit that screamed money. His tie was silk, his watch heavy, his accent unmistakably Russian when he spoke. Devin entered, cuffed, with the guards in tow. "Wait outside for a second, would you?" the Warden said, gesturing without looking. The guards ushered Devin back into the hallway, to a bench bolted into the floor. Officer Johansen leaned down, smirking. "Have a seat, hotshot." Devin sat. His hands rested calmly on his lap, but his mind raced. Who was the man inside? Why was a Russian businessman sitting in the Warden's office, speaking in low tones behind closed doors? And why did Devin feel like he had just walked into the center of the storm?

CHAPTER 16

OLIGARCH

The Warden's office always smelled faintly of polish and whiskey, a strange attempt at courtesy in a place where civility didn't survive long. Narrow bands of sunlight sliced through the blinds. Leather chairs sat stiffly in front of a heavy oak desk, and on the far side stood a man who didn't seem to belong.

Benedikt Oblonsky.

His suit was European-cut, sharp enough to slice the stale air. The watch on his wrist gleamed gold, thick and deliberate, a statement as much as an accessory. His shoes- polished black leather-clicked against the linoleum floor with every shift of his stance. And though he wore the required visitor's pass clipped to his breast pocket, nothing about him suggested submission. He looked at the Warden as though he were the hired help. "You promised me, Gary," Oblonsky said, his Russian accent bending the words into heavy shapes. "You promised me my men." He gestured with one hand, rings flashing under the light. His tone was part complaint, part threat, and entirely dismissive. "I have a fight club with no fighters. Do you know what that means? Empty seats. No bets. No money. And worst of all-" he jabbed a finger into the air—"no honor. Some of my best men sit in this… how do you say … shit hole." The Warden folded his hands on his desk, hiding his irritation. He has heard this type of arrogance before, but Oblonsky's brand of it was volcanic, a mix of wealth, power, and foreign disdain. "Your best man …," the Warden said carefully, placing emphasis on "man," "… is serving time. He's a criminal, Benedikt. This is not Russia." Oblonsky's mouth twisted into something between a smile and a snarl. "Dog fighting is illegal in America, yes? But my men are not dogs. They are men. Warriors. Fighters." He leaned in, lowering his voice. "And I know people in high places. People who take bribes. That is very American too, no?"

The Warden blinked, forcing his expression to stay neutral. The audacity was breathtaking. Oblonsky didn't bother with subtlety-he flaunted corruption like a badge. "I can't just open the gates and let him walk out," the Warden replied, tone dry, hands splayed across the desk. "You know that. But …" He let the word linger, rolling it like a dice. "I might arrange something you'd like. A compromise." Oblonsky straightened, then reached for the glass of liquor on the side table. He swirled the amber liquid lazily, savoring the smell before taking a slow sip. His eyes flicked toward the window. "What about the one you have out there? Big shoulders. Bald head. Looks like he can fight." The Warden chuckled, though the sound was hollow. "Gabe? No, no. He's going to be here a while. He's not for sale." "I didn't ask if he was for sale," Oblonsky muttered, lips curling. "I asked if he can fight." The Warden didn't answer right away. He moved to the window, parting the blinds just enough for the two of them to peer out. Below, in the yard, Aleksei sat like a king in exile, his table, a throne amid chaos. Lately Aleksei had become a thorn in Oblonski's side because he knew too much about the oligarch. The type of information the FBI may be interested in.

Oblonsky's expression shifted. His lips pressed together, his head shaking slowly as he shot a look at his old friend. "It's a shame," he said, voice thick with nostalgia. "He could have been great. Like Benedikt." The Warden smirked faintly, though it never reached his eyes. "Keep an eye on him," Oblonsky continued, the sharpness returning. "Every move. Every word. I want to know." The Warden nodded. "Consider it done." Oblonsky drained the last of his glass, setting it down with precision. He adjusted his cufflinks, the gold glinting. "I will go to Mother Russia for a few months," he said. "Business, you understand. But Gary…" He paused, his gaze stabbing the Warden like a blade. "…I am counting on you." "I'll see what I can do," the Warden replied. Oblonsky's eyes hardened. "Don't see, my friend, just do and I'd reward you." Oblonsky clears his throat. "New rule for fight club-" He leaned close, his breath reeking of liquor and expensive cigars. "We never shut down fight club." He held the Warden's gaze for a beat daring a backlash. When it didn't come, he adjusted himself and strode toward the door, every step echoing with control.

In the hallway, Devin sat chained to a bench, his wrists resting on his lap. He had listened through the thin wall, piecing together fragments of the Russian's voice, the cadence of power. The door opened. Oblonsky stepped out, his eyes landing immediately on Devin.

For a moment, silence stretched. Oblonsky's gaze traveled up and down Devin's frame, measuring him like livestock at auction. The disgust was written plainly across his face. "What a shame," Oblonsky muttered, his accent heavy. "I could use a man like you." Devin's jaw flexed a little as he tensed up. *What does that even mean?* he thought to himself. But he kept his expression flat, trying to sound disinterested. Oblonsky leaned slightly closer, lowering his voice. "Ya uvidim tebya," he said in Russian. I'll be seeing you. Their eyes locked, a silent duel of wills. Then the oligarch turned sharply, his shoes clicking as he strode down the corridor. From inside the office, the Warden's voice barked: "Bring him in!" The guards yanked Devin to his feet and marched him through the door.

The Warden stood behind his desk, one hand already reaching for the decanter on the side table. His face wore its usual smug calm, but his eyes flickered with a different light. Something calculating, something dangerous. "Sit," he said simply. Devin obeyed. The Warden poured two drinks, the golden liquid catching the light. He didn't offer it yet. He let the smell fill the room first, rich and sharp. "I see you've made new friends," the Warden remarked, eyes never leaving Devin's back. Devin didn't answer. Silence was safer. "You like music?" the Warden asked suddenly, a strange twist in tone. "Yes," Devin said cautiously. His muscles coiled, unsure where this was going.

The Warden smiled faintly. He lifted a bottle, holding it in the light. "Brandy?" Devin turned his head slightly. Relief, confusion, and the absurdity of the moment clashed in him. "Some say Monica," he muttered before realizing the mistake. He turned, caught sight of the bottle, and flushed. "Oh-yeah. Brandy. Definitely." The Warden chuckled, handing him a glass. Devin accepted it, fingers brushing the cool crystal. He didn't drink. "What do you want?" Devin asked flatly.

The Warden's grin widened. He sipped his own glass first, savoring the taste, before finally answering. "My friends on the outside would be very happy if you could help me keep an eye on Lebedev," he said. "All you gotta do is just listen and take notes. Report back if you hear anything … unusual." Devin let the words hang, his face unreadable. "What's in it for me?" he asked at last.

The Warden's reply came smoothly, without hesitation. "Congratulations," he said, raising his glass. "You've just got your own cell with a great view of …" He was lost for words. "Well, it doesn't matter, you now have what you wanted." Devin's chest tightened, he couldn't tell if it was excitement or anxiety. It was exactly what he had wanted indeed. Some peace and quiet. A chance to maneuver without a slob of a bunkmate breathing down his neck. But he forced his expression to remain flat, almost bored. He couldn't let the Warden see satisfaction. Not here. Instead, he adjusted the cuffs before lifting the glass to his lips, took a slow sip, and placed it back down with quiet precision. Inside, though, he felt the weight of the walls shifting. Everyone wanted something from him, the Russians, the Warden, the Bureau. And each drink, each handshake, each exchange was a new thread in a web tightening around him. *I've gotta be careful not to overplay my hand*, he thought.

Walls and Mansions

Devin's new cell was a stark contrast from the previous. It was a subtle improvement—sterile walls lined with grime, and yet he fought each day to impose order upon them. It wasn't much of a space, just a rectangle of cold cement and rusted bars, but he had rearranged what little he had until it reflected discipline. His blanket was folded with military precision, corners sharp as a knife's edge. His shoes sat side by side under the bed. Even the few books issued by the prison library were stacked according to height.

It was the only way he knew how to keep his mind intact— treating the cell like the barracks, like a place that could belong to him if he only forced it hard enough. But tonight, lying flat on the bunk and staring up at the peelings on the ceiling, all that discipline couldn't kill the boredom that gnawed at his brain. Hours stretched out like years, the silence broken only by distant shouts, the occasional bone rattling clang of a gate, or the muted cough of another inmate down the tier were all taking a tow on him.

He folded his hands across his chest, closed his eyes for a moment, and then snapped them open again. Sleep wouldn't come easy. With a grunt, Devin swung his legs over the side of the bed and reached under his pillow. From the hidden crease he pulled out a stub of chalk he'd bartered from the laundry crew. He got off the bed and walked to the wall beside his bunk; its surface already scarred with old carvings and graffiti from the men who had occupied it before him.

He pressed the chalk hard against the concrete and made another line. A tally mark Six. One for each day he had been inside these walls. He stared at the marks for a long while, the pale scratches catching the dim glow from the corridor light. Six lines, and each one felt like a weight dragging him deeper into this undercover life. He traced the first line with his finger, remembering the bus ride, the fear of the man beside him, the smell of sweat and metal. He traced the next, remembering the cafeteria and the fight that came that night, the moment he declared himself not to be trifled with. And then the next, remembering Aleksei's cold eyes across the yard. "Six days," he muttered under his breath. His voice sounded strange in the small space, swallowed quickly by the concrete. "Feels like six years."

Devin sat back on the bunk, resting his chalk between his fingers like a cigarette. He thought of Tanya, her ponytail bouncing as she jogged, the way her laughter filled their kitchen, her stubborn refusal to support this mission. He thought of his father, immortalized on the Bureau's wall, looking down at him with silent expectation.

What would you say, Pop? That I'm in over my head? That I should pull the plug before this goes too far? Or would you nod and tell me this is the job—hard and sometimes ugly, but necessary? Devin sighed and lay back again, eyes tracing invisible patterns on the ceiling until the sound of distant footsteps told him the night guard was making his rounds. He hid the chalk and closed his eyes, pretending to sleep.

Far away from the suffocating walls of MCC, the night painted a different picture. Oblonsky's mansion sat like a jewel on the edge of the city, a sprawling estate wrapped in marble and glass. The driveway glistened with freshly washed luxury cars, Mercedes, Bentleys, a Ferrari or two-all lined like obedient soldiers awaiting inspection. The pool in the backyard shimmered under lights, its surface so clean it reflected the stars above.

Bodyguards dotted the property, each one dressed in black, their hands never straying far from the concealed bulges at their waists. They were disciplined, watchful, trained to look invisible until the moment came to strike. And in the center of it all stood Benedikt Oblonsky, rolling up the sleeves of his tailored shirt. He was not a very tall man, but his presence filled the marble patio with a heaviness that made even his guards keep their eyes down. His hair was slicked back, silver streaks catching the glow from the lanterns. On his wrist, a gold watch caught and threw light with every movement of his hand. His phone buzzed. He picked it up with a flick of impatience.

"Hey... my main man Gary," Oblonsky said, his Russian accent lacing the words with a mixture of menace and excitement. He flashed a small grin. "What do I owe the pleasure?" On the other end of the line, the Warden's voice oozed smug satisfaction.

"I'm gonna make you a very happy man." The Warden said. Oblonsky chuckled, deep and guttural. "And I'm gonna make you a very rich man. Tell me, Gary, do you like money?" Across town, the Warden leaned back in a lawn chair on the deck of his suburban home. The irony of the question made him grin. His cigar glowed at the tip as he drew in smoke, exhaling it slowly into the late afternoon air. A glass of tea sweated on the table beside him. "In a Russian accent" he replied mockingly into the phone, "Do you like Mother Russia?" Both men erupted into laughter, their amusement as obscene as it was dangerous.

Intercut between them, the conversation crackled across miles but felt like they sat in the same room, drinking the same poison. "I am a very busy man, Gary," Oblonsky said at last, his tone snapping back to business. "So … tell me— what do you have for me?"

The Warden tapped ash off his cigar and smirked at the clouds. "Five men. All former fighters. They get out in three days. I'll have their names and outside contacts sent over on Monday." Oblonsky's face softened into satisfaction. "You are a good man, Gary." The Warden's grin widened. "Good for business." But Oblonsky's reply came slower, colder, cutting through the cigar haze like a blade. "Yes … you are good for business." The laughter had faded. The Warden felt it—an edge to the words, a reminder that in this world of deals and corruption, loyalty was only worth as much as the next payoff. His grin slackened, the cigar suddenly bitter in his mouth. His conscious gnawing at him.

At the mansion, Oblonsky ended the call with a flick of his finger, slipping the phone into his pocket. He exhaled through his nose, and the amusement drained from his face like water down a drain. "Enough business," he muttered. And then we finally see why he had rolled up his sleeves.

A man sat bound to a chair on the patio. His face was swollen, purple and red from hours of abuse. Blood dripped sluggishly from his nose, staining his shirt. His wrists were tied behind him, ankles lashed to the chair legs. He looked barely conscious, his chest heaving in shallow gasps. Oblonsky stepped forward and without hesitation drove his fist into the man's abdomen. The sound was sickening, a dull thud followed by a wheeze of air and a strangled cry.

The oligarch straightened his sleeves again, brushing imaginary dust from his wristwatch. "To goons," he said in Russian, his tone casual, almost bored. "Get him out of here and teach him what we do to rats." Two bodyguards moved instantly, lifting the broken man like a sack of trash. They dragged him away into the shadows of the estate, his moans fading into silence. Oblonsky poured himself a fresh drink from the bar beside the pool and lifted it toward the stars. "To fight club," he murmured, and took a slow sip.

Back in MCC Devin turned on his bunk, restless, unaware of the exact shape of the storm building outside. He only knew that every tally mark on his wall carried weight. Every day inside meant another move on a board he hadn't fully seen yet. And far away, Benedikt Oblonsky moved his own pieces with blood sweat and tears of others, and an occasional whiskey to forget his role in all of it. The two worlds, very different then the next were set on a collision course with destiny. Each passing day brought them closer than ever.

CHAPTER 17

FRACTURES

The garage smelled faintly of rubber mats and iron. Tanya's fists sliced through the air, the dull rhythm of her gloves striking and blocking, leather echoing back at her in the quiet garage. Kick, punch, block, pivot. Again. Harder. Faster. Sweat gathered on her brow, strands of hair clinging to her cheeks, but still she pushed herself further, as though each jab could knock away the loneliness that had rooted itself in her chest.

The heavy bag swung wildly under her kicks, thudding into the concrete wall with dull reverberations. Yet the more she struck, the hollower it felt. Her body worked, but her spirit was somewhere else entirely. At last, she stopped, her breath ragged, arms limp at her sides. She slid down against the wall and sat, the gloves heavy in her lap, icked off her shoes. Her eyes drifted toward the ceiling to floor pole in the corner—a remnant of another time with Devin crossed her mind, a better version of her life. She gazed at it long enough that her expression softened. For a moment, her lips curved into a faint smile, a memory tugging her backward. But the smile broke just as quickly, and a tear slipped free, tracing a clean path down her flushed cheek.

The silence pressed in, thick and unyielding. Then the doorbell rang. She rose slowly, peeling the gloves from her hands before removing her socks, and walked barefoot across the cool floor into the house. At the front door she hesitated, wiping hastily at her eyes before pulling it open. Mack stood there in casual clothes with badge hanging from his neck, posture uneasy but eyes steady. "Can I come in?" he asked. She nodded, stepping aside.

Inside the dining room, they sat across from one another, a half-filled water glass between them. Mack leaned forward, his voice low but firm. "I went to see him," he said. "He's doing fine. He wanted me to tell you that." Tanya's throat tightened. She managed only one word, choked out like a plea: "How much longer … is he—" Her voice cracked before she could finish. Mack's gaze softened. "I don't have the answer you want," he admitted. "But I promise I'll keep you informed. The second I know anything, you'll know too." Her fingers toyed with the glass, circling its rim. "Thank you." "Anything you need," Mack said, sliding a card across the table, "you call my cell." She took it carefully, as though it were fragile, then looked back at him with tired eyes. "You're a good man, Mack, and I appreciate the visit." He offered a half-smile, stood, and left without another word.

The apartment felt heavier once the door closed behind him. Later, steam filled the bathroom. Tanya's silhouette wavered behind the curtain as hot water poured over her skin. Her head bowed under the stream, eyes closed, the sound of the shower masking the tears that mingled with the water. She stayed there a long time, letting the warmth numb her thoughts, until her skin was flushed and the mirror fogged completely. But when she finally stepped out, toweling herself dry, her face was composed again- calm, resolved, though no less haunted.

The next morning, dressed in clean scrubs, Tanya locked the apartment door behind her. The key clicked, the sound final. She slung her bag over her shoulder and walked to her car. Her movements were deliberate, steady. To anyone watching, she was just another woman heading to work. But inside, she carried the weight of waiting, of uncertainty, of love stretched thin by silence. On the other side of the city, the world spun differently.

In the prison yard, Devin walked with Aleksei Lebedev. His beard had grown thick, his scalp still bare, his frame harder now, every muscle sharpened by the routine of survival. Beside him, Aleksei moved with the authority of a man who owned the ground under his feet, his henchmen trailing like shadows. Other inmates watched from a distance, their expressions a mix of curiosity, resentment, and fear. Whispers traveled fast behind steel bars, and the newest rumor was that the Russian had taken a liking to the bald brawler, a nickname that was catching steam around MCC. That Devin had risen faster than most men dared. It was true. And it made him a target. "So … tell me," Aleksei said, his accent thick, his tone almost playful. "How does a good hacker allow himself to get busted? Hmm? A man like you, he sees things coming before they arrive." Devin smirked, adjusting his pace to match. "Not everything. I hacked into the wrong system. Government stuff. Turns out they really hate that."

Aleksei barked a short laugh. "Yes, yes, I believe it. Government men are like spoiled children—they throw tantrums when you touch their toys." They stopped walking, the henchmen forming a loose circle around them. Aleksei's eyes gleamed with calculation. "I need a favor," he said. "You have certain computer skills, yes? And privilege I do not." Devin's brow furrowed. "What kind of favor?" The Russian leaned in, voice dropping to a growl. "Find out who the rat is. I need to know who put me in this place." The words hit Devin like a stone in the chest. His mind raced. *That's the Bureau's target. That's why I'm here.* But his face remained neutral, controlled. "That's government stuff," Devin replied carefully. Aleksei's expression hardened. "But we are friends, yah? And friends help each other."

The henchmen shifted, waiting for Devin's answer. He could feel their jealousy, their suspicion, burning holes into his back. One wrong move and the fragile trust

Aleksei offered would snap like a dry twig. Devin forced a smile, though his jaw stiffened. He realized the line he was walking was thinner than ever. And in that moment, two worlds stretched further apart—Tanya on the outside, fighting her loneliness with sweat and silence, and Devin on the inside, fighting his way deeper into the coils of a man who trusted no one.

The visiting area was colder than Tanya expected. Even with the heavy plate of glass between her and the rest of the room, the chill seeped into her bones, carried on the low hum of fluorescent lights. The plastic chair beneath her felt too hard, the linoleum floor too sterile. She sat still, palms pressed against her knees, her heart beating in uneven rhythm. Then the door opened. She saw him.

Devin!, The orange uniform hung loose on his frame, his shoulders leaner, his body stripped of softness. He looked older, sharper. His once-boyish face was now crowned with a thick stubble, his skull shaved clean, the contrast stark. A small cut marked his cheek, faint but undeniable. Her throat constricted. For a moment, she couldn't breathe.

Devin's eyes found hers. His expression softened, though his movements were measured, almost cautious. He sat across from her, separated by glass that seemed thicker than any wall she had ever known. Slowly, he lifted the receiver. "Hey, babe," he said, his voice tired but steady. "I guess you stayed, huh?" Her fingers trembled as she picked up her own receiver. The sound of his voice sent a wave of relief and grief crashing together inside her. "We're in this together now," she whispered. "When are you coming home?"

The question lodged itself between them, sharp and unavoidable. Devin looked past her, scanning the guards.

They were distracted, arguing with an inmate further down the row. He leaned forward, lowering his voice. "Look, I'm really close to solving my case. It won't be much longer now." He forced a faint smile. "How's Baxter?" Tanya swallowed hard. She had promised herself she wouldn't cry, but her eyes burned anyway. "He's at the vet and will be there for a few more days. He's not well, Devin," she said softly. Tearing.

A shadow flickered in Devin's eyes. He closed them briefly, picturing his best friend. "I need you to deliver a message," Devin said firmly. "Tell Mack I need to see him. ASAP." Tanya nodded quickly, wanting to say more, but the sharp bark of a guard's voice cut through the air. "Okay, time's up!" Her body jolted as Johansen strode over, his presence heavy, his grip rough on her arm as he ushered her away. She turned, fighting for one last moment. "I love you," she said quickly, almost too fast, but with all the force in her heart.

Devin's hand clenched around the receiver. He wanted to press his palm to the glass, to reach through the barrier, but all he could do was watch. His eyes darkened with rage at the sight of the guard pulling her so harshly, and though he stayed silent, the fire in him flared hot. He lowered the receiver slowly, jaw tight, eyes locked on her until the door shut behind her.

Outside, the sun hit Tanya like a slap. The parking lot seemed impossibly wide, the prison looming behind her, its walls too high, too thick, too permanent. She walked quickly, her breath short, until she spotted the SUV parked in the shade. April sat behind the wheel. The moment Tanya slid into the passenger seat, April shifted the car into drive. The tires crunched over gravel as they rolled out of the lot. "How is he doing?" April asked quietly. Tanya stared out the window, her reflection faint in the glass. "Good," she said automatically. Her hand tightened in her lap. "I gotta make a call." April glanced at her, then back to the road. Her eyes flickered again, studying Tanya's posture, her too-quick answer. "You alright?" Tanya forced a breath, nodding. "Yes. I'm fine." But she wasn't fine. Not even close.

She pulled out her phone, scrolling through her contacts. Each name passed in a blur until one stopped her finger cold. She tapped it, her pulse quickening. At the FBI's Chicago field office, the atmosphere was very different. The prep building, usually kept sharp and precise, looked worn that afternoon. Sweat clung to the agents training inside, their shirts sticking, their breathing heavy. A group workout had left the room scattered with water bottles, mats, and discarded towels.

Mack lay on a mat, chest rising and falling, his shirt soaked through. He was exhausted, the kind of exhaustion that came not just from training but from carrying burdens he didn't speak of. Around him, other agents sprawled, muttering complaints about the new instructor. The room lacked the crisp energy it once had with Crews at the helm. Mack's phone lit up on the floor beside him. The name on the screen made him sit up fast, grabbing it. "Hello," he answered, voice thick with exertion.

He listened. Then he stood, already moving away from the group. "I gotta take this," he called back to the female instructor. She nodded, wiping sweat from her brow, relieved at the break. Mack stepped into the hallway, pacing as he pressed the phone to his ear. "How's he doing?" Mack asked, his voice dropped, urgent. A pause. He ran a hand through his damp hair. "How soon?" His brow furrowed. Another pause. "I'll go see him first thing in the morning," he said finally. His tone was resolved, no hesitation left. When he hung up, he stood still for a long moment, phone heavy in his hand. The noise of the workout filtered faintly through the walls, but it felt distant, irrelevant. Devin needed him. That was all that mattered. The exercise was over. But something else was just beginning.

CHAPTER 18

FIGHT CLUB

The warehouse in the Englewood neighborhood pulsed like a living beast. Its corrugated walls rattled with the relentless thump of bass, each beat vibrating through the cracked pavement. Cars lined the parking lot—old and new alike, their owners streaming inside, drawn by the promise of a blood sport with gambling and anonymity. Inside, smoke clouded the rafters, the mingling stench of sweat, alcohol, and iron thick in the air. Men and women pressed shoulder to shoulder, shouting over one another, wagers exchanged with grubby bills or quick flashes of cash. In the middle of the chaos stood the ring, a makeshift patchwork square of ropes strung between steel pipes, its canvas already stained dark with blood.

Two fighters circled inside, stripped to the waist, their bodies tattooed with stories of survival and ruin. Every punch landed with a thud that was swallowed by the roar of the crowd. "Finish him!" someone screamed. A brutal combination followed a snapping jab, then a powerful left cross—and one man was hurled into the onlookers, scattering drinks and laughter alike. He staggered back in, grinning through a mask of blood. "You hit like a little bitch!" he taunted his opponent, spitting red onto the canvas.

The other fighter didn't flinch. He launched forward, knees rising like pistons, and caught the man square in the chest. The blow lifted him, stole his breath, and flattened him. This time, he didn't rise.

The crowd erupted, wild with approval. Bookies shouted, exchanging cash, pockets fattening. From the shadows near the entrance, Benedikt Oblonsky appeared. His tailored suit gleamed under the flickering lights, his gold watch catching stray beams as he slapped palms with men who admired him and women who sought his favor. He moved like a king among thieves, surveying the spectacle with the cool detachment of someone who owned it all. His phone buzzed. He frowned, stepped away from the cheering throng, and answered. His voice dropped, and though no one around him could hear the words, his pace quickened, his expression sharpening. The call ended as abruptly as it began.

He signaled his driver. The music thundered on, but Oblonsky slipped away unnoticed, sliding into the leather seat of a waiting car. The engine purred, tires screeched, and within minutes he was gone, the illegal fight club continuing its violent symphony without its chief patron.

The night air was crisp at the private airfield. A small Cessna sat ready, its nose pointed east as if impatient to cut through the sky. Oblonsky's car rolled directly into the hangar, headlights bouncing off the polished fuselage. He got out and strode across the floor, his suitcase unnecessary, his confidence absolute. The pilots straightened when he climbed aboard. "Take me to Moscow," he ordered, his Russian accent slicing through the hum of the engines. Within minutes, the aircraft was taxiing, its lights cutting faint arcs of red and green into the darkness of the rural airfield. The pilots eased their throttle forward and heard a guttural roar that vibrated through the airframe. Headlights illuminated the runway ahead, a tunnel of pale white stretching into the dark. The jet gathered speed, the rumble of its tires on asphalt growing to a steady drumming until, with a gentle heave of the yoke, the pilots watched the ground fall away lifting from the city of Chicago to Oblonsky's homeland.

Meanwhile, behind steel bars and concrete walls, Devin Crews sat across from Agent Mack in the prison visiting area. The glass separating them was thinner this time, less imposing than the thick divider Tanya had endured. They leaned close, voices low, careful not to draw the attention of the guards hovering nearby. Devin's beard itched, his face marked with small nicks from hurried shaves. His eyes carried the strain of endless calculation. "Just find out who the informant is," he said. His tone was calm, but urgency lurked beneath it. "We need to give Aleksei something, a taste. Otherwise, he won't talk." Mack leaned back, frowning. His casual attire couldn't mask the tension in his jaw. "You realize what he's going to do if you hand him that name? He won't hesitate ya' know. He'll whack the guy before you can blink." Devin's gaze hardened. He thought about his next words carefully with the gravity of his situation in mind. He hated what he was about to set in motion, but he had to do something. "Whatever it takes. I need to get out of here, Mack. The longer I'm inside, the more dangerous this gets. For me. For Tanya."

He didn't like the words he spoke. *Am I becoming a monster?* He thought to himself. Mack exhaled, rubbing a hand over his face. His friend's desperation was clear, but the line between duty and survival was blurring fast. "You're playing with fire," Mack muttered. "Yeah," Devin said quietly. "But at least I'm the one holding the match." Half a world away, Moscow stretched beneath a pale winter sun. The city was both ancient and alive, its golden domes gleaming against a skyline of steel and glass. Snow clung to rooftops, car tires hissed on icy streets, and steam rose from grates as people hurried by in coats pulled tight.

Oblonsky sat in the back seat of a taxi, his presence filling the cramped vehicle. The driver stole nervous glances in the mirror but said nothing, focusing instead on weaving through the traffic. Oblonsky gazed out the window, silent, the city reflected in his cold eyes. The taxi delivered him to the Federation Council. The building loomed, columns tall and unyielding, the Russian flag snapping in the wind above. He entered with the ease of a man accustomed to access, passing through layers of security until he was inside the grand chamber.

The hall echoed with the thunder of voices as Senator Lobanov, broad-shouldered and commanding, finished his speech at the podium. The language was Russian, the cadence fiery, each word striking chords of nationalism and defiance. Applause followed, swelling like a wave. Lobanov descended from the stage; his face flushed with conviction as he disappeared into the side corridor. Oblonsky followed at a measured pace until they met outside the senator's office.

Lobanov's office was a shrine to power. Heavy crimson curtains draped the tall windows, the oak desk gleamed, shelves sagged with books and framed photographs. A Russian flag stood proudly behind the desk, its gold crest vivid in the warm light.

Lobanov entered first, greeted his secretary, then shut the door firmly behind his guest. "Benedikt," he said, his accent thick. "Senator," Oblonsky replied with a faint bow. "That was a powerful speech, brought me to tears." Oblonsky grinned. Lobanov caught the hint of sarcasm. They embraced; two men bound not by friendship but by ambition. The senator moved to a cabinet, poured two drinks, and handed one across. The amber liquid caught the light. "You have the green light for Operation November," the senator said. "Came from the top." Oblonsky arched a brow. "You called me to Moscow for this?" The senator's expression grew serious. "Can't be too careful. You never know who's listening. The FBI's watching us more closely than ever."

Oblonsky swirled his drink, the ice clinking softly. "Can't blame them. Ukraine was sloppy work. Next time, leave it to the professionals." Silence stretched, thick and meaningful. "The American," the senator said at last. "You trust him?" Oblonsky smirked. "Nothing little money can't fix. You give an American enough money; he'd sell out his own country." The senator raised his glass. "Good work. The boss would be proud." Their glasses touched, the sound sharp as steel, sealing something dangerous in the quiet of that gilded room. The world tilted between two realities: Devin, trapped in the grinding gears of survival inside a prison where every alliance could kill him, and Oblonsky, orchestrating global moves from velvet offices and bloodstained fight clubs. And somewhere in between, the future of nations teetered on a knife's edge.

The Price of Names

The Warden's office reeked of expensive tobacco and cheap justification. Papers cluttered his desk, but he paid them little attention. Instead, his cell phone was pressed to his ear, his lips curling around words softened by whiskey. "Yes, Ben…" His voice lowered to something between gratitude and calculation. "I must say, that was very generous of you. Now I can finally buy Carrie that boat she always wanted." He leaned back in his chair, boots tapping against the floor, the thought of his wife cruising on Lake Michigan with a new toy already floating in his mind.

On the other end, Benedikt Oblonsky's accent was unmistakable, thick and jagged, like glass dragged across stone. "She likes boats…how come you don't tell me soona'?" The Warden chuckled and rose, wandering over to the liquor table in the corner. He selected a bottle of aged bourbon, poured a generous measure into a glass, and swirled it with the casual arrogance of a man who believed himself untouchable. "I wanted it to be a surprise," he said, sipping, savoring. Oblonsky's laugh buzzed through the line. "I am glad you are happy, my friend. Just keep giving me fighters and I will keep giving you…how you say in America…Finder's Fee."

The Warden parted the curtains with two fingers, peering out across the yard. His gaze swept past the cliques of inmates until it landed on a figure moving with precision, alone yet magnetic. Devin Crews. He wasn't just doing pushups or laps like the others. He was practicing fighting forms, sharp kicks and controlled strikes, a blend of discipline and fury etched into muscle memory. The Warden smiled. "Speaking of finder's fee," he murmured into the phone. "I think I've found a gem. He's really good. I'm asking double the price." He watched Devin finish a set of kicks, chest heaving, eyes distant as if his mind lived somewhere outside the fence.

The prison yard at midday was a carnival of contradictions: laughter laced with menace, cigarette smoke drifting lazily over tension sharp enough to cut flesh, and the quiet hum of alliances forming and dissolving with every passing minute. Aleksei Lebedev sat at a weathered table near the far fence, cigarette in one hand, checkers in the other. His men flanked him, guards in everything but uniform, their eyes scanning the yard with the indifference of wolves at rest.

Devin walked toward them with the deliberate calm of a man who knew too many eyes followed him already. When he sat down, the Russians switched their chatter from liquid consonants to careful English. "Gabe," Aleksei greeted, his accent thick but his grin smooth. He flicked ash to the ground, then glanced at his men. "Give us a minute." The henchmen obeyed, rising slowly, not straying too far. They lingered just close enough to remind Devin they could be back in an instant.

Devin leaned in slightly, lowering his voice. His heart pounded harder than he let show. "I did some digging … was able to get that information you wanted." Devin glance around with a swivel, then from his sleeve, with the subtlest movement he could manage, he slid out a tightly rolled scrap of paper. He passed it beneath the table with the ease of a man sliding a coin across a bar. Aleksei took it, hands steady, eyes flashing with a hunger Devin had seen in predators before. He unrolled the slip and stared. The name was plain, written in Devin's blocky scrawl: Adriane Pavlov. Aleksei's expression sharpened like a blade. He lifted his gaze across the yard until his eyes locked onto a thin figure sitting alone under a patch of sun. The man looked foreign in every sense—gaunt face, slouched shoulders, skin pale against the gray of prison garb. "That's him," Aleksei hissed. "Pavlov."

Devin followed his gaze, and recognition struck like a blow. It was the same Ukrainian who had offered him a seat in the cafeteria weeks earlier, the one who had extended an olive branch when others sneered. For a second Devin's stomach twisted. He hadn't thought through the weight of this moment but realized the name on a piece of paper was now a death sentence. Across the yard, Pavlov must have felt the pair of eyes on him. He turned his head, eyes flicked toward Aleksei, then Devin, and realization dawned. The man froze, as if caught in a sniper's sights. Panic rippled beneath his skin, subtle but unmistakable.

Devin broke eye contact first, shame threatening to crack his facade. He told himself it was necessary, part of the job, another piece of bait for Aleksei. But watching Pavlov, a man who had done little more than show kindness, suddenly mark himself as prey, Devin felt the guilt settle heavy in his gut.

Pavlov stood abruptly. He made no attempt to look casual, no slow stretch or feigned boredom. He walked straight to the nearest guard, muttering something too low for Devin to hear. The guard frowned, glanced at Aleksei's table, then led Pavlov inside. The Ukrainian's shoulders hunched with every step. Devin exhaled slowly. He had delivered the name, but at what cost? "You did good," Aleksei said, breaking the silence. His grin was sharp, his teeth yellowed by smoke. "Come back tomorrow and I will help you with your other thing." Devin nodded stiffly and rose. He wanted nothing more than to leave, to wash the stench of complicity from his skin. But as he turned, movement flickered at the edge of his vision. An inmate mouthing at the guard in English but with a thick Spanish accent, tattooed and smooth, drifted past Devin and slid onto the bench beside Aleksei. Their familiarity was casual but practiced, the kind born of long dealings.

Devin slowed his pace, careful not to appear too curious. He watched from the corner of his eye as the Spaniard, with a sleight of hand quick as a magician, pressed something into Aleksei's palm. A phone. Small, battered, its casing scratched but functional. Aleksei curled his fingers around it, tucking it away as if it were nothing more than a coin. Devin clocked the subtle transaction. The Spaniard stood, stretched, and wandered off in the opposite direction, whistling faintly as though nothing had happened.

Devin's pulse thudded in his ears. A cell phone inside MCC was more dangerous than any weapon. It meant outside contact, coordination, secrets slipping through cracks no prison guard could see. He kept walking, forcing his face blank. But inside, the truth roared: the game was spiraling, and every step pulled him deeper into a pit where one wrong move could bury him for good. Devin walked towards Big T, keeping his head on a swivel, lest another skinhead catches him off guard. The afternoon sun was drifting away, and darker clouds were forming in the sky. Devin kept his gaze on Big T, the only alliance he had come to trust thus far. Big T was a smack talker, but he was honest with his friends. He was the only true confidant Devin had in this new world defined by constant scrutiny. With every stride, the crunch of gravel under his slow, deliberate steps was amplified in the oppressive quiet, a tiny sound in the vast, open space that felt utterly confining. High above, in the east tower, a shadow moved behind the glass, always watching the inmates and ready to respond with use of force if necessary. He knew a pair of binoculars were trained on him as he embraced Big T.

"What was that all about with the Russian?" Asked Big T.

"Nothing, don't worry about it." He responded flatly.

Together they approached the guard posted by the entrance and asked to be let back into the building. The guard gave them a once over, then nodded in permission.

CHAPTER 19

GUNS, MURDER AND SIRENS

The small cell had become Devin's world—a box of concrete and steel that pressed against him no matter which way he turned. Yet in its forced stillness, he had carved out something resembling order. The floor was mopped clean. A makeshift curtain made from torn bedsheets now hung where bars once made his life an open theater. Books, magazines, and manuals stacked neatly on the shelf above his bunk.

That night, he lay stretched out on the thin mattress, a fitness magazine balanced in his hands. The glossy pages glared under the dim fluorescent light, filled with men sculpted like statues, bodies as disciplined as machines. Devin stared at them but couldn't focus. The words blurred. His mind was elsewhere, clawing at something nameless.

He shut the magazine with a sharp slap and swung his legs off the bed. Crossing to the steel bars, he peered out into the dim corridor. The prison was restless even in silence—distant coughs, the echo of boots from guards performing their routine rounds, a verbal abuse, a muffled laugh, all feeding into a hum of unease that never stopped.

Devin exhaled, pressed his forehead briefly to the cold iron, and then stepped back. His chest tightened with helplessness. He hated all of it—the waiting, the watching, the pretending, especially for a man who hasn't committed a crime. He threw himself down on the bed again, eyes shut, fists clenched against the pillow. The curtain shielded him from prying eyes, but not from the storm in his own head.

The thunderous scream came the next morning. It cut through the cell block like a blade, raw and jagged, a sound that made every inmate freeze for half a second before the chatter rose in waves. "Help!" a voice shrieked, breaking off into gurgles. Guards thundered down the hall. Keys jangled, boots slammed against concrete.

Devin jumped off the bed and was at his bars in an instant, craning his neck in the direction of the chaos. Guards flew by, radios chattering. The other prisoners pressed close too, faces crowding the narrow gaps. The commotion erupted at Pavlov's cell. When the door swung open, the scene that unfolded made even the hardest men recoil. The Ukrainian dangled from a noose made from a bed sheet, his body grotesquely altered. His shirt clung dark with blood, riddled with punctures. His right hand hung mutilated, a finger missing, the stump jagged and raw. His head lolled forward, eyes glazed in lifeless resignation. "Christ," one guard whispered, backing away. Officer Johansen barked over the chaos, his voice slicing through the chatter. "Open the cell! Get him down!" Two guards rushed in, fumbling with the knot, struggling to lower the body. But it was already too late. Pavlov's skin was pale, his limbs stiff. The cold of death clung to him like frost. The air buzzed with murmurs and accusations. "They gutted him!" One inmate shouted. "No way he did that to himself!" Another inmate assisted with the investigation from inside his cell. "A message. That's what that is." The first inmate added. "That's enough," Johansen shouted at the inmates. Devin watched every detail with a stone face. His stomach churned, but his eyes stayed sharp, scanning not just Pavlov but the crowd, the guards, the reactions. And then he saw Aleksei.

The Russian was standing further down the corridor, hands clasped, his expression painted in shock. He shook his head slowly, even muttered a curse under his breath. But to Devin, it was too polished, too deliberate. The man was acting for an audience, not reacting to a tragedy. Four nurses rushed to the scene, one of them carrying a red duffle bag. An attempt at CPR was futile, forcing the lead nurse to call a DOA. The nurses stepped back as the guards zipped Pavlov into a black body bag. The heavy sound of the zipper closing sent a chill down Devin's spine. As the body was carried out, Devin's gaze met Aleksei's across the way. For a heartbeat, the world went quiet. Aleksei's face shifted into a mask of practiced grief. Devin's jaw tightened. He knew better. Every fiber of his being was sure that the Russian had something to do with it. Guilt befell Devin as he recoiled back into his cell.

By lunchtime, the prison cafeteria buzzed with rumors, whispers skittering like rats across the long tables. Devin carried his tray, his steps deliberate. His eyes swept the room until they landed on Aleksei, seated with his men, calmly working through his meal as if nothing had happened.

Devin set his tray down and slid onto the bench beside him. The tension was electric, a murmur of silence sweeping the table as others pretended not to notice. "We need to talk," Devin said low, his voice taut. Aleksei didn't look up immediately. He chewed, swallowed, wiped his lips with a napkin. Then, only then, he tilted his head toward Devin. "Not now," he replied, his accent thick, words measured. His eyes flicked to the guards stationed across the room, their gaze scanning but disinterested. "Meet me outside later." Devin clenched his jaw, pushed himself up from the bench. He turned to walk away but paused mid-step. Without glancing back, he said, "Thanks for the books." A beat of silence. Then Aleksei's voice, calm and steady. "You are welcome." It wasn't gratitude. It was ownership.

Far from the prison walls, in a clean, fluorescent-lit conference room, the mood was no less tense. Special Agent Benson stood at the head of the long table, manila folders and half-drunk coffee cups scattered across its surface.

Back at the bureau, agent Mack sat next to the boss, posture casual but eyes alert. Around them, several agents filled the seats, their faces weary with too many late-night operations. Benson opened the meeting with the weight of a man carrying too much. "What's the status on Crews, Mack?"

Mack leaned back slightly, arms folded, a crease forming between his brows. "Sir, we haven't made contact in a week. Last time I checked, he didn't have any solid intel. I can reach out to him, see if he's got anything brewing." Before Benson could respond, another voice cut through the room. The Distinguished Agent didn't waste time with introductions. He was the kind of man who didn't need them. "How soon can we get that info?" he demanded, his voice echoing. "Time is running out. We've got an election in two months. We can't afford to drag our feet." The weight of his words settled over the table like heavy lead. He pointed a finger, not at anyone in particular but at the whole room. "I need daily updates on this. Something I can take upstairs. The entire election is riding on this, fellas." And just like that, he turned and strode out, his polished shoes striking like gavel blows against the floor.

The silence he left behind was thick. Benson rubbed his temples, exhaling. Then he turned to Mack, his tone clipped. "Get me something. Let's bring our guy home." He, too, stormed out, leaving Mack alone with the others. Mack's eyes drifted to the screen at the end of the room, where Devin's file and image glowed in digital light. The bald head. The beard and fresh scars. The hardened eyes of a man pretending to be someone else. Mack muttered under his breath, barely audible. "What're you up to in there?" He wished his friend could hear his voice.

The Blood in the Yard

The prison yard pulsed with a strange kind of rhythm—the thud and muffled squeaks of sneakers on cracked asphalt, the clank of weights from the corner station, the low rumble of conversations in a dozen accents. Above it all, the ever-watchful eyes of the guards in their towers, rifles dangling, made the whole place feel like a stage set for violence. Devin paced across the yard, his steps sharp, restless. He had rehearsed what he would say, but the closer he drew to Aleksei, the less certain his words felt. Every second wasted was another moment his cover could unravel. He needed answers, not tomorrow, not next week. Today.

Aleksei sat near the checker table, broad shoulders draped in the casual confidence of a man who had learned long ago that power didn't need shouting. His goons hovered around him like satellites, their eyes narrowing as Devin approached. "Beat it," Devin said, his tone clipped but steady. The words dropped like a stone in water. The goons stiffened. Their hands twitched, eyes flicking to Aleksei as though waiting for permission to pounce. Aleksei's gaze lifted, calm, and unreadable. After a pause that stretched like an eternity, he gave the faintest nod.

The men hesitated, threw Devin a few murderous glares, *he is now giving us orders,* they thought, then reluctantly peeled away. They didn't go far, only far enough to give the illusion of privacy. Devin didn't care. He sat across from Aleksei, leaning forward. "When is the next attack coming?" he asked, voice low but urgent. "And who's behind it?" Aleksei studied him, his expression neither hostile nor friendly. He spoke slowly, like a man weighing every word. "I have a granddaughter and she's … my world." He said, then paused for a beat. "The state won't let her come visit. The Warden is behind it. This I know."

The pivot jarred Devin. He had expected names, dates, something tactical. Instead, Aleksei offered a wound, personal and raw. "My attorney is the best; I can get your granddaughter on the visitation list." Devin replied without missing a beat. Aleksei's eyes lit up like a Christmas tree. "You do that and I owe you everything." The Russian replied. Aleksei glanced to the right, then to the left, and then back to Devin, his eyes narrowed. He tilted his head, smoke-colored suspicion in his stare. "Gabe, this thing you ask," he said, tapping his chest, "you know it implicates me, yeah? Why do you want this information anyway?" Devin's throat went dry. For a second, he faltered. Then he forced a swallow, masking the panic with practiced calm. "They can't try you twice for the same crime," he said. "That's double jeopardy." Aleksei's gaze sharpened. "How do you know so much about the law?"

The question hung like a snare. Devin felt his pulse kick. Too much knowledge was dangerous, a spotlight on secrets he could never afford to reveal. He forced a laugh, soft and dismissive. "I read," he said. "A lot." He leaned closer, lowering his voice so only Aleksei could hear. "If more criminals paid attention to the law, we could put these places outta business. Checkmate." For the first time, Aleksei's mouth twitched into something resembling a smile. He liked the thought. It was sharp, subversive—the kind of thinking that set Devin apart from the average inmate. "The Warden," Devin continued, pressing the advantage. "He wants to retire. It's election year. He wants to go out like a hero. If we can help him stop the interference coming down the pipeline, he'd be untouchable. A hero. And us? Me and you? Our stay here becomes very pleasant."

The Russian leaned back, the weight of the proposal settling into him. His silence was heavy as he pulled out a small box of cigarettes. He tapped one free, lit it, and took a long drag—smoke curling between them. Devin waited, pulse steady but every muscle on edge. "When was the last time you saw your grandchild?" Devin asked, gently but firmly. "The Warden can make that possible. Help me help him." Aleksei's eyes softened, just for a flicker, like a crack in armor. The cigarette trembled between his fingers before he drew on it again. "I'll tell you," he said finally, voice rough. Then his head jerked to the side. His eyes widened. "Oh no," he muttered. Devin turned, instincts snapping.

Across the yard, a member of the Six-Nine gang had broken formation, striding straight toward a cluster of skinheads. His fists were clenched, rage written across his face. "No," Devin whispered under his breath. From the blindside, a skinhead lunged. The flash of metal caught the sunlight—a shank.

The blade sank deep into the Six-Nine's gang member's side. The man's body jerked, then collapsed. Blood gushed through his shirt as he clawed at the asphalt, gasping, his eyes wide with disbelief. He tried to crawl, dragging himself inches, but his strength ebbed with every second. The yard erupted into chaos. Shouts split the air; feet pounded the ground. A wave of Six-Nine members surged forward, faces twisted with vengeance. They charged the skinheads like a storm, fists, feet, and fury ready to tear everything apart. Then the sharp crack of gunfire split the chaos. POP! POP! POP! The guard tower spat bullets. The sound echoed like thunder in the yard. A siren wailed overhead, piercing, merciless. "Down! Down! Down!" Voices roared as officers rushed to the scene. The inmates knew the drill. They dove to the ground, sprawling across the dirt and pavement, hands clasped behind their heads. The riot team poured in, shields raised, batons ready, boots pounding like drums of war.

Devin hit the dirt beside Aleksei. The dust bit his lungs, the ground pressed cold against his cheek. For a moment, there was only silence between them—silence filled with everything unspoken. Their eyes met, inches apart. Neither moved. Neither dared. In that stillness, Devin understood: the prison wasn't just bars and walls. It was a chessboard. And the game had only just begun.

CHAPTER 20

STICKS AND BALLS

The dive bar on North Lincoln Avenue was the kind of place that didn't need a name. Its sign out front had lost and replaced some of its neon letters years ago, leaving only a faint red glow that sputtered in the night like a dying heartbeat. Inside, though, the walls carried the weight of a hundred unspoken stories. The air was thick with the smell of spilled beer, charred burgers, and the faint tang of old smoke soaked into wood paneling. It was a watering hole for most law enforcement due to the owner being a retired officer himself. A neutral ground where detectives, FBI agents, and even the occasional private eye came to drink, laugh, and forget, if only for a night, about the ugliness waiting for them outside.

At a corner table near the bar, Mack leaned back in his chair, a half-empty glass of whiskey in front of him. Beside him sat agents Lowrey and Dodson, their jackets slung over the backs of their seats, ties loosened. The day had been long, and the night promised little reprieve.

The door swung open, letting in a rush of cool air from the street. Tanya stepped in first, her hair pulled back, her expression a careful mask of composure. Behind her came April, radiating her usual energy, and Jen, who was quieter, her eyes sweeping the room with curiosity. Mack spotted them instantly. He stood and raised a hand. "Over here!" The women made their way through the bar, drawing more than a few looks. Tanya had a quiet elegance about her, something that didn't quite fit in the dim haze of the room, while April's presence was a spark—vibrant, alive. Jen followed, a soft smile tugging at her lips, the kind of smile that suggested she was taking in everything without giving much away.

Mack gestured broadly as they approached. "Agents, you remember Tanya." He pointed. "That's April. And that's …"

"Jen," Tanya said smoothly, finishing his sentence. They all exchanged handshakes—some firm, some perfunctory—a ritual of acknowledgment more than warmth. For a brief-moment, the circle at the bar felt complete. Mack clapped his hands together. "How about some pool … ladies?"

The Hustle

The pool tables were in a separate room at the back of the bar, lit by hanging green lamps that cast glowing circles over the felt. The clack of billiard balls carried through the air like gunshots softened by distance. Mack, Lowrey, April, and Jen grabbed cues, while Tanya lingered near Dodson, who leaned against the wall with a beer in hand.

Mack lined up his shot with the swagger of a man who had done this too many times before. He sank the ball cleanly into the corner pocket and pumped his fist. "Anybody want lessons?" he boomed, grinning wide. "I charge by the balls." Dodson snorted into his beer. "I believe you." He shouted. "I saw your last girlfriend. She looked like she had balls." Laughter broke out around the table. Mack, though, winced, his grin faltering as color rose to his cheeks. April leaned against her cue, tilting her head at Lowrey. "Is he always this confident?" Lowrey smirked. "You ain't seen nothing yet." April shot Tanya a glance—a conspiratorial spark—and Tanya answered with a small smile, the kind that carried more history than words.

Mack kept at it, sinking shot after shot, his confidence ballooning with each success. But then he leaned into one, lined it up too eagerly, and missed. The ball rattled in the pocket and rolled back out. "Ohhh! Nooooooo," he groaned, throwing his arms up. "Somebody moved the pocket. Who did that?" April laughed. "Guess you're not as good as you think." Her tone carried just enough bite to stir him.

Mack's eyes narrowed, a grin tugging back at his lips. "You wanna put your money where your mouth is?" he challenged. Jen piped up before April could answer, pointing straight at Tanya. "No, but she will." Mack blinked. "No way." "Yes way," April chimed in, her grin wicked. The air shifted, tension turning playful. Mack dug into his wallet, produced a credit card, and slapped it onto the table. "I'll make it interesting." Jen shook her head, laughing. "We don't take cards; it might be stolen. Cash only." Mack rolled his eyes, pulled out a twenty, and set it down with a little more force than necessary. "You got it."

The Game

The balls were racked tight, the triangle neat. Mack leaned over, lined up his cue, and let loose. The break was loud, the balls scattering wildly, but not a single ball was sunk. He grimaced. "Well, that's disappointing." "Don't worry," Tanya said softly, stepping forward. "I'll take it from here." She chalked her cue, fingers steady, her movements almost graceful. The room seemed to stand still as she leaned into her first shot.

POWH! The cue ball smacked hard into the pack, sending one solid ball spinning into the corner pocket. "Solid it is," she said before leaning into her next shot. As she lines up her shot, her face became an intense focus. The overhead bulb amplified a furious concentration with sweat beads forming slowly on her forehead. Her opponent, Mack, settled for a wide stance across the table, arms folded, watching Tanya like a hulk. The music and loud voices in the bar reverberated off the felt. Tanya remains unfazed. POWH! She sank a ball with a thunderous crack leaving the cue ball spinning in the middle of the pool table. It looked good—too good. She followed it with another. And another. Mack folded his arms, watching closely, suspicion growing in his eyes. "Beginner's luck," he muttered. But Tanya didn't stop. Her shots were precise, deliberate, the kind of play that spoke of muscle memory, of hours spent at tables just like this one. She sank a long shot with a clean angle, bringing the cue ball back and freezing inches away from the last shot. She was lined up perfectly, the eight-ball had a direct path to the corner pocket. Mack gulped, seeing this. A collective groan rose from onlookers; Tanya smiles at Mack as she rubs chalk on her pool stick one last time. With a smooth flick of her wrist, CRACK! The eight-ball rolled home.

The room was silent for a heartbeat. Then April clapped, grinning like a child at Christmas. Tanya straightened, twirling the cue lightly in her hand. She looked at Mack and cleared her throat. "You alright?" she asked, her voice laced with mock concern. "You need another drink?" Dodson nearly spit his beer out laughing. Lowrey chuckled into his sleeve. Jen gave a polite little clap.

Mack's face darkened, the bravado slipping. He leaned his cue against the table, staring at Tanya with new calculation. "Tell me again," he said quietly, almost too quietly, "how did you and Crews meet?" Tanya's smile softened, turning wistful. "At a pool tournament in college," she said. "I won that night too." For a moment, the noise of the bar faded for her. She imagined Devin's face again—younger, laughing, his eyes bright with admiration as she sank shot after shot. He hadn't cared that she beat him. He had loved her more for it. Mack, though, only grunted. It wasn't just that he had gotten owned by a girl, but he had gotten owned in front of a crowd, and he knew his buddies at the bureau would never allow him to hear the end of it. He knew the jokes were coming, he just didn't know how much. "Crews is one lucky man." He pulled the twenty-dollar bill that he had pocketed when the match started, still crisp and clean with only a single fold along its length and held it out to her. "Here. You earned it." Tanya took it, her fingers brushing his. She met his gaze squarely, refusing to look away. Behind them, April practically bounced with glee. "Hey Mack, I've got a suggestion for you!" she crowed, unable to resist twisting the knife. But Mack ignored her. He wasn't in the mood for jokes anymore. He turned, walked toward the bar, and let the noise of the room swallow him whole.

CHAPTER 21

FRIENDS AND FOES

The prison corridor continued to reeked of sweat and cleaning agents—the stale air that never seemed to move. Devin had grown used to the rhythm of the place: the clang of gates, the heavy boots of guards, the murmurs of inmates that carried like ghosts through the halls. But tonight, that rhythm shattered.

WHAM!

The blow came out of nowhere, catching him square across the jaw. His head snapped sideways, his body sprawling against the cold concrete. Stars burst across his vision. He hit the floor hard, tasting blood almost instantly, copper flooding his tongue.

He forced himself up, his knees trembling, only to feel the hot sting in his side. His hand darted down. A jagged shank was buried in his flesh. His prison blues were already blooming red. Pain seared through him, but instinct pushed him upright. He blinked against the blur and saw them: the skinheads. Not just the trio he had humiliated in the showers weeks ago, but more. Reinforcements. Five of them in total, their faces lit with hatred, eyes wild with vengeance. They wanted him broken.

The smallest one charged first, cocky, certain he'd see Devin crumble. Devin pivoted, letting instinct and muscle memory guide him. His left hook connected with the man's jaw like a hammer. The skinhead dropped instantly, teeth clattering against the floor. Two more rushed. Devin braced himself, pain flaring in his ribs, but rage drove him. The first met a vicious kick to the neck—Devin's heel striking bone with a sickening crack. The second ran into a hard right fist that sent him crashing against the wall, crumpling like paper. Devin bent, wincing, clutching his wound.

Every movement sent fire rippling through his torso, but he refused to give them the satisfaction of seeing weakness. The last two hovered, their hesitation thick in the air. Then the alarm blared.

The shrill, merciless wail filled the corridor. Inmates shouted, a dozen voices rising in chaotic chorus. Metal gates slammed open. Guards thundered in, barking orders. "On the ground! Everybody down!" The skinheads scattered, dropping like obedient dogs. Devin's body finally betrayed him. He staggered, the world tilting sideways, and he collapsed onto the floor like dead weight. The cold concrete pressed against his cheek as darkness nipped at the edges of his vision.

The Infirmary

When consciousness returned, he was sitting on an examination table, the sterile smell of antiseptic burning his nose. A fluorescent light buzzed overhead. A nurse leaned close, she was strikingly attractive, her dark hair tied back, her eyes focused on her work rather than him. She wrapped bandages around his torso with practiced efficiency, her fingers firm, unflinching. "Keep that on for a few days," she said, her voice steady, almost detached. "Come back if anything changes." Her hands pressed against the wound, testing for stability. Devin winced, a hiss slipping through his teeth. She glanced up briefly, meeting his eyes. For a second, he thought he saw something softer there—pity, maybe—but it vanished as quickly as it came. She looked over her shoulder at the guard standing nearby. "He's ready." Devin slid off the table gingerly, his movements stiff. The pain was manageable, but the fatigue was bone deep. He muttered, "Thanks," his voice rough. The nurse didn't reply. She was already preparing for the next inevitable patient.

Back in the Cell

The cell welcomed him with silence. Neat, orderly—his doing. He had worked hard to carve some semblance of control out of chaos. The small stack of books in the corner, the curtains he'd made from bedsheets for privacy, the tally marks on the wall. He sat on the bed and stared at the chalk scratches. Six had grown into twenty. Almost three weeks. Each line was a scar, each day a reminder. He lay back, staring at the ceiling. The pain in his side throbbed with every heartbeat. But it wasn't the wound that kept him awake. It was the thought of time slipping, of his cover wearing thin, of the noose tightening. The man known inside the walls as Gabe, needed something miraculous to happen, now.

A Dangerous Meeting

The next day, the visiting area felt colder than usual. Metal table, bolted chairs, thick plexiglass, the faint smell of disinfectant that couldn't quite mask sweat and fear. Aleksei sat cuffed on one side, his expression carved from stone, anger simmering in his eyes. Across from him, Benedikt Oblonsky lounged like he owned the place, a visitor's pass dangling from his expensive suit.

His gold watch caught the harsh light, gleaming with arrogance. The guard stayed by the doorway, distant but watchful. Oblonsky's voice cut through the tension, harsh and mocking. "Eto byl ne moy zvonok. Eto prishlo sverkhu." He switched to English, his accent thick, deliberate. "It wasn't my call. It came from the top." He leaned in slightly, his smirk widening. "You are…how do you say…sloppy. Sloppy men get caught. Just remember to keep your mouth shut." Aleksei's face faltered, pride collapsing under the weight of the threat. Oblonsky's voice dropped lower, colder. "If you ever feel like talking…remember, I know where your granddaughter goes to school." The silence that followed was deafening. For the first time, Aleksei looked small. Powerless. Oblonsky leaned back, satisfied. He smirked, the kind of smirk that carved scars into memory. It wasn't the smirk that rubbed Aleksei the wrong way, he had dealt with men like these his whole life. It was the overt threat to bring harm to the man's granddaughter that presented as the final straw from all the disrespect he had endured.

The Yard

Later, Devin found him in the yard. Aleksei looked better—or at least, he wore the mask of someone trying to look better. His men hovered nearby, loyal shadows. "My friend," Aleksei said, his accent thick but playful. "You look like shit. If shit had muscles and charm." The goons laughed on cue, mocking but not unkind. Devin dropped onto the bench beside him. Aleksei nodded, sending the men a few feet away. "I'm gonna give you this info," Aleksei said, his tone shifting. "Because I don't want to see you killed." Devin leaned in, every nerve sharpened.

"My former partner," Aleksei continued, bitterness dripping from every word. "He has been screwing me over. He has direct connection to the motherland. KGB ties. He pulled me into this misinformation campaign against U.S. elections. The pay was good, so I went along." His jaw clenched. "Now I sit here. And he? He mocks me. He doesn't even give me a real visit." He spat out a string of Russian curses, his hands trembling. Devin kept his face neutral, but inside, his pulse quickened. Aleksei's voice dropped, heavy. "Benedikt Oblonsky. He's your guy. But…"

He scanned the yard, lowering his voice further. "Be careful who you give that information to. He has the cops in his pocket. Those pigs." His eyes narrowed. "Don't you just hate them?"

Devin hesitated. A wrong word could unravel everything. He nodded subtly. "Yeah. I hear you." Aleksei coughed violently, harsh and wet. His men tensed, their eyes darting nervously. He waved them off, wiping his mouth with a napkin he pulled from his pocket. When he lowered it, Devin caught the red smear of blood.

"You okay?" Devin asked quietly. "I'm fine." Aleksei crumpled the napkin and tossed it away, his face hardening again. "No one crosses Aleksei and goes free. Eventually, I found them. Always." But there was something brittle in his voice now, a crack in the armor.

The rumble of a diesel engine coming from outside the walls drew their attention. Aleksei pointed toward the gates. "Look. Fresh meat." Devin followed his gaze. The bus pulled into the yard, steel doors groaning as they opened. Inmates filed out, shackled, their faces hard or hollow, their eyes darting. "How many you think?" Aleksei asked. "A packed house," Devin replied.

The Warden was already standing in position like a football coach watching practice. When the convicts got off the bus, the warden immediately went into action, delivering his usual spiel, his voice booming across the yard with a smug on his face. The gate clanged shut behind the bus, sealing the newcomers in. Among them, Devin spotted a face he recognized—Hector. Older now, covered in tattoos, gold glinting in his mouth. Confidence radiated from him, a swagger that hadn't dulled despite the chains.

Aleksei leaned back, his eyes never leaving the new arrivals. "You ever heard of fight club?" He asked. Devin's gaze lingered on Hector as the guards ushered the men into the building. The word echoed in his mind. Fight club. Another layer to the prison's underworld, another piece of the game he was trapped in. And somewhere in that mess, Oblonsky's shadow loomed larger than ever. "No, tell me about the fight club," Devin insisted, never taking his eyes off Hector. *What are the odds,* he thought to himself. "I can't talk about fight club, not now. Maybe some other time." Aleksei responded. He then saw the stern look on Devin's face and had to ask. "Hey Gabe, is everything alright?" "Yeah…yeah…yeah." Devin replied.

The Thin Line

The prison yard was alive with the dull roar of activity, a restless energy that never seemed to fade. Men lifted weights with guttural grunts, others played makeshift games of handball, and knots of gangs huddled together, whispering in their chosen corners. Above it all, the guards loomed in the towers, rifles slung lazily but ready, their eyes sweeping for trouble.

The inner gates clanged open, and a line of new inmates spilled out into the chaos. The sound of chains scraping, the shuffle of cautious steps, the hum of a thousand stares falling on fresh meat—it all combined into an almost ritualistic initiation. Among them walked Hector. He moved with swagger, his gold tooth flashing in the sun, tattoos running like a road map across his arms and neck. Two other new inmates flanked him, laughing and nudging one another as they tried to mask their nerves. Hector was talking, gesturing wide with his hands, already staking a claim in a world that swallowed most men whole.

Devin had his back to the gate, sitting at a table with Aleksei and his crew. Aleksei, ever the predator, noticed the trio heading their way. His lips curled into a sly grin. "Which one you think will drop the soap first?" he muttered, his thick accent slicing through the noise. His goons chuckled. Devin turned casually, just enough to acknowledge the joke—and froze. His eyes locked with Hector's.

The world seemed to still. For a split second, it was only them—no barbed wire, no gangsters. Just recognition and three guards trailing the new inmates. Hector's face lit with shock, then excitement. "Yooooooo" Devin's pulse spiked. He leaned forward, his voice sharp, cutting Hector off before the word could form. "Beat it…fresh meat." The words came out with practiced disdain, laced with enough venom to pass for authentic prison hostility. But inside, his heart was pounding against his ribs. Hector hesitated, his smile faltering. He lingered, squinting at Devin as if he couldn't trust his own eyes. "Yo, homes!" he tried again, louder this time.

Devin rose to his feet, forcing himself to look annoyed rather than panicked. He stepped away from the table, turning his body as if dismissing Hector's existence. "I know you, Ese!" Hector pushed. "I said beat it!" Devin snapped, more forceful now, his voice low and dangerous.

The Russian goons stirred, their curiosity piqued. Aleksei leaned back in his seat, eyes narrowing with interest. He smelled blood in the water. Hector wasn't letting go. His voice carried across the yard now, drawing ears from all directions. "You're that cop!" Devin's stride faltered. He stopped, turned slowly. It was a stare-down now, silence gathering like storm clouds. Devin fought to keep his face neutral, but his nerves buzzed. Hector pressed on, gesturing to his buddies. "He's a cop. He took me to jail before. That's him. I'm not loco. He's a pig." His words spread like wildfire. Inmates nearby lifted their heads, murmurs rippling outward. Cop. Pig. Snitch. Three dangerous labels a man could wear behind bars.

Devin caught sight of Aleksei whispering to his men. Their eyes lit with sudden clarity and hunger. The mob began to form. Goons stepped closer, their shadows falling over Devin. Other inmates drifted in, eager for spectacle, some eager for blood. Devin backed away, forcing each step to look deliberate even as his instincts screamed to run. The crowd thickened. Voices rose. Fingers pointed. His cover, the fragile mask he had worn so carefully, was crumbling. He turned suddenly, breaking into a double-time stride toward the nearest guard post. The mob followed, boots scuffing on concrete, jeers rising like a wave. And there, waiting like a vulture, was officer Johansen. Devin's stomach sank.

The guard watched him approach, saw the mob closing in and did nothing. His lip curled into something between a smirk and contempt. Devin reached him, chest heaving. "Open it! Get me inside!" The guard folded his arms, deliberately blocking the entrance. Behind Devin, the roar swelled, the mob nearly on him. Hands reached, voices shouted, the promise of violence seconds away.

"Open the damn door!" Devin barked, panic threading his tone, despite himself. The guard didn't budge. Then, almost lazily, he raised his hand and hit the alarm. The siren blared across the yard, sharp and shrill. Guards above trained rifles down. The mob slowed, some ducking instinctively, others raising their hands in mock surrender. Devin didn't wait for second chances. Another guard rushed over, shoving Johansen aside just enough to drag him inside. The heavy door clanged shut, cutting off the roar of the crowd. Inside, the silence pressed against his ears.

The Corridor

Officer Johansen stormed in moments later; fury etched into his face. He jabbed a finger at the men holding Devin.

"Take him to his cell." "No!" Devin shot back, adrenaline still coursing. "You can't do that. You've gotta get me outta here." The guard sneered. "Take him to his cell!" Devin jerked his arm, yanking free from the grip of one guard. His voice rose, desperate but sharp. "Take me to the Warden! Now!" A younger guard leaned close to Johansen, whispering something in his ear. Johansen's eyes hardened. He stepped forward, inches from Devin. "Inmate. There is no Warden. It's your cell or the SHU." "That's easy," Devin muttered. Before anyone could react, his fist lashed out. CRACK! The punch connected with the guard's jaw, sending him sprawling to the floor. Blood sprayed from his lip. For a brief moment, silence. Then chaos.

The guard scrambled to his feet, rage consuming him. A baton cracked against Devin's ribs. The pain exploded through his side, forcing him to double over with a gasp. "Get him to the SHU! NOW!" Johansen bellowed. Two guards seized Devin, with two other nearby, dragging him down the corridor. His feet scraped against the floor, his body wracked with pain, his mind spinning.

The Hole (SHU)

The door slammed behind him, locking with a metallic thud that echoed through his bones. The SHU. Solitary. A concrete box no larger than a walk-in closet. No furniture, no window, just walls that pressed in on every side. The air was heavy, stale. The light above buzzed faintly, flickering like it might die at any moment. Devin staggered forward, falling against the wall. His ribs screamed, his side burned where the shank wound was still healing, and his knuckles throbbed from striking the guard.

The silence was absolute. No voices, no footsteps, no clanging of gates. Just the sound of his own breathing, harsh, ragged—and the occasional drip of unseen water. It was a mindfuck, just like they said. The stench of smeared feces from past visitors still lingered in the cracks of the walls. He slid down, sitting on the cold floor, his knees pulled to his chest. He closed his eyes, but the darkness behind his lids was worse than the buzzing light. He saw Hector's face, Aleksei's smirk, the mob's hungry eyes. His cover wasn't cracked—it was shattered. How long could he survive in here?

The Warden

Miles away, the Warden's car tore down a dirt road, gravel spitting beneath its tires. His phone was pressed to his ear, his voice sharp with disbelief. "He did what?" he barked. His knuckles whitened against the steering wheel. A pause. "Nobody moves. Lock it down. I'm on my way. Jesus!" He jerked the wheel, the car spinning in a U-turn that sprayed dust into the sky. He sped back toward the prison, cigar smoke curling from the ashtray.

Through the Window

Later, the Warden stood with two guards outside the SHU, peering through the tiny slot in the heavy steel door. "Impersonating and officer is a crime that could be added to your sentence, son...do you know that?" Inside, Devin's voice echoed from the hole, raw and urgent. "I'm a cop. You've got to believe me." The guards glanced at each other, their faces etched with doubt. The Warden didn't blink. "You work for who, again?" Silence stretched. "I don't buy it," he said finally, his tone cold as iron. "Enough games, inmate. See you tomorrow." Devin's voice rose again, desperate, muffled by the walls. "I'm telling you the truth!"

The Warden shook his head, turning away. "I'll make a few phone calls. If what you say checks out...well, just sit tight." The guards followed as he walked down the corridor, his polished shoes clicking against the concrete. Behind the steel door, Devin sank deeper into the void. The walls felt closer already.

CHAPTER 22

BREAKING COVER

The prison's interior had a strange pulse at night. The halls echoed with restless voices, the clanging of metal bunks, the occasional shout that carried the sharp edge of violence. Even the air itself seemed to vibrate, thick with tension, sweat, and anticipation. Inside his dimly lit cell, Aleksei Lebedev stood by the bars, his gaunt face pressed to the steel as his sharp eyes scanned the corridor. The cacophony around him was louder than usual. Inmates were calling across tiers, banging cups against doors, stirring in ways that felt orchestrated rather than random. Something was off.

Aleksei's "Spidey sense" was going haywire. He had been in enough prisons, both in Russia and America, to recognize when the storm was coming. A guard strolled by, unconcerned, his keys jangling like a cruel reminder of who held the power here.

"Hey!" Aleksei called, his thick accent curling around the single word. "Where is my good friend Gabe? I would like to see him. If that is his real name." He followed in a snarky tone.

The guard didn't break stride. "Piss off inmate!" he spat, not even looking at him. Aleksei's eyes narrowed, and his voice dropped lower, colder, more deliberate. "You don't want to do that." The guard's boots clicked away, but Aleksei's words lingered in the air, heavier than steel. He reminded the guard with another shout, "you don't want to do that! Do you know who I am? The guard was long gone and had turned down another corridor.

The Warden's Office

Devin sat in a stiff wooden chair, his wrists red from the cuffs that had only just been removed. He rubbed them absently, as though trying to erase the memory of iron. Across from him, the Warden paced, his shoes thudding softly against the floor. Confusion registered in his gaze.

"Story checks out," the Warden finally said, his voice betraying more relief than confidence. He glanced at Johansen standing in the corner who was equally bewildered. "Get him a bottle of water, would you? Do you need anything else?" The warden asked. Devin shook his head. "No." But the way he said it carried an edge—clipped, taut, simmering with distrust.

The Warden kept pacing, his brow damp with sweat despite the cool night air. His hands fidgeted, tugging at the edge of his jacket, smoothing his tie, adjusting himself. He looked less like a man in control and more like one trying desperately to hold on to it. He stopped abruptly, turning to Devin. "Are you sure you don't want anything else?" he asked. The question hung strangely in the air, more like a plea than an interrogation. Devin studied him, his jaw tight, eyes calculating. He could tell the Warden was going through an internal dilemma. The warden's shirt was now showing huge sweat stains.

The Convoy

Far from the prison, two black SUVs roared down a dirt road, their headlights cutting through the darkness like knives. The engines growled, spitting gravel as they devoured the miles. Inside the lead vehicle, Agent Mack gripped the wheel, his eyes locked on the road, his jaw set. The radio crackled with urgency. "Yes, sir," he said into the speakerphone. "Our ETA is ten minutes." The voice on the other end was snappy, commanding. "Make that five and get there now." "You got it, sir."

Mack cut the call, his knuckles tightening as he pressed harder on the accelerator. The SUV surged forward, the second vehicle following close behind like a shadow. Inside the cabin, silence pressed down, broken only by the growl of the engine. Every agent in the car knew what was at stake.

The Transformation

Back in the Warden's office, Devin stepped out of the private bathroom. The prison orange was gone. In its place were clean street clothes, freshly pressed, borrowed but fitting well enough to erase the image of the broken man who had been dragged into solitary. He adjusted the collar, squared his shoulders. For the first time in weeks, he looked like himself again—maybe even more so.

The nurse from the previous engagement was tending to Devin once more. She hovered, checking him over quickly. Her hands were gentle but professional, dabbing at the still-healing wound on his side. She nodded. "You look good, that should heal in no time." The Warden offered words of encouragement, trying for camaraderie. Devin's reply was sharp, cutting through the pretense. "Save it, Gary. You'll get your Yelp review."

Johansen smirked at the jab, quickly hiding it when the Warden shot him a glare. The embarrassment flushed the Warden's cheeks, but he forced a chuckle. "Any suggestions before you leave?" he asked, feigning interest. Devin's eyes burned into him. "Yeah. Lebedev incited a riot and killed the Ukrainian. He should probably go to the SHU. And take his damn phone." The CB radio on the desk crackled to life, saving the Warden from having to reply. "Sir, the FBI is here." The Warden grabbed the receiver. "Thank you, Jim." He turned back to Devin, trying to lighten the moment, though the sweat on his forehead betrayed him. "So… the name is Devin, huh?" Devin said nothing, his silence heavier than words. "No hard feelings, right?" the Warden tried again. "I like to keep things live around here. It's all just one big game to lighten the mood." Devin leaned forward, his voice low, dangerous.

"I'll come back with my friends so we can all play. Checkmate, asshole." The Warden swallowed hard, suddenly wishing for the comfort of his liquor cabinet. Agent Mack and crew burst into the office. One by one they embrace Devin and when they were done, Mack retrieves Devin's badge from his pocket and gently bestows it around Devin's neck. Gary, Johansen and the other COs stood by, watching in amazement. They said their goodbyes and exited one by one. When Devin reached the doorway, he paused beside officer Johansen and took one last sip of his water then handed the empty bottle to Johansen. When their eyes met, Johansen seemed meeker this time around. He hesitated to take the empty bottle from Crews but a look from Gary told him to play ball. He stuck his hand out with reservation, Devin shoved the empty bottle in his hand and held it there for a beat, maintaining direct eye contact. They spoke nothing but a lot was said in the moment.

Freedom

The roar of the SUV engines outside was like music. Devin climbed into the passenger seat of Mack's vehicle, sinking into the leather as if he hadn't sat on anything soft in years. Mack grinned, relief washing over his face. "Welcome back, buddy." "Thanks," Devin murmured.

He turned his head to the window, eyes lifting to the vast expanse of sky. A million stars burned above, cold and clear, reminding him of everything he still had to fight for. Tanya. Baxter. The future. For the first time in weeks, he counted blessings instead of tally marks on a wall.

The Fall of Aleksei

Meanwhile, in the dim confines of the prison, Aleksei was startled when officer Johansen and another CO appeared at his cell. "Inmate," one barked, "where's the phone? Aleksei looked dumbfounded. Hands behind your back!" Johansen instructed before whipping out a pair of handcuffs. Aleksei hesitated, then slowly complied, his wrists sliding behind him. The guards moved fast, tossing the cell with trained precision. Within seconds, one pulled a battered, hidden cell phone from the pillow. Aleksei's eyes flashed with rage as they began to drag him out of his cell. "What is going on? Where are you taking me?" "The SHU," the guard said flatly. "For inciting violence in the neighborhood. Courtesy of your friend Gabe." The name hit him like a blade. Gabe.

As the cuffs snapped around his wrists, Aleksei's fury boiled beneath the surface. His eyes followed the guards, his mind already calculating revenge. But for the first time, he felt the ground shifting harshly beneath his feet.

CHAPTER 23

DEBRIEF

Alarm clock was still the way to go. The one on Tanya's nightstand shrieked into the cold silence of the early a.m.. Its red digits glowed faintly against the morning light filtering through the blinds. Tanya groaned, rolled over, and slapped the snooze button with a tired hand. For a moment she stayed there, her hair spilling across the pillow, her breathing heavy. Then, almost instinctively, she rolled over toward Devin and nestled her head against his chest. His warmth, his steady heartbeat, grounded her in a way nothing else could. "Good morning," he murmured, his voice still heavy with sleep. "Good morning indeed," she replied, smiling faintly. Devin motioned towards the clock. "What was the alarm for?" "Work," she sighed, eyes still closed. "But that can wait. I miss this." He kissed her forehead, slow and gentle, before pushing himself upright. The sudden movement brought a sharp twinge of pain. He winced, one hand going instinctively to his side. "Let me see that," Tanya said quickly, sitting up beside him. She pulled at the hem of his shirt and gently examined the bandaged wound beneath. Her fingers traced the edge of the dressing, careful not to hurt him. "You're still tender." "It'll heal," Devin muttered. "Do you have to go in today?" she asked, though she already knew the answer. "Yes. Debrief…standard procedure."

Tanya pursed her lips, reluctant to argue. "Then let's at least clean it up first." Her tone carried more than practicality. It was her way of holding on, of caring for him in the small spaces life still allowed. Examining the wound carefully, she said, "that nurse did one heck of a job. What was her name, again? It sounded like a question, but it wasn't. Devin grinned; he wasn't falling for the trap. He knew her too well. "Don't know…I didn't ask." "Good answer." She replied. They both shared a chuckle and a light kiss. For weeks she had lived with the uncertainty of whether she'd see him again. Now, every second mattered.

Back in the Fold

The FBI's Chicago Field Office buzzed with its usual mix of urgency and banter, but when Devin stepped through the doors, freshly shaven, his beard gone, the place seemed to shift. Heads turned. Agents paused mid-conversation. Smiles spread. He had walked out of MCC prison not just alive, but intact with some valuable information that carried national security implications and that made him a quiet legend. "Crews!" someone called, clapping him on the back.

Another agent offered a high five. A pair shook his hand like they hadn't seen him in years. Devin nodded, shook hands, exchanged greetings, but never let the attention linger too long. He appreciated the love, but he was still carrying too much of the prison in his bones. Special Agent Benson's voice cut through the crowd like a whip. "Mack, Crews, Lowrey!"

Devin followed Mack and Lowrey down the hallway. Their footsteps echoed against the tile floor until they reached the heavy door of the secured briefing room.

The Briefing Begins

Inside, the atmosphere was thick. Around the long table sat three figures who radiated authority. At the head was the Director they had seen earlier, stone-faced as always. Beside him sat Mallory Johns, a supervisor in her fifties whose presence filled the space without her having to raise her voice. Her sharp eyes missed nothing. On the other side was Phil Donohue, another veteran supervisor, his expression neutral but his fingers drumming faintly on the tabletop. Benson dropped into a chair with his usual lack of ceremony. "It's your show," he said, gesturing at Devin.

Devin hesitated for a beat, then got up and stepped behind the lectern at the front of the room. He picked up the clicker, pressed a button. The screen behind him flickered alive, casting a faint glow over the room. The first image appeared: MCC Federal Prison, stark and imposing. "I entered MCC on…" Devin began. "Hold on there for a sec," Mallory interrupted, leaning toward Benson. She pointed to the corner of the projection. At the bottom right of the screen, a small imperfect video feed was visible, the words VEGAS stamped beneath it. The image was fuzzy, distorted, but recognizable: Director Marc Stevens from the Vegas Field Office. Benson leaned forward, fiddling with a control box.

"Hey, Stevens, can you hear us?" Static. No answer. "Stevens?" Benson repeated. He glanced at Mack. "Do you know how to fix this?" Mack shrugged. "No. I'll get Sherry." Devin stepped away from the lectern, his hands finding the keyboard at the side of the room. He typed quickly, trying to coax the feed into clarity.

Mallory and Phil exchanged a look, subtle but telling. Mallory's suspicion lingered on Devin longer than the screen. Mack returned with Sherry in tow. She brushed past Devin with a confident smirk. "I got it. You just have to touch it the right way, and you will get the response you were looking for. Let me show you how to be gentle with it." Devin couldn't tell if that was a sexual innuendo or professional instructions. Her words earned a ripple of suppressed amusement around the table. Mallory arched an eyebrow, the corner of her mouth twitching. To her, the comment sounded like more than technical talk. Sherry settled at the keyboard. Her fingers danced quickly, her posture relaxed as though she'd done this a hundred times. Within seconds, the bottom feed sharpened.

On screen, Director Marc Stevens appeared in crystal clarity and with him was something peculiar, something none of them expected to see. He wore a sock puppet on his right hand, bobbing it up and down while making high-pitched animal noises. The man was imitating dinosaurs. Benson shot up from his seat, leaning over the table, his face flushing red. "Stevens! We can see you!" But Director Stevens carried on, oblivious, now prancing behind his desk like a pony. "Somebody fix this thing?" Benson groaned, wanting so much to spare his friend the embarrassment, pressing the control box again-and-again. "We need that audio feed." "Trying, sir," Sherry said, biting her lip to hide her grin. "We're close."

Devin, now back at the lectern, shook his head, resisting the urge to laugh. He raised his voice deliberately. "Marc?" The word cut through the static. On the screen, Stevens froze, sock puppet still raised. His eyes widened as realization dawned. For a beat, the entire room held its breath.

CHAPTER 24

ROAD TO VEGAS

The feed cleared at last, and Director Marc Stevens' face came into focus. He froze, eyes widening, realizing the entire Chicago team could now see him—sock puppet still perched on his hand. "Harold!" he blurted. "Are we on?" Benson's voice cut through the speaker. "Yes, Marc … and we can all see you." Stevens blinked once, then yanked the sock puppet off as though it had betrayed him. He glanced at his right side, where a little girl in a pink dress, tiara tilted slightly on her head, was giggling uncontrollably. The words HAPPY BIRTHDAY glittered across her sash. "Here, sweetheart," Stevens muttered, thrusting the puppet into her small hands.

The child grinned, slipping it on her arm. "Mommy, are we coming back?" she chirped as a woman in her forties hurried forward, scooping her up without answering. They disappeared out of frame, the little girl craning her neck back toward the camera, the puppet waving like it knew more than it should.

In Chicago, Mallory chuckled softly, shaking her head. The absurdity of national security riding on men like Stevens wasn't lost on her. Devin, standing at the lectern, resisted the urge to smirk. Timing was everything. "Kids, huh?" Stevens' voice finally came, too loud in the speaker. He straightened his tie, trying to regain composure. "Okay. Let's begin."

The Prison Connection

Devin clicked the remote, and a new image filled the screen: Aleksei Lebedev, the man whose shadow still haunted Devin's sleep. "That is Aleksei Lebedev," Devin began, his tone steady, his eyes sharp. "He's been sitting in MCC for about two years. Convicted as the mastermind behind the foreign interference in our last election." Devin paused for dramatic effect, scanning the room. Mallory's brows knit, Phil leaned back with crossed arms, and Benson gave a subtle nod, urging him on. "But he didn't work alone," Devin continued. Another click. A new face appeared: Benedikt Oblonsky. "Benedikt Oblonsky," Devin said slowly, "first in command. A Russian businessman with deep ties to the Kremlin. While Aleksei took the fall, Oblonsky walked free. Their relationship fractured months ago. That's when I moved in close." There was silence in the room, the kind of silence that meant people were listening hard. "Aleksei ran more than politics," Devin went on. "He was the point man for an underground fight club in Englewood. Brutal. Illegal. He controlled it with precision. When Aleksei went down, Oblonsky didn't hesitate—he seized control. That operation is still running." Another click. Grainy photos of the fight club flashed onscreen—men bloodied, cash exchanging hands, a ring of smoke and violence.

Mallory leaned forward, her eyes narrowing. "You witnessed this?" Devin nodded. "Firsthand. These weren't just fights. They were auditions—ways for Oblonsky to find muscle, intimidate rivals, and funnel cash. I've seen men broken in seconds while the crowd cheered." Even Mack shifted uncomfortably in his chair. He had seen his share of violence, but the casual way Devin described it carried a weight that made the room colder.

The Vegas Threat

Devin pressed the clicker again. The next slide appeared: bold letters spelling Muscle-Mania over a slick promotional photo of men mid-pose, veins popping, muscles glistening under bright lights. "Oblonsky is planning something big," Devin said. His voice lowered, heavy with certainty. "And it's happening at Muscle-Mania, in Vegas. That's weeks away." Stevens' voice came through, sharper now. "That's practically tomorrow in our world." "Exactly, sir," Devin replied. Another click. This time, an image of a sleek Cessna jet gleamed on the screen. "This is how Oblonsky travels," Devin explained. "Intel places him in Ontario. He'll be stateside soon for the event. But we can't just nab him at the airport. We need evidence. Hard, irrefutable evidence. Otherwise, he walks." Phil finally spoke, his voice measured. "So, what's the play?" Benson leaned back in his chair, almost theatrically. "Crews," he said, pointing at Devin like the man was both answer and weapon. Devin swallowed, nodded, and clicked again.

The screen now showed video footage of a bodybuilding competition: contestants strutting across the stage, skin bronzed, muscles flexing under spotlights. They posed in practiced unison while judges scribbled notes. Mack shifted uncomfortably in his chair. "Do we really need to watch this?" he muttered, half to himself. Mallory smirked. "Uneasy, Agent Mack?" "Let's just say I'm more of a basketball guy," he replied, drawing a few chuckles.

Devin didn't break stride. "This is how we get him. Oblonsky trusts the world of muscle. He sponsors competitors, scouts talent, hides behind the glamour of bodybuilding. If I'm inside that circle, with all-access, I can get close enough to gather what we need."

Old Habits

Stevens' voice cut back in. "Are you suggesting what I think you're suggesting?" "Exactly," Devin replied without hesitation. "I'll be a walk-on. I'll have unrestricted backstage access." There was a pause. Stevens sounded skeptical. "I see muscles, Crews, but have you actually done this before?"

Before Devin could answer, Benson leaned forward with a grin that was almost smug. "Show them." Devin clicked one last time. The final image projected across the wall: a much younger Devin Crews, shirtless, standing tall under bright stage lights. His body was carved, lean, competition-ready, but the image was three years old. He was mid-pose, confidence radiating from his younger self.

The room reacted in unison—surprise, disbelief, and a grudging respect. Mallory raised an eyebrow. "Well," she said dryly, "the man got the goods, that explains the confidence." Mack let out a low whistle. "I don't know whether to be impressed or worried about how long you've been hiding that." Devin allowed himself the smallest smile. "I just need a few weeks to get back in shape. It's like riding a bike. The muscle remembers." Phil leaned forward, adjusting his tie. "Muscle memory and high-level espionage. Quite the mix." Benson slapped the table with excitement. "Any further questions, ladies and gentlemen?" The room stayed silent, tension and anticipation thick in the air. Benson's grin widened. "Good. Because I guess we're going to Vegas."

CHAPTER 25

VEGAS

The FBI private jet hummed in the Chicago hangar, its silver frame reflecting the morning light. Detective Crews climbed aboard with the rest of the team, his duffel slung over his shoulder. He carried little clothes, essentials, a few books, and the weight of a mission that could define his career or end it.

The cabin was plush compared to the standard commercial flights he remembered. No bustling families or overhead announcements, just quiet leather seats and an aisle that seemed to narrow with the gravity of what lay ahead. Mack dropped into the seat beside him with a groan, stretching his legs like a man who already regretted the trip. "I can't believe you're making me do this," Mack muttered. Devin smirked, leaning back. "You're gonna love it." Mack didn't answer. Instead, he pulled a manila folder from his briefcase and handed it over. "Package from Stevens."

Inside was a glossy photo of a sleek desert mansion. Palm trees flanked the driveway, and its edges glowed like a mirage against the sand. Devin stared at it longer than he intended. "That's our safe house outside Vegas," Mack explained, pointing out every detail of the locale. "Undisclosed location. Stocked with everything you'll need—weights, food, training plans. Even a hot tub." Devin didn't look up. He kept studying the photo, as if the house already contained answers to questions he hadn't voiced. Mack leaned closer, lowering his voice with a grin. "You're even allowed to have Tanya over. Unless, of course, you'd prefer the company of naked guys in tiny outfits." Devin shot him a glare that could have cut steel. Mack chuckled nervously and raised his hands in surrender. "Kidding. Relax."

The Desert Fortress

The jet sliced through the sky and later dipped low, crossing over the neon sprawl of Las Vegas. The iconic Welcome to Fabulous Las Vegas sign glowed beneath them, gaudy and magnetic as ever.

Hours later, a black SUV wound through the desert night, headlights bouncing across the rocky terrain until the safe house came into view. It wasn't just a mansion. It was a fortress—walls high, cameras watching, the kind of place where secrecy thrived. Devin whistled under his breath. "Looks like someone's compensating here." There was a long pause until the SUV came to a stop at the gate. Mack stretched, opening his door. "Are you staying?" Devin asked. Mack shook his head, grinning. "Oh no. I'll be on the strip. This is Vegas, baby. Do you think I'm wasting it on protein shakes and push-ups?" Devin did not respond. When he was out of the SUV with luggage secured, they hugged briefly, Mack clapping Devin on the back before hopping back into the vehicle and slipping away into the night. Devin stood in the driveway, bag in hand, the desert air pressing close around him.

The compound was silent when he stepped inside, too quiet. The house had a nice touch. Granite countertops, leather couches, polished wood floors—it had all the warmth of a model home. He was alone. He dropped his bag, walked through the rooms, and found the backyard. There he located a hot tub steaming under the desert sky. "Hot tub. Nice," he muttered, though his voice carried more loneliness than excitement.

Pillow Talk

Later, stretched across the king-sized bed, Devin pressed his phone to his ear. Tanya's voice filled the space, soft but cautious. "No, I'm serious," Devin pleaded. "You can come. I'm here all alone. The competition's in four weeks. It'll help." Silence stretched across the line. He listened; eyes fixed on the ceiling fan whirling above him. "Please," he tried again, the word breaking into something softer, almost boyish. "You gonna' make me beg?" Another pause. He sighed. "Wait," he exclaimed, "Baxter is back at the vet?" After a while he said, "Oh poor guy, I hope he gets better. Do they know what's wrong with him?" After a beat. "Oh. Alright. I understand. Back at ya'." He hung up, the silence in the room even heavier now.

Training Day

The days bled together. His world narrowed to sweat, repetition, and discipline. When he ran out of food, he took the pick-up truck that was tucked away in a detached garage and went shopping at the supermarket. He shopped for lean cuts of meat, towering bags of spinach, endless cartons of eggs and protein shakes. At the counter, the cashier raised an eyebrow at the absurd pile, but Devin only smiled faintly, as if the food itself was classified.

His routine was designed to be brutal with mass exhaustion. Mornings began on the treadmill. Hood up, music low, he ran until sweat soaked through his shirt. Afternoons were weight training; bench presses, curls, deadlifts, his body remembering the rhythm of a life he had long abandoned. Nights were for abs, planks, the burn that told him he was inching closer. Outside, he sprinted dirt roads, dust rising beneath his shoes, the desert stretching forever. Alone in the vastness, he fought not just the gravity of his current situation but painful memories; the cold stares of Aleksei's men, the riot sirens, Pavlov's lifeless body and the attack in the shower that seems to be playing on repeat in his thoughts. The mirror became his companion. First, he trained under layers of hoodies, hiding progress even from himself. Later, he stripped down, muscles tightening, veins rising. Day by day, the man who once competed reemerged.

Four weeks later, he stood shirtless before the full-length mirror. His body was lean, hardened, his eyes steady. He smiled for the first time in weeks. "Back in business," he whispered, even though the emptiness of the house felt like a prison.

But far away, behind bars, the past wasn't idle. In the SHU, Aleksei Lebedev's voice carried through the slot of his door. "Guard!" He shouted as officer Johansen walked the corridor, his shadow cast long across the floor. "What do you want? Make it quick." Aleksei's eyes glinted in the dim light. "I heard you need money. I need a phone. Maybe we help each other." Johansen studied him, lips curling. Deals made in shadows were the currency of survival. As much as he wasn't a big fan of the Russian, he appreciated the man's audacity.

The Vegas Glow

By the time Devin's training wrapped up, Vegas was pulsing with its usual upbeat. Outside a glittering hotel, a marquee screamed in bold letters: **MUSCLE MANIA TOMORROW**. Cars swarmed the Vegas strip. Tourists snapped photos. The air buzzed with anticipation. In a dark stakeout van across the street, FBI agents packed shoulder to shoulder. The smell of coffee and nerves filled the space. Benson cleared his throat. "Listen up. Tonight's just the benefit—for former competitors." He glanced at Devin. "You might even see some old pals." Mack folded his arms, trying not to laugh. The van was too small for his long legs, and the cramped space made him irritable.

Benson continued, his voice stern. "Remember, tonight is recon only. Intel gathering. Nobody makes a move unless I say so. Understood?" Everyone nodded, though nerves flickered in their eyes.

Inside the Hotel

The hotel lobby gleamed under chandeliers. Guards posted at the entrance checked passes, while others sat casually at the front desk, disguising vigilance with small talk. Devin walked through inconspicuously, his Access Pass swinging around his neck.

Mack slouched in a corner chair with a newspaper shielding his face, his eyes scanning every movement, every inch of the lobby. Devin navigated the flow of guests; tourists, competitors, sponsors—blending into the tide. Then a tap on his shoulder froze him. "D.C.!" a familiar voice boomed. He turned. "Mikey!" Mike grinned wide, pulling him into a hug. "How long has it been, brother? When I saw your name on the list, I couldn't believe it." Before Devin could answer, a young woman appeared at Mike's side. Stunning, restless, she looped her arm through Mike's. "Hey," Mike said proudly, "meet my lady." Devin smiled, shaking her hand. "Pleasure." But the young woman tugged Mike's arm impatiently. "Sorry, we gotta go." Mike gave Devin a quick pat. "Good seeing you, D. Tomorrow, yeah?" "Tomorrow," Devin agreed, watching as they disappeared into the crowd.

Behind the Curtain

Devin drifted backstage, where hotel staff bustled with last-minute preparations. He scanned the hallways—doors labeled EMPLOYEES ONLY, CONTROL ROOM. He tried one. Inside, two startled technicians spun in their chairs, blinking at him like deer in headlights. Devin muttered an apology, closing it quickly. Wrong place. He kept moving from one door to the next. He found a door that led to the underground garage. Another that opened to a tangle of phone lines, humming quietly. Every door was a possible lead, every hallway a possible thread in Oblonsky's web.

Finally, Devin circled back to the lobby. No other agents were in sight. He pulled out his phone and dialed Mack. "We all left," Mack's voice came, casual. "No action tonight, D. See you tomorrow." Devin lowered the phone slowly. His reflection in the polished marble floor looked back at him, distorted. He felt the pulse of the mission tightening around him. Tomorrow will be different. Tomorrow, everything begins.

CHAPTER 26

THE GREEN LIGHT

Special Housing Unit was quiet that night, save for the drip of a leaky pipe and the muffled snores of men locked in concrete boxes. Aleksei Lebedev stood near the barred slot of his door; the glow of a smuggled cellular phone pressed against his cheek. He watched as Johansen walked away, seemingly satisfied with doing business. His voice was low but sharp, carrying the weight of menace across the line. "You have the green light," he muttered in his thick Russian accent. "Make it loud. I want to hear about it on the evening news."

There was no hesitation, no second thoughts. He ended the call with a decisive snap, sliding the contraband phone beneath his mattress just as distant footsteps echoed down the corridor. His gray eyes glimmered with satisfaction. Even from the belly of a prison, his reach extended far beyond those steel walls.

The Hitmen

Miles away, in the darkness of a dim lit side street, a dark green SUV sat idling, its engine purring low like a predator waiting for the right moment to strike. At this time of the night, this street was mainly quiet. Two men sat inside the SUV, waiting, silhouettes beneath the faint glow of the dashboard. One of them, thin with sharp cheekbones, lowered his phone and slipped it into his tracksuit pocket. He spoke in Russian, his voice casual, as though he were discussing groceries rather than a kill. "The boss gave the green light and no, you don't have to come," he said, turning to the driver. "It's just a girl; I don't need no help with this one. Look out for cops." He spoke with light trace of his Russian accent. The driver nodded, adjusting his rearview mirror to scan the deserted street. His jaw was set, his fingers drumming impatiently on the steering wheel. They were professionals, used to this sort of work; quick, clean, decisive. As his partner was crossing the street, the driver yelled, "Petehr." When his partner turned around, he said, "make it quick, we have another job."

Petehr cracked his neck, tugged at the collar of his Adidas tracksuit, and let out a short breath. Confidence radiated from him, but it was the kind of confidence sharpened by years of violence. With a casual motion, he hopped over a jersey barrier and landed on the other side of the street. The vehicle eased forward like a vulture in the night, pulling onto the shoulder of the road.

Safe House

At the FBI safe house on the outskirts of Vegas, Devin Crews lay on his back atop the oversized bed. The sheets were too crisp, the silence too heavy. Even with weeks of training behind him, a coil of unease refused to loosen inside him. His phone was pressed to his ear, and Tanya's voice filled the void. She was back at their apartment, her tone warm, teasing, a lifeline to normalcy he craved more than he admitted. "Look for a folder that says DePaul University," Devin said, rubbing a hand over his face.

On the other end, Tanya sighed dramatically as her fingers clicked across his laptop keys. "You kept files from college? Are you some kind of hoarder?" Devin chuckled, the sound loosening some of the tightness in his chest. "I just keep the important stuff." He paused, then added softly, "Like you." There was a beat of silence before Tanya laughed, the sound softer this time, more intimate. After a few clicks through several folders on the laptop, she said, "Aww…Okay, okay…I think I got it." Papers shuffled faintly in the background. "But you're going out on stage to this? Baby, you need some new music. This is ancient." "It's all I've got," Devin admitted. "Email it to me. I can't go on stage without my music."

The Apartment

Tanya leaned closer to the screen, scrolling through the mess of old folders. She smiled at the sight of Devin's college essays, photos from campus, even half-finished music mixes from his younger days. It was a glimpse into the man he used to be, a dreamer, a competitor, someone not yet burdened by the weight of responsibilities. Her hair spilled over her shoulder as she typed, biting her lip. "You know," she teased, "for a guy who lives his life undercover, you sure don't know how to cover up your digital footprints." Devin laughed again, though faintly distracted. "Don't expose me. Just…send the file." She rolled her eyes, but her smile lingered. "You're lucky that I love you." "I know, and I love you too." He replied.

The Shadow Arrives

Outside the apartment, the green SUV was parked on the shoulder a few houses down Tanya's street. The street was quiet, only the hum of a streetlamp overhead and the distant rumble of a train. Petehr glanced up at the building, mapping every shadow, scanning for potential eyewitnesses, nothing stirred. Clementine was purring somewhere in the bushes. With casual ease, Petehr slipped a small pin from his pocket. It glinted briefly in the glow of the streetlight. In one smooth maneuver, he approached the front door, inserted the pin, and twisted. The lock gave way with a satisfying click, a sound too low for Tanya to hear over the hum of her laptop. The hitman pushed the door open just enough to slide inside, the night swallowing him whole.

Two Worlds Collide

Back in the safe house, Devin was still talking, unaware of the danger converging on Tanya. "You know what the worst part is?" Devin said quietly. "It's not the training. It's not the mission. It's…this. Laying here, not being able to see you." Tanya's fingers paused on the keyboard. Her throat tightened, though she tried to keep her tone light. "You'll see me soon. And when you do, you better be ready to actually relax for once."

Devin closed his eyes, imagining her there beside him, her warmth chasing away the cold desert air. For a fleeting moment, the mission, the Russians, the looming Muscle-Mania event, all of it disappeared. Neither of them knew that at that exact moment, danger had slipped into the night and was converging on Tanya's.

Shadows at the Door

Tanya leaned against the headboard; one hand wrapped around the phone pressed to her ear. Her breathing had steadied after their laughter, but her voice carried a quieter weight now. "I really admire your commitment," she said softly, almost as if she were afraid of the words. "Is there anything you wouldn't do to be FBI? You even went to jail for Christ's sake." On the other end of the line, Devin chuckled faintly, though his reply was quick. "Prison, I went to prison…there's a difference."

"Exactly! I guess that answers my question." Tanya shot back. She let the word hang for a beat, her eyes staring at the framed photograph on her dresser—Devin in uniform, back when he was fresh out of the academy, clean-cut, and smiling without shadows behind his eyes. "They'd be fools not to hire you." She told him directly. But then, something shifted. Her body went rigid. The phone, still pressed to her ear, picked up nothing but her sharp inhale. "Tanya?" Devin's voice sharpened immediately. "What's wrong?" She didn't answer at first. Her gaze flicked toward the darkened hallway. The apartment, usually her sanctuary, suddenly felt cavernous and unsafe. A creak, faint but unmistakable—cut through the silence. "I…I think I heard something," she whispered. Devin's voice turned urgent, stripped of warmth. "Dial nine-one-one. Now." Her fingers trembled, but she obeyed. She tapped the digits quickly, sliding the phone into her pocket without ending the call. The line remained open—Devin could still hear everything.

Tanya's bare feet made no sound against the floor as she crept toward the hallway. She pressed her back against the wall, peeking around the corner. Nothing. Just darkness. Her pulse hammered in her ears. She glanced around for something—anything, to use as self-defense in case there was an intruder. Her instincts were telling her that she was not alone. A lamp sat on the end table, but it was too small. It could do no damage. The hallway was empty, offering no weapons, no cover. Then she saw a shadow. Not the shifting kind that came from the trees outside, but solid. Human form. Her body froze for half a heartbeat before instinct kicked in. She bolted toward the kitchen, toward the knife block on the counter. But she didn't make it.

A violent shove came out of nowhere, slamming her to the floor. The impact rattled her teeth, stars exploding across her vision. Her head cracked against the hardwood, and a hot sting split open across her forehead. Disoriented, she tried to crawl backward, but heavy footsteps advanced. From the other end of the line, Devin's voice was frantic. "Tanya! Talk to me! What's happening?" His cries were loud, but Tanya couldn't reply, she was now fighting for her life. Her breath came ragged. The figure loomed over her, a man, tall and wiry, with eyes cold and flat. His accent cut through the silence. "I have a message from the boss." Tanya was too afraid to even process what the intruder had said. Fear surged, but something else followed, anger—she felt exposed and violated. She screamed, pure, primal, then decided to fight. She wasn't going to be another nameless victim. Not tonight. She let him get close, let him bend down and grab a fistful of her hair. The sting of his fingers on her scalp made her wince, but it also gave her the opening she needed. With all her strength, she drove her thumb into his left eye.

The hitman howled, staggering backward, hands clutching his face. He swore in Russian, shaking his head as though trying to clear it. Tanya scrambled to her feet. The counter. The knives. She lunged for them, but he charged. His shoulder collided with her midsection, sending her stumbling backward. Petehr grabbed Tanya from behind wrapping his arms around her neck, but Tanya wasn't the easy mark he'd clearly expected. A lightning-fast hip toss, sent Petehr airborne, forcing him to release his grip, his body went tumbling to the floor. Petehr shrieked in agony from the pain he felt. Pain flared through Tanya's body, but adrenaline kept her moving. She was in survival mode. She reached for his leg and he heel kicked her in her right knee. She retreated and rubbed her knees. He got up and lunged towards her. As he reached for her again, she lashed out with her fist, slamming it into his throat. He gagged, wheezing. She followed with a sharp kick to his groin. His knees buckled as he folded over, both hands grabbing his private part. He felt the pain and there was no denying it. Tanya saw fear flicker in his eyes. "The cops are on the way," she spat through heavy breaths. For a moment, they stared at each other, predator and prey—though it was no longer clear which was which.

Still holding his groin, Petehr's confidence faltered. He backed up a step. Then another. But Tanya wasn't done. With a burst of momentum, she lunged, tackling him. They both crashed into the glass coffee table, shards exploding around them. The sound was deafening.

Pain bit into her arms and legs with deep cuts, but she didn't stop attacking. Something metallic skidded across the floor. The intruder's handgun, previously hidden in his waistband, spun into the floor and came to a stop in a corner a few feet away from them. Both of them froze for an instant, eyes darting to the weapon. Tanya moved first. Her hand darted down, closing not around the gun, but around a simple ballpoint pen among the debris. With a sharp thrust, she drove it into his thigh. The hitman screamed, collapsing onto one knee, clutching his leg.

Tanya didn't wait. She scrambled across the floor, glass cutting into her skin, until her hand closed around the gun's cold grip. She spun, raising it, her arms shaking but steady enough. Petehr's wide eyes locked with hers. For a second, time froze. She had him dead to rights. She could end it. But her finger hesitated on the trigger. Her breaths increase, heart slamming in her chest. She wasn't a killer. The hesitation cost her. He staggered upright and bolted, crashing through the doorway. She followed him but by the time she reached the threshold, gun still raised, the night swallowed him. She had lost the shot.

Failed Attempt

The hitman sprinted away from the apartment, blood soaking through his tracksuit. He hopped the jersey barrier than felled over to the ground. He picked himself up and stumbled toward the waiting SUV, lungs burning. "Go! Go, go, go!" he shouted as he flung himself inside. The driver's eyes went wide at the sight of him—battered, bleeding, glass embedded in his skin. "She's not a girl," Petehr struggles with his words, He was breathing heavily. "She's a demon. Drive!" The SUV roared to life, tires squealing as it tore down the street. Just as they rounded the corner, red-and-blue lights flared. Police cruisers sped past in the opposite direction, sirens blaring, missing the SUV by seconds. Inside the fleeing vehicle, the two men sat in silence, the weight of failure pressing down on them.

Back in Prison

At MCC, Aleksei's cell phone lit up in the darkness of the SHU. He answered immediately, listening. The voice on the other end was Petehr. As Petehr relayed the information of how the night had turned out, sparing no detail. Aleksei's face twisted in fury. "You got beat by a girl?" he growled in Russian. "How could this happen? This is embarrassing." Aleksei shouted into the phone before hanging up.

He paced the small confines of his cell, muttering curses under his breath. His fists clenched so tightly his knuckles turned white. After a long beat, he stopped, exhaled sharply, and forced composure back into his tone. "New plan," he said. "Gather everybody. You're going to Vegas. Don't screw this up. Everyone must pay." He ended the call and sat in the shadows, his mind already moving pieces on the board. The game wasn't over. Not by a long shot.

CHAPTER 27

IT'S SHOW TIME

L as Vegas was already awake by the time the black Escalade glided down the Strip . The desert sun hadn't yet scorched the pavement, but the city pulsed with its own kind of heat—a relentless thrum of slot machines, laughter, taxi horns, and the flicker of giant LED screens promising jackpots and endless entertainment.

The Escalade belonged. It was sleek and stylish just like the myriads of luxury cars zooming in and out of the hotel. Among the chaotic spill were some minivans, limos, and rental cars toting patrons to and fro. The tinted windows of the Escalade hid its passengers from prying eyes, but even through the glass, it radiated a certain presence, and the license plate said everything: B.O. for "Benedikt Oblonsky." Valets in crisp uniforms jogged to keep up with the steady traffic in front of the grand hotel marquee. The sign had been changed overnight. In bold red letters it screamed: MUSCLE-MANIA TONIGHT.

The Escalade slowed, turned left, and peeled away from the flashing facade. It slipped into a side entrance like a predator moving back into the shadows, unseen but very much aware of everything. Inside, the tinted rear window caught the sunlight just enough to reveal a pattern: three bars, red, white, and blue—the Russian flag, a quiet declaration of allegiance to the Slavic nation.

The SUV descended the ramp into the parking garage. Its hum echoed off concrete pillars as it rolled to a stop by the service elevator. Four doors flew open in unison. The front passenger stepped out first. His polished shoes clicked against the cement floor. He adjusted the cuff of his designer suit, revealing the glint of a heavy gold watch. His expression carried the same weight as the watch, expensive, deliberate, meant to be seen.

Benedikt Oblonsky.

The man who walks free while his formal partner Aleksei Lebedev rots in a cell, the formal mastermind of past election interference who for some reason remains untouchable. The man Devin Crews had been sent undercover to expose. Three other men followed him, remaining close by as if rehearsed. They weren't dressed like bodyguards, but the way they moved—quick, alert, in perfect formation, said everything. One scanned the garage while another tapped the elevator button, eyes sharp. The group entered without a word, swallowed by the steel doors that slid shut behind them.

The Lobby

Above, the hotel lobby buzzed with activity. Tourists dragged rolling suitcases across marble floors polished to a mirror sheen. Families posed by oversized flower arrangements, couples argued softly at the check-in desk, and the faint whir of slot machines bled in from the casino floor.

Devin walked in through the main doors, just another face in the crowd. At least, that's how it had to look. He wore a gray sweatsuit and a baseball cap pulled low. A duffel bag swung casually from his shoulder, though every item inside had been chosen for strategy—clothes, supplements, cover stories. His gait was relaxed, but his eyes were always moving, cataloging every detail: the uniform of the security at the front desk, the positioning of cameras, the exits and blind spots.

The lobby smelled faintly of chlorine from a nearby pool, the air layered with cologne, perfume, and the faint tang of espresso from the café. On the surface, it was ordinary. But

Devin knew better. This wasn't just a hotel. For him and his crew, tonight the hotel is going to represent a command center, aware that it could turn into a battlefield.

The Auditorium

He slipped through a side hallway into the auditorium, where workers bustled to prepare for the evening's event. The space was massive with rows of chairs fanning out toward a stage framed with glittering lights. Audio techs tested microphones. A stagehand dragged a ladder across the floor. Somewhere above, spotlights flicked on, one by one.

Devin let the duffel drop by a chair and stretched his arms, feigning a competitor's casual looseness. But his gaze swept the entire room. Sightlines. Entrances. The space behind the stage curtains where shadows could conceal more than lighting equipment. Right now, this was more than just an auditorium, it was a maze of vulnerabilities. "D.C.!" The voice cut through the clamor. Devin turned and broke into a grin as his buddy Mike strode toward him, arms spread wide. Mike hadn't changed much—same easy swagger, same bright energy, though time had added a few creases around his eyes. He wore gym shorts and a tank top, his physique still competition ready.

They clasped hands, pulling into a half-hug, half-slap on the back. "Mike," Devin said, the warmth in his voice genuine. "Damn, it's been too long." "Too damn long," Mike agreed. "I saw your name on the roster and thought, no way. Crews? Back in the game? I couldn't believe it." Devin smirked. "You know me. I don't do half measures." They laughed, the familiarity a welcome relief. But the moment didn't last.

A hard shoulder collided with Devin's back as someone brushed past, sending him off balance for a step. He turned sharply, eyes narrowing. The culprit didn't stop. Mike's voice rose, half-annoyed, half-mocking. "Hey! Uri! Wassup man!" The man glanced back briefly—dark eyes, a scowl sharp enough to cut glass. Then he kept moving, ignoring them. Devin frowned. "You know him?" "Uri Katznov," Mike said with a dismissive wave. "Not really. Just another contestant. Those damn Russians, man. Always starting some shit."

Devin's instincts tightened like a coil. Uri wasn't just another contestant. The brush hadn't been casual; it was a test, a warning, or maybe a signal. His gaze followed Uri as the man joined a cluster of other competitors. They were an odd sight: bodies bronzed with spray tan, some flexing in mirrors, others lifting dumbbells, their muscles slick with oil. Laughter and trash talk filled the room, but underneath, Devin felt something colder, a current that tied these men together. "Never mind him," Mike said, clapping Devin's shoulder. "C'mon, let's do some curls. Gotta get these guns ready for tonight."

Devin forced a grin, following him backstage. Behind the curtain was chaotic yet intensely focused on the art of body sculpting. There was an aroma of oil and spray tan that hung in the air. Competitors, some pumping up with resistance bands and light dumbbells, others meticulously checking the posing routine in full length mirrors. Amid the scattered weights, empty water bottles, and discarded protein bar wrappers, coaches give final critiques and instructions. Devin moved towards the dumbbell rack. It was a solid steel bed holding about thirty dumbbells. The rack was compact yet sturdy, maximizing floor space while keeping the weights neatly organized. Devin picked up a pair, the iron felt cold and familiar in his hands. His arms pumped mechanically, but his mind wasn't on the reps. "Uri…huh?" Devin muttered, staring at Uri and two other bodybuilders whom he assumed to be Russians as well. Mike laughed, oblivious. "Yeah, man. Forget him. This is Vegas. We're here to shine." But Devin's eyes stayed locked on the Russians, memorizing every movement. Because in this room, among the clatter of weights and the haze of tanning spray, the real game had already begun.

Eyes in the Crowd

The nondescript FBI van sat like an uninvited guest on the edge of the Strip, parked in the shadow of a palm tree that did little to hide its presence. Inside, the air was heavy with the smell of fast-food wrappers and the stale sting of black coffee. A faint hum of electronics filled the cramped space, monitors casting pale light across tense faces, displaying every inch of the hotel they were monitoring. Benson leaned forward in his seat, headset pressed tight against his ear. His jaw was locked, his patience razor thin. "Crews, come in," he barked. Static.

"Crews," he repeated, louder this time, his voice grinding with irritation. "I said come in." Benson ripped the headset halfway off and glared at one of the younger agents hunched over a screen. The guy's eyes darted nervously between data streams, not daring to meet his superior's stare. "Is he wearing his damn earpiece?" Benson asked no one in particular.

The agent hesitated, checked another monitor, then shook his head. "Uh… signal's active, sir, but…it's not in motion. Just…blinking." Benson's nostrils flared. He didn't need the translation. Devin had ditched his comms, probably stuffed it somewhere carelessly. The man was a hell of an operative but infuriating in the way only lone wolves could be. Across the van, Mack sat with his arms folded, trying not to look amused. He'd been partnered with Crews long enough to know the man's habits. Some rules were mere suggestions, and communication was optional. Benson snapped his gaze at agent Mack. "Go check on him." Mack raised his eyebrows. "Me? You're sending me in there?"

"You're the only one he won't brush off." Benson responded as he motioned a hand toward the door. "And keep it clean. Eyes only." Mack muttered something under his breath but slid out of the van, adjusting the jacket that hid his concealed firearm.

Backstage

Inside the hotel auditorium, the energy had shifted. What had been a quiet, sterile hall hours ago was now alive with motion. Contestants filled the backstage area, the air thick with the smell that had intensified. The tanning spray, body oil, and nervous sweat. Metallic clanks of dumbbells echoed off concrete walls, mixed with bursts of laughter, shouts, and the occasional guttural grunt of determination.

Devin stood with Mike by the dumbbell rack, their muscles pumping under the harsh fluorescent lights. His duffel bag sat a few feet away, a tiny red light blinking unnoticed inside. Benson's voice echoed faintly from the earpiece buried within, a frustrated ghost lost under the noise. Devin was completely oblivious to the situation. "C'mon, one more set," Mike urged, curling a dumbbell with practiced ease. "You're looking solid, man. Vegas is gonna' love you." Devin smirked, rolling his shoulders. He kept his focus on the movement, but his peripheral vision was everywhere— noting clusters of contestants, spotting the Russians gathered in a corner, tracking exits like second nature.

Mike didn't notice any of it. To him, it was just another show. For Devin, it was an intelligence gathering minefield disguised in pageantry. Mack slipped in through a side hallway, his expression betraying immediate regret. The sight hit him like a slap: a sea of oiled-up men, bronzed bodies gleaming under the lights, most stripped down to posing trunks that left absolutely nothing to the imagination. The chatter was loud, the air humid with testosterone and chemicals.

Mack froze in place, his eyes darting everywhere except at the competitors. He looked like a man who had stumbled into the wrong room at the wrong time. "Christ," he muttered under his breath. *This is worse than basic training open showers*, he thought to himself. He wove through the crowd, stiff as a soldier trying not to draw attention, though his discomfort made him stand out all the more. A contestant flexed beside him, spraying himself with bronzer, and Mack recoiled like he'd been splashed with acid.

Finally, he spotted Devin and waved him over with a desperate flick of the wrist. Devin caught the signal, grinned, and strolled over, towel slung around his neck. "You okay there, buddy?" Devin asked, lowering his voice but not hiding his amusement.

Mack's expression was one part horror, one part disgust. "I've just never seen so many guys in bikinis before. If I drop my piece right now, I won't even bend down to pick it up. I'll kick it all the way into the hallway." Devin chuckled, clapping him on the shoulder. "You need to talk to somebody about that. I know a good therapist." "Don't joke," Mack said sharply. "Benson's climbing the walls out there. You left your comms in your bag again, didn't you?" Devin shrugged. "Can't exactly pump iron with a wire hanging out of my ear, can I?" Mack shot him a glare. "Yeah, well, next time try not to give our boss a stroke. C'mon. They're ready for you." Devin nodded, slipping into professional mode. But as he followed Mack, his eyes flicked once more toward the Russians. Uri was watching him; not openly, not enough to call attention, but Devin felt it. A weight in the room. A silent dare. The show hadn't even begun, and already, the real contest was in motion.

CHAPTER 28

THE G-SUIT

The hotel hallways smelled faintly of carpet cleaner and cigarette smoke, the residue of thousands of tourists who had passed through, chasing luck or distraction. Tonight, though, the corridor outside the corner suite was quiet, sterile. Mack rapped his knuckles against the door, short and authoritative. It opened immediately, revealing a woman with sharp eyes and a confident grip. "I'm Tammy," she introduced herself, shaking Mack's hand firmly before turning to Devin. She was a natural beauty. The kind of woman who knows she looks good but has no intention of weaponizing it. "And you must be Crews." Her head held high, her smile held recognition, the way one might greet a face seen often in briefing files and whispered conversations. Devin was a professional though, he returned the shake, measured but warm. "Good to meet you," he said.

The room beyond hummed with controlled chaos. Tables were stacked with laptops, wires coiling across the carpet, monitors displaying multiple camera angles of the hotel. Agents with headsets leaned over equipment, murmuring into microphones, testing comms. The space had been transformed into a forward-operating command post, less hotel room than temporary war room.

Devin and Mack wove through the bustle, eyes taking in every detail. The glow of screens lit up tense faces, coffee cups balanced precariously on stacks of paper, technicians hunched over blinking consoles. It was an army of shadows preparing for a type of operation that no one in the casino would ever know existed. From the back room emerged the leadership: Benson, all sharp angles and coiled authority; Stevens, his demeanor more bureaucratic but carrying the weight of a field director; Davis and Oliver, supervisors whose presence lent gravity to the scene.

Benson clapped his hands once, the sound cutting through the noise like a starter pistol. "Everybody, listen up!" His voice was firm, practiced, and filled with the certainty of command. "We are going to do this by the books. No improvising, no cowboy stunts. We are not going to turn this into an international incident." He paused, scanning the room, making sure the junior agents caught every word. "The goal here," he continued, "is that no one gets hurt. Understood?"

A chorus of nods followed. The younger agents, fresh-faced and wide-eyed, nodded perhaps too eagerly, their nerves thinly veiled beneath the veneer of professionalism. Benson let the silence hang a moment longer before adding, "Your country will thank you for what you're about to do. We promised the American people zero foreign interference in the upcoming election, and by God, we're going to deliver." No applause. No cheers. Just the steady hum of electronics and the shuffle of agents checking their gear. Gratitude, after all, was a promise often made, seldom delivered. Benson straightened, his tone sharpening. "It's show time."

Like a switch had been flipped, the room erupted into movement. Agents snatched up radios, technicians ran final tests, and the energy shifted from planning to execution. Amid the flurry, Agent Stevens approached Devin carrying a small black bag. "Here," he said, passing it over with the kind of nonchalance that made Devin suspicious. "I made this for you."

Devin unzipped the bag and reached inside. His fingers brushed against something soft, elastic. He pulled it out— and froze. It was tiny. A sliver of spandex, barely enough fabric to qualify as clothing. A posing suit, the kind worn by bodybuilders under stage lights, except this one had been custom-modified. He held it up for the room to see. "Oh, come on," Mack groaned, already anticipating humiliation.

Devin grinned wickedly and waved the fabric in Mack's face. "What do you think? My size?" Mack recoiled and stumbled backwards shielding his face, as though he'd been sprayed with poison gas, nearly tripping over a chair. His embarrassment set the room into ripples of laughter. Even the stone-faced junior agents cracked smiles. Devin examined the suit more closely, his amusement giving way to curiosity. "Wait a second. Is that…a built-in mic?" Stevens nodded. "And a camera. State-of-the-art. Don't worry—it only faces outward." Devin shook his head in disbelief, muttering, "Only the Bureau would bug a bikini."

Bathroom

The fluorescent lights buzzed overhead as Devin stepped into the bathroom, closing the door behind him. He held the item in his hands, running the fabric between his fingers. For a moment, he was back in college—the smell of chalk and sweat, the adrenaline of competition. The roar of the crowd when he'd taken the stage for the first time, bronzed and ready, his heart hammering like a war drum. It felt like another lifetime, and yet the old confidence stirred in his chest as he slipped into the tiny trunks. "Some things never change," he murmured at his reflection, the absurdity of the mission weighing against the familiarity of the uniform.

Bedroom

When he stepped out, conversation in the room screeched to a halt. Agents froze mid-movement, eyes drawn in disbelief. Devin stood nearly naked, the posing suit clinging to him like a second skin. Years of training and the recent weeks of preparation had carved his body back into an ancient Greek form—a figure both ridiculously sculpted and undeniably imposing. Everyone but Mack looked impressed.

"We need a mic check," Benson said, deadpan, as though this were any other briefing. Devin smirked and sauntered directly over to Mack, planting himself inches away, hands on hips. He swayed side to side, deliberately taunting. The room erupted into muffled chuckles. Mack's face turned crimson. He glanced around at the staring eyes, realizing escape was impossible. "No way," he muttered, shaking his head. "It's standard procedure," Benson said flatly. "Your job," Stevens added, unhelpfully.

Mack shot a look at Tammy, who stood in the corner biting her lip to stifle a laugh. Her shoulders shook with silent amusement. Defeated, Mack sighed and slowly crouched down toward Devin's waistline, his face a portrait of pure misery. "Mic check, one-two," he muttered in the lowest voice possible. The room held its breath. Mack shot back up instantly, as though the floor had shocked him. His ears burned. From the corner, Stevens gave a disapproving grunt, like a father watching his son fumble an easy catch.

Benson turned to the technicians at the control table. "Did you get that?" The two men shook their heads side to side in unison. "You gotta' do it again," Benson ordered. The color drained from Mack's face. Devin, meanwhile, looked delighted with the biggest grin yet. Mack crouched again, his pride dying a slow death. As he leaned in, Devin suddenly thrust his hips forward with exaggerated flair. "Ewww!" Devin exclaimed, mock horror in his tone. Mack yelped, stumbled backward, and landed flat on his backside. The room exploded. Laughter roared through the cramped space, agents doubled over, Tammy folded over bursting with laughter. Even Benson's lips twitched with a petite smile, though he quickly masked it.

Mack sat on the carpet, staring up at Devin with a look that was half fury, half humiliation. Pretending to shield his eyes, he muttered, "I've seen enough nightmares to last a lifetime." The technicians raised their thumbs in triumph. "We got it!" Devin extended a hand and pulled Mack up, leaning close to whisper, "Never, huh?" Mack's jaw clenched, but he said nothing.

Hallway

The mission was set. Seven suited agents filed out of the hotel room, their movements synchronized, their expressions grim. And then came Devin. Clad in the posing suit, body gleaming under the fluorescent light, he stepped into the hallway like a superhero conjured from some surreal comic book. The other agents parted instinctively, making a hole for him and Mack at the front. For a heartbeat, no one laughed. The absurdity melted into awe. Whatever else could be said, Devin Crews looked ready for war.

Vegas Streets

Outside, night had fallen, and the stars danced in the sky. The neon glow of the Strip painted everything in Technicolor and vibrance. The strip was well-lit and dazzling, to say the least. The entire boulevard was an electric dreamscape on display and the hotel was drawing in huge crowds. Tanya and April climbed out of an Uber, their eyes catching the marquee flashing above the hotel entrance: MUSCLE-MANIA TONIGHT. They exchanged a look—half excitement, half trepidation. Inside, in the long hallway leading to the stage, the FBI's secret weapon was on the move.

CHAPTER 29

ALL IS LOST

The hotel auditorium pulsed with energy. Large bodybuilding posters served as backdrop to the essence of the competition. From above, bright stage lights bathed the room in a golden glow, bouncing off oiled skin and glittering trophies lined up on a side table. Rows of spectators leaned forward in anticipation, some clutching programs, others holding up their phones to record. The scent of hairspray, cologne, and the faint tang of metal from the weight racks backstage mingled in the air, making the space feel both glamorous and suffocating.

At the judges' table, five men sat like kings on a dais. All were veterans of the sport—thick-necks, wide-chests, and killer physiques even long past their competitive prime but still visible beneath tailored suits and t-shirts. They held clipboards and pens like weapons, every stroke of ink a judgment on months, even years, of sacrifice. The fluorescent bore down as the lineup of colossal physiques awaited their next command. "Gentlemen," the head judge called out, "we need to see some triceps pose. "Quarter-turn to the right," the judge bellowed, his voice cutting cleanly through the auditorium.

Onstage, five contestants pivoted in unison, their bodies gleaming under the lights. The crowd gave an appreciative murmur, cameras flashing as lats and obliques flared with mechanical precision. Muscles swelled and hardened; every fiber engage as the competitors twisted their upper bodies to form. A few seconds of intense scrutiny passed before the next, equally demanding instruction. Backstage, Mack shifted uncomfortably. He leaned toward Tammy, the female agent who had joined them earlier. "Come with me," he muttered. His voice was tight, uneasy. Tammy didn't budge. Her eyes were locked on the stage, amusement curling at the corners of her mouth. "No," she said confidently, her tone teasing. "I think I see something suspicious."

The sparkle in her eye told Mack she wasn't talking about Oblonsky. Mack scowled and turned on his heel, stalking out of the auditorium. "Quarter-turn to the right," the head Judge repeated. The men pivoted again, now facing the crowd, smiles plastered to their faces despite the strain in their limbs. The judges scribbled notes, their poker faces betraying nothing. Tammy clapped politely, clearly enjoying the spectacle.

The air backstage was warm from the heat of stage lights and alive with the chatter of competitors pumping themselves up, stretching, or nervously pacing. Mack found Devin hunched over a weight bench, his expression carved with frustration. "We don't have eyes on Oblonsky," Mack said grimly. "We looked everywhere. Nobody has seen him." Devin lifted his head slowly, eyes sharp. "Nobody?"

"The crew on 10th said they saw his black SUV enter the underground parking. We checked, the vehicle's gone." Mack shook his head. "Sorry, man. We have to abort. That's coming from the top." The words hit like a gut punch. Devin sat down heavily on a bench, elbows on knees, head in his hands. "Fuck," he hissed. "This is not good." "I'm sorry, man. This one's out of our hands." But Devin wasn't listening. His mind raced, trying to stitch together another way forward, another opening. He couldn't let the mission die here, not when Oblonsky was so close. By now, he wasn't sure who he was trying to please, his new superiors, himself or his late father. Devin was determined to succeed at all costs.

The sound of footsteps pulled his attention. Tanya appeared, April trailing close behind her. The sight of Tanya and her girlfriend caught him off guard, he wasn't expecting to see them at this time. Tanya, her hair loose and resting on her shoulders, her eyes blazing with determination, and support for her man, pulled Devin upright. "Tanya!" Mack greeted immediately, a look of surprise written across his face. "Hello," Tanya said dryly, giving Mack only a glance before her gaze landed firmly on Devin. "What's going on?" Devin's throat tightened. "We lost him," he admitted. Tanya's brows drew together, and she turned to Mack. "What is he talking about?"

Mack moved quickly, gripping her arm and steering her a few steps away, past April, who lingered, her eyes fixed on Devin with unnerving intensity. Tanya caught it immediately. Jealousy flared like a match. "You," Tanya snapped at April, her voice cutting like glass. "Stay close to me." April blinked, startled, but obeyed, stepping beside her friend. Mack studied them both, suspicion narrowing his gaze. Something was bubbling under the surface between the two women and maybe even between April and Devin. "We are out here on an operation and Crew's is our lead guy, but our mission got called off," Mack explained, eyes flicking between the women and Devin. "We lost our target and he's taking it hard. Go easy on him."

Tanya folded her arms, considering. "So…not a good time to bring up Sherry?" she asked flatly. Mack nearly choked. "No! Definitely not." He leaned closer, dropping his voice. "How did you find out? Tanya shot Mack a look, "let's just say, I see everything." Mack decided to come to his friend's rescue. "Look," he said softly, "they had a thing back in the academy. He told me all about it. That was a long time ago and it didn't work out. They both wanted different things.' He said, when I asked him…" Mack paused for a beat and continued, "…she was moving too fast and he just wanted to be a cop, wasn't ready to settle down." Before Tanya could respond, a booming voice called over the loudspeaker: "Devin Crews, report to the stage!" All eyes swung to Devin.

Tanya turned back to him. "That's you. They're calling you. What are you going to do?" Devin sat there, weighing his options. The thought of quitting crossed his mind for a brief second. With a newly found energy, Devin stood abruptly, purpose flooding back into his posture. "Grab that bottle right there," he said, pointing. Tanya lifted the spray bottle of posing oil from a table. Devin planted his feet shoulder-width apart, arms stretched, palms parallel to the floor. "Hit me." She hesitated only a second before stepping closer. The mist of oil shimmered as it landed across his chest and arms, tracing every ridge of muscle, highlighting weeks of training. She worked slowly, methodically, almost reverently. April watched silently, her eyes drinking in the sight. Mack noticed and stiffened, his jaw tightening.

Tanya's hands glided lower, smoothing the sheen across Devin's abs, down to his thighs. "Okay," she whispered, her voice softer now. "You're good." Devin leaned forward and kissed her quickly on the forehead, firmly, grounding himself. "Excuse me," he murmured. "I've got a show to do."

Onstage

When Devin arrived next to the stage, the show's producer, a balding man holding a clipboard nodded briskly. "You're up next." Devin lingered a moment in the wings, watching Mike finish his individual set. Mike flexed his biceps with confidence, the crowd cheering, judges scribbling furiously. "Front lat spread!" The head judge commanded. Mike shifted, expanding his chest and flaring his lats like wings. "Side chest!" Mike hit the pose with a breathtaking display, holding it with a grin until every inch was scrutinized. "Back double biceps!" Turning slowly, Mike flexed again, his back a tapestry of muscles. After a collective inhale, the crowd erupted. Applause thundered through the auditorium as Mike waved to the crowd and exited the stage, grinning and soaked with sweat. Devin swallowed hard. His turn.

The announcer stepped forward, voice booming over the speakers. "The next round is going to be unusual," he declared. "Something we've never done before." Agents in the audience stiffened. Mack muttered under his breath, "No, Crews. Don't blow your cover." "Our next performer," the announcer continued, "is coming to you virtually.

The agents exhaled in unison, relief loosening the knot in the room. A giant projector screen descended from the ceiling, drawing gasps from the crowd. On it, appeared a ballroom decorated with bodybuilding paraphernalia. Competitors stood ready, Judges leaned forward eagerly. "I want to see this," one judge whispered to another.

As the virtual competitors struck their poses, Devin decided to tie all loose ends. He refused to let all his effort in the mission slither away for good. Time was slipping away. He darted from the wings, heart hammering, slipping out of the auditorium and into the hallway, the roar of the crowd fading behind him.

CHAPTER 30

CHECKMATE

The underground parking garage of the hotel was a cavern of concrete and echo, the kind of place where secrets thrived. Fluorescent lights buzzed overhead, casting long pools of white that only deepened the shadows between cars. A white van rolled slowly across the slick surface, its tires hissing in the damp air. Inside, the atmosphere was tense, like a pressure cooker. The men in the front seat didn't speak much; silence was their ally, focus their weapon.

The driver suddenly stomped the brake, screeching his tires when they saw the familiar black ESCALADE that belongs to Oblonsky. The license plate read only two letters: "B.O." It sat like a predator at rest, gleaming, waiting. The insignia of the Russian flag shimmered faintly in the tinted glass of the back window.

The passenger door swung open. Petehr climbed out, his face marked with scratches that hadn't yet healed. A thick bandage wrapped his left hand. He walked with a slight limp, each step a reminder of the humiliation he had suffered in a one-on-one fight with the demon, as he referred to her. But his eyes burned with vengeance. The sliding door at the back of the van opened. Two more figures dropped to the ground. One was Luca, late thirties, silent, with the blank face of someone who had long ago stopped asking questions about morality. The other was Kat.

Kat wore a plain housekeeping uniform, the kind of disguise that made her invisible in a hotel this size. A dark wig framed her sharp face, and her eyes glittered with cold intent. She dragged a piece of luggage on wheels across concrete, the rattling echoing across the garage like a ticking clock.

Luca pulled a Beretta M9 from under his jacket. He clicked the safety off, checked the chamber, and slid it back into his waistband. "Let's move," he muttered. His voice was low, hard, the accent was Slavic. Kat crouched near the SUV, her movements calm, precise. With a flick of her wrist, she unzipped the suitcase. Nestled inside was a block of steel and wires: a bomb. She ran her hand over it like a craftsman inspecting fine work, then slid it under the ESCALADE, fastening it tight against the undercarriage. She paused, scanning the garage. No witnesses. No sound but their breathing and the hum of the overhead lights. She rose, brushed her hands off, and nodded. Without a word, they walked toward the service door, their footsteps casual, almost lazy. Just hotel staff, nothing more. But in the garage, death now waited by a ticking timebomb, waiting to be called because somebody wanted Oblonsky dead. But who?

Desperation

Devin's feet slapped against the polished floor of the hotel hallway. He was still in his competition thong, sweat gleaming on his skin, but he didn't care. Embarrassment was nothing compared to the urgency clawing at his chest.

He yanked open a service door he had scouted earlier. The heavy steel swung wide, and there it was, a black Escalade with a Russian flag visible in its rear window. His breath caught. Oblonsky. *He's here.* His pulse thundered in his ears. He slammed the door shut and sprinted back down the hall, dodging startled hotel staff who gawked at the half-naked man barreling past them. His lungs were on fire, a searing, desperate match to his feet with every impact. He bursts through the stairwell door and enters a landing area. He looked up, then decided to go for it. The smell of damp concrete filled the air, and Devin had long forgotten about the competition going on upstairs on the fifth floor.

Every muscle screamed a protest as he hammered his way up, passing up various levels. A couple stood aside as Devin came flying up towards them, a slick sheen of sweat blooming on his forehead, but he kept going. One last flight of stairs stood between him and the fifth floor. Atop the final landing area, he braced himself against a steel rail, palming it, the steel was cold to touch. It was the only anchor in his dizzying ascent, and with a final, gasping surge of adrenaline, he rounded the last turn and burst through the fire door, staggering onto the fifth floor. After catching his breath for a brief-moment, he darted down the hallway and into the command post.

The Post Awakens

The room was thick with stale coffee and exhaustion. Two technicians were already packing up, wrapping wires and powering down monitors, their shoulders slumped in defeat. Benson leaned against a table, his face drawn, while Stevens hovered beside him, silent, waiting for orders that had never come. The door crashed open. Devin stormed in, chest heaving. "He's here!" Devin shouted. His voice cracked with urgency. Benson's head jerked up. Stevens froze. The technicians stopped mid-motion, cords dangling in their hands. Devin stepped forward, eyes blazing. "He's in the building. Confirmed."

For a moment, no one moved. The silence was heavy, like the breath before a storm. Then Benson's lips curled into a grin. He pumped his fist. "We're back on!" Stevens let out a sharp breath, relief breaking into a smile. "Yes," he said. "Let's go get the son of a bitch." Energy surged back into the room. The technicians scrambled, plugging wires back in, and with the click of power buttons, the hum of electronics filled the air again. A motherboard of connectivity for the computer systems lit up. Soon, a flicker appears on the first monitor, then the next and the next. Benson snatched a headset from the table, his voice sharp as a blade. "Attention all units," he barked. "The target is in the building. I repeat, the target is in the building. We're back on!" Across the hotel, agents stiffened at the order. The hunt had resumed.

Kat's Infiltration

On the luxury floor at the very top of the hotel, the trio of hitmen moved like sharks in dark water. Petehr limped, carrying his pain like a badge of honor. Luca hauled the suitcase now, its weight a silent promise. They slipped into a men's bathroom and locked the door.

Kat kept moving. She pushed a dining cart draped with a white cloth, her posture was that of a weary hotel maid just doing her rounds. She stopped by the control room overlooking the auditorium. Voices swept past behind her—guests, staff, but none looked twice at her. She fiddled with napkins and plates, waiting. The hall cleared. She knocked lightly and pushed the door open.

Inside, a fat man with glasses sat hunched over a bank of computers and switchboards. Tiny lights blinked like stars in a private galaxy. He jumped at the sight of her but quickly relaxed when he saw the cart. *Food*, he thought to himself. His lips stretched into a grin. "About time." Kat smiled back. It was not a kind smile. She wheeled the cart inside, closed the door with a click, and lifted the lid. The man's grin faltered.

Nestled on the tray was a pistol with a silencer beside it. His mouth opened, panic surging across his face. Kat moved quickly, screwing the silencer onto the barrel with steady hands. He tried to speak, to plead. "Pew. Pew." Two muffled shots whispered through the room.

The man collapsed forward, his blood splattering across the glowing lights of his equipment. Red mingled with green, dripping down the switches. Kat didn't flinch. She bent beneath the cart, pulled out another bomb, and planted it among the wires. She adjusted her uniform, smoothed her wig, and stepped to the thick glass overlooking the auditorium. Her eyes scanned the crowd. And then she saw him. Oblonsky, seated with his entourage, laughing, oblivious. Kat's lips curled into a scowl. "Benedikt Oblonsky," she whispered. "You're a dead man." She pocketed her weapon, primped her uniform, and clutched the detonator like a secret talisman. Then she slipped back into the hallway.

Kat knocked softly on a men's restroom door. It cracked open. Petehr scarred face peered out. She slipped inside. "It's done," she said, her accent thickening. They gathered around the suitcase, opening it to reveal more bombs. Luca leaned forward, his voice a growl. "The hard drive. Go." Kat nodded. She smoothed her uniform again, hid the pistol beneath her apron, and walked down the hall. At Oblonsky's suite, she knocked. "Housekeeping," she called sweetly.

The door opened a crack. A man stood there, gun hidden at his side, eyes cold. He blocked the doorway with his other hand. Kat counted in her head. One. Two. Three. She smiled. "So, only three towels then!" The man frowned. "What?" Before he could react, the hallway erupted. Three shadows surged from behind Kat. Guns blazing, POP! POP! POP! The man at the door jerked backward, blood painting the walls and the floor beneath him. His limp body dropped with a heavy thud.

Inside the suite, two more Russians scrambled for weapons. Too slow. Bullets tore through them, bodies collapsing onto expensive furniture. Glass shattered, rounds ricocheted, the air filled with the metallic sting of gunpowder and blood.

In seconds, silence. All of Oblonsky's men lay dead. Luca scanned for a quick inventory then pointed toward the corner, where a massive computer tower hummed. "The server," he said. They went to work, pulling drives, stuffing evidence into bags. "Where's the…" Luca started to ask a question before he was interrupted. Kat answered by holding up the detonator. His grin was sharp. "Good. Go downstairs. Wait for the signal." Kat nodded, her eyes flicking once more with fire. The hotel was now a powder keg. And the fuse had just been lit.

Suite Victory

The tiled walls of the backstage men's bathroom echoed with a sterile hum. Mack stood at the urinal, staring straight ahead, shoulders rigid beneath the dark cut of his tailored suit. The chatter in his earpiece was faint, Benson's voice drifting in and out-but his concentration was broken when the door creaked open.

Two blonde-haired bodybuilders lumbered in, skin bronzed and glistening with oil, torsos bare save for the strips of fabric clinging to their hips. They looked like Norse gods on steroids, their heavy footsteps shaking the floor tiles. Without hesitation, they took the two urinals beside Mack-one on the left, one on the right. He was boxed in, their massive shoulders dwarfing him.

Mack froze. He didn't dare glance sideways, though he could feel their presence, the heat radiating from their oversized frames. His jaw clenched. One of them leaned ever so slightly, a smirk curling his lips. "You look tense," the man said, his voice a low rumble. "Need a shoulder rub?" The second bodybuilder snorted, and both burst into loud, unrestrained laughter. The sound bounced off the tiles, a cruel chorus. Mack's ears burned red. He zipped up, stormed to the sink, and scrubbed his hands at lightning speed. Soap, water, towel done. His reflection looked rattled, his tie slightly crooked. He didn't care. He shoved the door open and fled the bathroom, panting as if he had just run a marathon.

Hallway Collision

The hotel's labyrinthine hallway stretched before him, patterned carpet swallowing his footsteps. As Mack steadied his breath, Devin appeared from the opposite direction, striding toward him like a vision from a nightmare. Devin was still in his bikini, the tiny fabric straining over his muscular frame. Sweat glistened under the hallway lights. A badge swung from his neck, a gun gripped firmly in his hand. "Follow me," Devin said, urgency in his voice. Mack blinked, thrown by the surreal image of his partner half-naked with a weapon. "Where're we going?" "Oblonsky's got a suite on the top floor. Intel just pinged suspicious activity from there, computer traffic we can't ignore. We've got a warrant … and there's more." Devin swallowed, "shots fired." Mack nodded, adrenaline washing away the remnants of his bathroom humiliation. Mack quickly drew his weapon and fell into step beside Devin, their pace quickening.

Elevator Ride

They slipped into a service elevator, its steel walls closing around them. The cab shuddered as it began to rise, making stops along the way. The silence was heavy, filled only by the whirring machinery. At the tenth floor, the doors slid open. An elderly couple stood waiting. The old man's eyes widened as he took in Devin's nearly naked body, the badge, the weapon. His wife gasped, clutching his arm. "We'll take the next one," the man muttered, pulling her away as if fleeing a dangerous animal as she cranes her neck to get another look. The doors closed again.

The elevator groaned upward. Another stop. The doors parted, revealing two young women dressed for the night. One staggered slightly, clearly drunk. Her gaze locked on Devin and refused to let go. Devin made sure that his firearm was concealed from the civilians. "Whoo whoo!" the drunk friend muttered, her laughter bubbling. "Look at that! I think he's happy to see us." Her friend tugged her arm, trying to pull her inside. Mack reacted instantly, sweeping open his jacket to reveal his badge and firearm. The drunk girl's laughter died on her lips. Both women stumbled back, sobered by the cold glint of authority.

The doors closed once more. Silence again. Mack kept his eyes forward, lips moving faintly, muttering something under his breath. He wanted to speak but bit back the words. Devin gave him a quick sidelong glance, then looked away, smirking faintly. Finally, Mack cleared his throat. "Do you want my jacket?" "No thanks," Devin said flatly. "Please," Mack insisted. "Take it."

Luxury Floor

When the elevator doors opened at the luxury floor, Devin was wearing Mack's suit jacket. It stretched awkwardly across his broad shoulders, barely containing him, but at least it lent a semblance of decency. Devin stood tall, gun hidden behind his back, posture stiff as if at parade rest. Waiting outside the elevator was Kat. She looked composed, her disguise immaculate, the wig neat, her uniform crisp. But her eyes flickered when they met Devin's, scanning him quickly, dismissively.

She gave a half-smile, unimpressed. Mack, however, was instantly taken by her. His eyes lingered, shamelessly drinking her in. She stepped into the elevator as they exited. Mack turned his head for one last look. She caught his gaze and smiled. He smiled back, foolishly, unaware of the storm that followed her. As soon as the doors sealed her inside, Kat's composure cracked. She slammed the button for another floor, exhaled sharply, and pressed her palm to her chest. Panic etched across her face.

Breach

Devin and Mack moved down the luxury hallway, their footsteps deliberate. A trail of blood spatter caught their attention, streaked across the patterned carpet like breadcrumbs to a nightmare. They drew their guns, flicked the safeties off, and took positions on either side of a large door. From inside came muffled movement—the scrape of chairs, hurried voices. Devin counted down with his fingers. Three … two … one. They kicked the door open. "FBI! Freeze!" Mack bellowed. "Don't move!" Inside, the Russians flinched at the intrusion. Luca and Petehr were bent over a large computer server, cables and drives scattered around them. One lunged for a pistol on the table.

Devin fired first. His burst of bullets clipped the gun, sending it skidding across the floor. Both Russians threw up their hands, eyes wide. "On your knees!" Mack barked. Reluctantly, they complied, lowering themselves beside three white-draped bodies already sprawled on the floor. The smell of blood thickened the air. Mack slapped handcuffs onto their wrists. The men knew better than to resist, fearing repercussions.

Devin tugged at the sheets, confirming his suspicion. Three of Oblonsky's men lay dead beneath, faces pale, eyes staring blankly. "Ewww," Devin muttered, covering his nose. Petehr glared up. "You FBI?" He asked in his thick accent, "Not yet," Devin shot back. He tilted his head, smirking. Devin to return his own set of questions. "You KGB?" The man frowned. "I don't know what that is." Devin mimicked the accent, mocking him: "I don't know what that is." Mack pulled out a notepad, scribbling. "Field interview. Names. Start talking. First and last." The Russian sneered. "Jon. Jon Doe." Mack's face tightened with anger, pen stabbing into the pad.

Suddenly, a sound from within the suite. The bathroom door creaked. A third Russian emerged with a large studio headphones clamped over both ears, music pulsing, accompanied with a head nod. He carried a newspaper in one hand, oblivious until his eyes locked on the agents. He froze. Then his arm shot behind his back. A Glock appeared in his hand. Devin didn't hesitate. His instincts screamed. He swung his gun up, sighted, and fired.

The shot cracked like thunder. The Russian slammed back against the wall, blood spraying as his pistol clattered to the floor. His right arm hung limp, crimson spreading fast. He howled in agony, clutching the wound. Mack yanked his weapon up as well, but Devin's was still smoking. Devin approached cautiously, barrel trained on the man writhing on the floor. "It's just a flesh wound," Devin said dryly, lowering his aim. "Good shot," Mack admitted, eyes flicking with reluctant respect. "I'll sweep the rest of the place."

After a few minutes, the suite swarmed with reinforcements, four agents came rushing in, weapons drawn. One of them was a data analyst, he holstered his weapon and moved over to the massive server blinking red and green. His fingers danced over the attached keyboard. "I got something," he muttered, eyes wide. Devin leaned over his shoulder. "What is it?" The analyst clicked through folders, each one revealing dark web troughs. Propaganda. Election files. Evidence of manipulation on a global scale.

On the screen: "KKK" propaganda. "BLM" propaganda. Fake Facebook accounts by the hundreds. Instagram identities cloned and twisted into hate machines. IRA operations. Even files exploiting the Proud Boys—all part of a coordinated web of lies. "Look at this," the analyst said, voice grim. "Lotsa fake advocacy groups. They were getting ready to unleash it." Devin's eyes hardened. He turned to Mack. "We got him." Mack's phone buzzed. He answered, listened. His eyes widened, locking on Devin's. He snapped the phone shut. "He's downstairs, it's time to take him down."

CHAPTER 31

DENOUMENT

Rows of spectators leaned forward in their seats, eyes glued to the spectacle. The auditorium held a large crowd; some with signs showing support for the athletes, others with foods and drinks holding side conversations. The judges sat like royals at their table, clipboards ready, pens twitching. "Gentlemen, this is the final round, are you ready?" The head judge boomed into the microphone, his voice echoing across the packed hall. The ten finalists stood in a straight line, shoulder to shoulder like living bronze statues in bikini bottoms—chests puffed up, veins bulging, jaws relaxed, forcing a smile for the camera. Devin lingered in the wings, still wearing Mack's jacket over his bikini, a duffle bag tucked at his side, waiting for his moment. "Quarter-turn right!"

The competitors pivoted in unison, muscle choreography. Shoulders rolled, lats flared, calves flexed. The crowd responded with gasps, whistles, and camera flashes. Four more turns followed, each more dramatic than the last. "Front double-biceps!" The synchronized explosion of arms made the crowd erupt. Whistles pierced the air. Women screamed names, men clapped, and a storm of cellphones captured every second. "Front lat spread!"

They widened themselves into impossible wingspans. The judges scribbled furiously. And in the front row, in the velvet-lined VIP section, sat Benedikt Oblonsky. He was draped in wealth and arrogance as usual, his gold watch glittering, a row of women wrapped around his arms, each like an ornament. His hulking bodyguards hovered close, eyes scanning lazily. To anyone else, he looked untouchable, the king of his own twisted court. But then his phone vibrated.

Oblonsky's lips curled into a frown as he read the screen. He answered, muttering in Russian. His composure faltered. Whatever he heard made him jolt upright. His eyes darted, searching. Without hesitation, he shoved the model on his arm to the side. She yelped, tumbling back into her seat. He barked a signal with two fingers. His bodyguards immediately moved. Together, the three tried to slip through the crowd toward the exit. They didn't make it. The auditorium doors burst open.

Standing there, illuminated by the light spilling in from the hall, was Devin Crews. His half-naked form drew stunned gasps, but his badge hung proudly from his neck, and in his hand was a gun steady as stone. Behind him, Mack charged in, firearm raised, expression hard. "Oblonsky!" Devin shouted, his voice carrying over the panic rising in the room. "Freeze! You are under arrest for conspiracy against the United States!" Screams tore through the audience. Chairs scraped, people tripped over each other. The orderly spectacle of muscle and glory collapsed into chaos.

Oblonsky's bodyguards froze at the sight of multiple weapons trained on them. Embedded agents rose from their hidden positions in the crowd, guns drawn, circling like wolves. The bodyguards decided against reaching for their weapons, they froze. There was no escape. For a split second, Oblonsky's lip curled with disgust. His men were cowards. He yanked a model by the arm, pulling her against him. She gasped in shock, struggling, until the cold barrel of a Walther P38 pressed into her spine. She sobbed. "Please-don't hurt me," but her cries were ignored, he was now using her as a human shield while he contemplated his next move.

Kat's Dilemma

Downstairs, in the women's restroom, Kat trembled. Her wig stuck to her damp forehead. In her hands, the detonator gleamed like a cursed relic. Her thumb hovered, shaking. Sweat ran down her temples. She glanced at her watch. Seconds ticked away. Her mind racing as her chest heaved: *Do it. Don't do it. You'll die too. No, you'll win. You'll finally matter.* Her knuckles whitened as she gripped tighter.

Hostage Standoff

Back upstairs, Oblonsky sneered across the room, locking eyes with Devin. "You look familiar," he growled, accent heavy. "I've seen you before. Yeah?" Devin kept his aim straight, calm under the tension. He caught sight of Tanya and April crouched near the control booth, eyes wide with terror. He subtly motioned for them to move away from the scene. "Put your hands up!" Devin ordered. "Drop the gun Oblonsky, don't make me do it!"

The hostage whimpered, tears streaking her face as Oblonsky pressed the barrel harder into her back. "At MCC, yeah?" Oblonsky remarked, his memory surfacing. His voice was bitter. "That's where I saw you." One of his guards muttered in Russian, drawing Oblonsky's attention for half a second. That was all the opening Devin needed. Two quick shots rang out—POP! POP! Oblonsky screamed, his shoulders jerking violently as the bullets tore into him. His Walther pistol clattered to the floor. The model shrieked and scrambled away. For one breathless second, relief swept the room. His bodyguards instinctively reached into their jackets but were both shot before they could brandish their guns. Then—

BOOM!

The control room exploded. Glass shattered, fire bloomed, and the air filled with choking smoke. Screams echoed, bodies dropped, debris rained down. Visibility collapsed into chaos. When the haze cleared enough to see, Oblonsky was gone. Devin's stomach dropped. He scanned frantically, no sign of Tanya. Heart pounding, he tore toward the exits. Mack was already moving, and together they bolted into the hallway.

Hot Pursuit

Blood stained the stairwell door. A trail smeared down the steps, leading like a breadcrumb trail into darkness. Devin and Mack followed, guns raised. As they burst onto a service floor, bullets ripped through the doorframe above them. Splinters showered down. They ducked, pinned by the barrage. Other agents swarmed in, crouching behind concrete pillars.

Oblonsky, coughing blood, staggered at the far end of the hall. His suit was torn, crimson spreading across his chest. Beside him lay Kat, lifeless, the detonator still clutched in her hand. Another bodyguard sprawled nearby, bleeding from the shoulder. Oblonsky alone remained standing, fueled by rage. He raised his pistol, coughing violently. His eyes burned with defiance. "Stop," he croaked. "Or I will shoot." Devin and Mack exchanged a glance. Then, step by step, they advanced. Oblonsky squeezed the trigger-click. Nothing. Again-click. Empty. His arm trembled. His body shook. Finally, he hurled the gun away and dropped to his knees, defeated.

Mack moved swiftly, cuffing his wrists. The Russian winced, bleeding, powerless. Devin lowered his weapon, stepping so close he could feel the man's breath. He leaned down, whispering in Oblonsky's ear. "What a shame," Devin said softly. "That fine suit is now ruined." Oblonsky's face twisted with fury as he knelt helplessly. Devin straightened, eyes hard. "Checkmate, asshole." Paramedics rushed in with a stretcher. Agents secured the scene. Oblonsky was hauled away, cuffed and humiliated.

Aftermath

Back in the auditorium, the crowd had thinned to a nervous trickle. Police cordoned off sections, interviewing shaken contestants and staff. The bodybuilders reemerged, still glistening, still nearly naked, trying to look dignified in the aftermath of violence. Mack spotted the two familiar blondes he met in the bathroom earlier. They looked pale, eyes darting nervously as they passed. "What?" Mack snapped, flashing his gun. "You look nervous? Never seen a gun before?"

He waved it toward them. The two grown men jumped like startled children, nearly whimpering. "Get outta' here," Mack barked. "And put some damn clothes on!" He barked. Devin caught movement at the edge of his vision. Uri Katznov, the Russian contestant, was sneaking toward the exit, shoulders hunched, hoping to disappear. "Hey, Katznov!" Devin's voice cracked like a whip.

Uri froze. His body stiffened. Slowly, reluctantly, he turned. "Come back here," Devin ordered, stepping forward. "You and me-we need to talk." Uri shuffled forward, his swagger gone. Devin toyed with his gun, spinning it idly in his hand, eyes never leaving Uri. "Have we met before?" Devin asked dryly, his tone mocking. Uri's lips trembled. The man who once strutted the stage looked like he was about to piss himself. And Devin smiled.

CHAPTER 32

BADGE OF HONOR

Las Vegas smelled of smoke and burnt wiring. Sirens cut through the chaos, red and blue lights spinning against the glowing skyline. Fire trucks screamed down the boulevard, followed by ambulances and squad cars. The Grand Hotel that was once alive with the glitz and glamour of bodybuilding competition was now wrapped in barricades, reporters swarming like bees to a hive.

Devin Crews stepped onto the street, no longer in his ridiculous posing suit but dressed in pants, shoes, and a crisp shirt. The adrenaline of the fight had drained from him, leaving something heavier. He tugged the shirt collar, still smelling faint traces of oil and gunpowder on his skin. Across the way, Benson and Stevens stood by the bureau's stakeout van, watching the fire crews sprint toward the blast site. Mack and two other agents flanked them, waving badges at cars and pedestrians to clear a path.

Devin's face was unreadable as he approached. "I can't believe he made me shoot him," he muttered, more to himself than to anyone else. His words carried the mix of disbelief and inevitability. Mack clapped a heavy hand on his shoulder. "You did the right thing," he said. "I was getting ready to take him down myself if you hadn't."

They crossed the street together, traffic stalled as sirens wailed. Flashbulbs from news cameras lit their faces like lightning. Mack glanced sideways at him, his tone softer now. "You're gonna' make a great asset to the bureau, just like your old man." The words lingered in Devin's chest. His father. The shadow he'd carried all these years. For the first time, the weight felt a little lighter.

A white news van screeched to a stop in front of the hotel. A crew spilled out, setting up a camera and lights within seconds. When they were ready, the reporter, Kelly, smoothed her blazer and signaled to her cameraman. "Good evening," she began, voice sharp and clear. "I'm standing outside the Grand Hotel in downtown Las Vegas, where authorities believe a plan to interfere with the upcoming elections has just been thwarted."

Sherry's Living Room

Miles away in Chicago, Sherry sat curled on the couch, her partner beside her. They had planned for a quiet night, but the TV screen stole their attention. The local news had been interrupted by national coverage. Onscreen, Kelly continued: "Authorities believe Russia is behind this election tampering campaign. They name Benedikt Oblonsky, a Russian businessman, as the ringleader. The FBI has him in custody-thanks to a very special team." The camera cut to the street outside the hotel. Amidst the chaos, Kelly stood with a microphone, joined now by a man in a clean shirt, looking tired but resolute. "Detective Crews," she said, turning to him, "I'm hearing that you led this operation to bring this man down. What can you tell us about the operation?"

Devin's eyes went straight into the camera. For a second, it felt as though he were looking into every living room in America, into Sherry's, into the eyes of the men and women who doubted him, into the ghosts of his own past. "It's still an ongoing investigation…," he said, steady and professional. "…so, I can't comment on the details. I hope you understand." Kelly smiled. "I sure do. Either way, we thank you. Our country thanks you." Devin gave a simple nod. "You're welcome." On her couch, Sherry pumped her fist into the air. "We did it!" she exclaimed, a spark of pride in her voice. Her partner turned to her with a raised brow.

"Who is we?" Sherry smirked but didn't answer, eyes still glued to the screen.

Two Weeks Later

The FBI Chicago Field Office buzzed with energy. A cold Midwestern wind whipped outside, but inside, the hallways brimmed with warmth and chatter. It had been about two weeks since the failed attack in Las Vegas. Devin walked in through the main doors, Tanya on his arm. He was sharp in a tailored three-piece grey suit, hair trimmed neat, shoes polished. Tanya wore a fitted black dress that turned heads the moment they entered. As they stepped into the long hallway, a ripple of clapping rose from the corner. "There he goes!" Lowrey shouted. "He's the man!" Dodson added, pointing at Devin like a sports star entering the arena.

The hallway filled with applause and laughter. Devin grinned wide, soaking it in, though his cheeks burned slightly. Tanya squeezed his arm tighter, pride radiating off her. "How was your vacation?" Dodson teased. Tanya tilted her head toward Devin, about to answer, when Lowrey cut in with a sly smirk. "Vacation? I thought he was in jail!" The hallway erupted in laughter, the kind that stung just a little but carried affection. Then Benson stormed in, voice booming. "Hey! What's all that noise-" He stopped mid-sentence as his eyes landed on Devin. His stern face cracked into a grin. "Well, look at that. It's Crews." Behind him, Sherry stepped into view. Her eyes darted toward Tanya, and in that single second, the two women read volumes to each other. Tanya stood taller, radiating beauty and quiet confidence. Sherry blinked, then looked away. Benson waved Devin forward. "Come in here. The crew's waiting." A female agent touched Tanya's arm. "Come on, let me show you around." Tanya glanced at Devin. He gave her a reassuring nod before stepping into a secure room.

The Briefing Room

The conference room was packed, agents shoulder-to-shoulder, some with coffee mugs, others with bottled sports drinks. The chatter dropped instantly when the Director entered. He stood at the front, posture straight, eyes scanning the room. "I heard we have someone special with us today."

Every finger pointed toward Devin. He cracked a smile, rising slowly to his feet. "Well then," the Director continued, "step up here with me, Detective Crews." Devin joined him at the front, standing at parade rest, the weight of the moment pressing down. "A few weeks ago," the Director said, voice ringing with pride, "we received credible intel of foreign interference in our upcoming election. As of now, the mastermind is behind bars." He turned to Devin. "And I hear you had something to do with that." Devin grinned faintly, trying to mask the rush of emotion.

The Director studied him for a moment. "How long ago did you apply to join our team?" "Whoo … it's been a while now," Devin admitted. "Well," the Director said, walking to the side table, "I have something special for you." He picked up a dark blue folder. Gasps rippled through the room. Everyone knew what was coming.

The Badge

Moments later, Devin stood with his right hand raised. "…so help-me-God," he finished, voice steady. The Director extended his hand. "Congratulations, Agent Crews." The room erupted in applause. Devin shook the Director's hand, then looked down at what lay in his palm: The real thing, a gleaming FBI badge, the crown jewel of law enforcement. The edges caught the light, and for a moment the room blurred around him. His throat tightened. He blinked fast, fighting the tears.

He clipped the badge to his belt. Solid. Real. His. Agents lined up to congratulate him, clapping him on the back, shaking his hand. Someone shouted, "About damn time!" The room filled with laughter and joy.

Sherry's Office

Later, Devin, Tanya, and Mack stood in front of Sherry's desk. The office was pristine, a sharp contrast to the clutter Devin remembered from before. Even the old academy photo was gone. Sherry sat with perfect poise. Her eyes scanned the trio. "What do we have here?" she asked, voice dry. Devin opened his mouth, but Mack cut him off. "This time, it's permanent." Devin handed her the blue personnel folder. She reached for it with her left hand, her wedding ring glinting under the light, the diamond catching Tanya's eye. Relief passed between Devin and Tanya in a silent glance.

Sherry laid the papers beside her keyboard, cracking her knuckles with exaggerated drama. She looked up at them. "First and last name!" she demanded. All three froze, wide-eyed. Then she smirked. "I'm just kidding. Relax. All of you." The tension broke into laughter. Even Tanya chuckled, shaking her head.

The Exit

The hallway was lined once more, about twenty agents and staff forming a gauntlet. Devin walked through, high fiving left and right, his grin stretched wide. At the end stood Mack, Tanya, and the female agent. "Welcome to the team, buddy," Mack said, clapping him hard. "Thanks," Devin replied. Tanya's eyes shimmered. She threw her arms around him, planting a long kiss on his lips. Mack handed Devin another blue folder marked Personnel Office.

"You know what we gotta do, right?" Mack said with a grin. Mack then retrieved a windbreaker jacket he had been holding behind his back. He unfolded for all to see, the letters "FBI" emblazoned on the back. He threw the jacket around Devin's shoulders. Devin slipped his hands in the sleeves and adjusted himself. He looked official, a federal agent at last. The three large golden letters emblazoned on the back.

Celebration

As they stepped outside together, Mack asked, "So how are you two gonna celebrate?" Tanya looked up at Devin, her smile sly. "I know a spot." She uttered. Devin pulled her closer, whispering just loud enough for Mack to hear. "I know a spot too." He grinned. Tanya pushed him playfully. "Boy, you're nasty, get away from me." Mack let out a guffaw, shaking his head as Devin winked at him. For the first time in a long while, the future felt wide open, bright, and entirely theirs.

CHAPTER 33

THE FINAL MOVE

The bar was familiar now, the kind of place that collected memories as easily as it collected spilled beer on the counter. Tanya loved that about it—the low amber lighting, the faint hum of a jukebox in the corner, the sound of laughter rising above the clinking of glasses and not to forget, the sound of pool balls clacking across the tables allowing the sound to reverberate through the air. It wasn't crowded tonight, but it was theirs. This time, they were alone with two other friends for a more intimate evening.

Devin and Tanya sat at a small round table across from Mack and April. The air between the four of them buzzed with the strange energy of a first double date, it was half comfort, half nerves, and all the possibilities that lie ahead on their new journey. Devin leaned back in his chair, pointing his glass at Tanya, eyebrows raised. "Wait…you really took his money?" Tanya sipped slow, letting the suspense hang before answering with a smirk. "Sure did."

April burst into laughter, almost spilling her drink. "That's bold," she said, covering her mouth. Devin chuckled, shaking his head. Tanya's grin widened, enjoying the attention. Mack, however, looked less than amused. His stare, blank, eyes narrowing like a man who'd been outplayed at his own game. Reminded of his old wounds, Mack remembered his competitive edge, "I want a rematch," Mack declared boldly. Tanya leaned forward, her eyes twinkling. "Oh, you're still sore about that?" "It's not about being sore," Mack insisted. "It's about principle." Devin raised a hand, shaking his head at his friend, "not a smart move Trust me on this one." Before Mack could fire back, a waitress walked by, she was young and good looking, balancing a tray of drinks with practiced grace. Devin caught her eye. "Another round for us, please," he said. She nodded with a quick smile and disappeared into the crowd.

The conversation shifted. Mack leaned his elbows on the table, fixing Tanya with a curious gaze. "So, Tanya. How did you find out about Sherry? Crews told me he didn't mention her at first." Devin lowered his glass, *Mack, what are you doing?* He thought to himself. his lips tightening just slightly. He spoke with a calm, almost cocky confidence. "Not that there was anything to talk about." Tanya tapped her finger against the rim of her glass. "Just a little detective work… that's all. I put two and two together." April giggled and raised her hand. Tanya smacked it in a playful high five, both women laughing like conspirators.

Devin rolled his eyes. "Oh, so you're a detective now? Alright. If you're such a good detective…" He leaned forward, voice lowering into a challenge. "…tell me where we're all going next Saturday?" The table went quiet. Tanya blinked, caught off guard. Devin took a long sip from his glass, enjoying her silence. Mack broke it with a curious glance at Devin. "Are we still on for that?" Devin grinned. "Ohhh yeah." Tanya folded her arms. "Wait. What are we talking about?"

The Hyatt

Saturday came sooner than Tanya expected. The four of them sat front row at a bodybuilding event, the Hyatt auditorium buzzing with energy. Bright stage lights swept over competitors coated in oil, their muscles catching the glow like polished bronze statues. Devin wore a simple white T-shirt tucked into slacks; he settled for a pair of white sneakers, clean and casual. Tanya had picked a navy dress with a slit, pairing it with heels that clicked against the auditorium floor. April wore a red dress that demanded attention, while Mack leaned into denim and floral, his shirt loud enough to announce itself from across the room.

The crowd cheered as a contestant struck his final pose and walked off the stage. April leaned toward Devin, eyes wide. "What was the name of that last move?" Devin smiled, slipping easily into the role of teacher. "That was the lat spread. We call it…the wings." April nodded as if memorizing it for a test.

Mack slurped loudly from his cup, pointing at the stage. "The abdominal flex is the best. When they're oiled down just right, the whole-body glistens from across the room. I think the first guy's gonna' win. I like him." Devin, Tanya, and April turned in unison, staring at Mack like he'd just confessed to being a secret pageant judge. "I would've never guessed," Devin deadpanned. Mack blinked. "What? What did I say?" Devin shook his head slowly. "Nothing." Tanya laughed, covering her mouth, while April nudged Mack's arm with playful affection.

The Ride Home

Later that night, Devin drove with Tanya in the passenger seat. The city lights blurred past the windows, exhaustion settling into their bones after the long day. Neither spoke at first, content in the quiet.

Finally, Tanya sighed, leaning her head against the seat. "That was…surprisingly fun." Devin smirked. "Surprisingly?" She shot him a look. "I couldn't tell though…between you and Mack, who had the most fun." Devin grinned, Mack is now a fan, I think I created a monster." Devin paused. "His critiquing of oil application was golden." Tanya laughed. "Fair enough." She paused, her smile softening. "I liked seeing them together, though. April looks happy." Devin nodded. "Yeah. Can't believe they hit it off that quickly." "Well," Tanya said, grinning, "she always wanted a cop. I just hope he can dance." Devin barked out a laugh, shaking his head. "Oh, that I gotta see."

They pulled into the lot, parking in front of their apartment. Tanya stretched her hand toward him as they got out. He locked his fingers with hers, giving a gentle squeeze. She leaned in, stealing a kiss that lingered. "Thanks for the date. I had a really great time."

Home

Inside, Baxter bounded toward them, tail wagging furiously. Tanya bent down to ruffle his fur, purse sliding off her shoulder. "Finally, we're home," she said with relief. "Yeah," Devin replied, shrugging off his jacket. Devin came up behind her, slipping his arms around her waist. He pressed soft kisses against her neck, then her cheek, then her lips.

Tanya turned in his arms, wrapping hers around his neck. Their kiss deepened, slow and searching at first, then hungry. They were standing in the same spot where he'd once performed his routine for her birthday—a memory that flashed between them like static electricity. Her fingers trailed up his chest, tugging at his shirt. He lifted his arms, letting her peel it away. In return, he reached around to unzip her dress, the fabric sliding to the floor. Baxter whimpered, offended, and dragged the dress away like a guilty thief.

Tanya kicked off her heels, laughing. Devin slipped off his sneakers without even looking, a practiced ease that made her shake her head. She glanced over his shoulder suddenly. "What's that?" He turned instinctively. She darted toward the bedroom, her laughter echoing down the hall with every step.

The Bedroom

The room was dim, the soft glow of a bedside lamp outlining Tanya stretched across the bed. Devin had love in his eyes. She looked at him with mock seriousness. "No sir, Mr. FBI," she said, pointing toward the foot of the bed. "You haven't performed yet." Devin's eyes flicked to the newly installed stripper pole, their private joke, their game. He shook his head in disbelief, a grin tugging at his lips. "Oh, really?" he said, voice low. "Really," Tanya replied, leaning back on her elbows.

Devin slipped into stage mode, gripping the pole, moving with exaggerated flair. Tanya laughed, biting her lip, watching him wiggle out of his jeans. He clapped his hands, and the lights dimmed further. With a final playful spin, he leapt onto the bed, Tanya pulling him close. Their laughter tangled with their kisses, passion taking over, filling the room with warmth and fire. Between breaths, Tanya whispered, "What's that?" Devin grinned against her skin. "Checkmate." Their laughter spilled into the night, sealing the chapter not with gunfire or chaos, but with intimacy, joy, and the promise of something lasting.

www.ingramcontent.com/pod-product-compliance
Lightning Source LLC
Chambersburg PA
CBHW051239050726
47594CB00001B/229